# Schrödinger's Dog

Allan Brewer

Copyright © 2017 Allan Brewer

All rights reserved.

# DEDICATION

This book is dedicated to Demelza's parents, Zoe and Jerry, both of whom were writing novels before their premature deaths.

# ACKNOWLEDGMENTS

Thanks to Sandra and Tina for proofreading, and facilitating in me the confidence to publish. Thanks to Anni for support, advice and narration on the audio book version.

## CONTENTS

| | | |
|---|---|---|
| Chapter 1 | Cometh the hour, cometh the man | 1 |
| Chapter 2 | There is no word or action but has its echo in eternity | 15 |
| Chapter 3 | Perhaps that suspicion of fraud enhances the flavour | 40 |
| Chapter 4 | Of boots, guns, clocks and sparks | 53 |
| Chapter 5 | An unwelcome weapon | 75 |
| Chapter 6 | Paradox lost | 109 |
| Chapter 7 | Ambiguity about causation | 124 |
| Chapter 8 | A 20th Century cup, and a late 19th Century bulldog | 152 |
| Chapter 9 | The Moving Finger writes | 163 |
| Chapter 10 | There's one great advantage in living backwards | 182 |
| Chapter 11 | And there came wise men from the east | 192 |
| Chapter 12 | The aftermath | 206 |

# Chapter 1
## Cometh the hour, cometh the man

<u>*MONDAY 14th November*</u>

The dull and damp November morning seemed to perfectly match the equally grey, nondescript building as I crossed the road to enter it for the first time. However, the dullness of the weather and the building did not douse the excitement I was feeling inside to find out about this new job. I had been up, dressed, and breakfasted so early that, although they had told me that this would not be a *'9 to 5'* job, I only managed a token few minutes later than the traditional 9 o'clock start to the working day.

It had been just two weeks previously that the head-hunters had visited me at my Oxford home, and talked to me for the first time. They had invited me to be on the GCHQ payroll until the end of my sabbatical year, another 10 months, to give them unspecified advice on unspecified subjects, whilst still leaving me plenty of time to write the two academic history books that I had planned for the year. (GCHQ, for readers who may not be familiar with the acronym, is the British intelligence and surveillance organisation, which covertly monitors communications around the world for security purposes. The organisation is famously housed in a massively impressive purpose-built doughnut-shaped building, though my new job, I had been told, was located in this unimpressive and anonymous annexe nearby!)

As I was a modern historian specialising in ethnic groups and national boundaries, and had interviewed many players and journalists from the Middle

East, their request had not been all that surprising, but the speed with which the arrangement had been concluded was rather startling. The idea, though, was very welcome to me. I had taken the sabbatical because I had grown rather weary of the undergraduate work, and although researching and authoring books was very satisfying, the intrigue and involvement with a completely new, non-academic set of colleagues promised to be very refreshing. Indeed, they had made it quite clear that I could still spend most of my time on the books, so what did I have to lose? A sinecure on top of a sabbatical - the additional salary could probably help support me away from undergraduates for another year or so after that.

The annexe was a single storey building, set a couple of roads away from the main GCHQ complex - an unimposing, fairly modern concrete building, with no logo or nameplate indicating what was inside. I could see one or two security staff inside the main door, searching people, in similar style to airport security. I entered and handed the appointment letter that I had been sent, to the first security officer. He glanced at it, and then politely explained, "OK Professor Tremaine, we have to check your bag and your pockets on the way in, and then I'll show you to the security chief, who will want to see you before you do anything else." My brown, worn leather bag was one of the old-fashioned Gladstone sort, with a wide bottom and pleated side, a nod back to the identity and comfort zone of the academics of my father's day. Indeed the bag *had* belonged to my father. The security officer lifted out the three books, which I had brought with me, flicked through the pages of each slowly and checked the spine for any concealed mischief, before replacing the books in my bag. Meanwhile, I emptied my pockets into the tray in front of me. I felt a tinge of vulnerability and resentment, like I always felt at airports, as my personal belongings were rifled through. Keys, money and our bags - these things give us our own security, if not identity, I mused. And how easily and quickly we have been persuaded to repress our objections to being searched, as a necessity, in this modern era. At least he had not asked me to remove my belt.

There were three other people ahead of me receiving similar treatment - the first a young woman, confident-looking, with natural dark loose-curling hair, and two rather geeky-looking young men behind her. "And what have you got for us today Miss Gosmore?" the security officer was cheerfully bantering to the young woman as she emptied the considerable contents of her rather hippie-looking bag into a tray with a noisy flourish. She grinned at him, challenging but friendly, as he went through the motions of sifting through the contents.

"Do you want to know what those are for Fred?" she asked loudly as he pushed aside a few loose tampons. The act was clearly aimed more at embarrassing the geeks behind her than the security officer, who was obviously used to her manner.

"OK Miss, I think that's all in order, you can go through now, have a good day," he replied, clearly content to terminate the interaction. She turned slightly to see if she had achieved the desired result of embarrassing the geeks, and shot a glance at me, the slight movement in her eyebrows betraying that she did not recognise me. Then a fraction of a second later the confident and mischievous expression returned. She turned back and strutted on down the corridor. A couple of minutes later, I too was past the handheld metal detector, and escorted to the office of the man whom, I assumed, was the security chief.

He welcomed me in, checked my letter, sat me down and started to talk. He had obviously given this induction talk very many times before, emphasising the nature of work at GCHQ, the necessity and obligation of security, and the actual details of that security - he managed to make the lecture last 47 minutes by my watch. (I still wear an analogue watch, another nod to the old academic comfort zone.) Although he was clearly reeling all the information off largely by rote, I could tell that here was an intelligent man, looking me over and watching my reactions as he spoke. He asked me almost no questions; presumably, they already knew everything they wanted to know about me, before bringing me here. The monologue was boring, but it only managed to increase my curiosity and intrigue about why I was here. After signing the documents of the official secrets act, I was given an identity badge to wear, and a phone number for security that I could ring in case of problems. Then I was escorted down the corridor, which seemed to be lined with offices on one side, and with Laboratories or workshops on the other side, to the office of the person who was in charge of the project, to which I had been assigned.

I knocked on the door and entered, walking into a comfortably furnished, but not extravagant office, to be greeted by a man who epitomised middle management, in a dull suit with white shirt and tie. He was overweight, not extremely so, but enough to make his shirt look ill-fitting, and his suit look uncomfortable. His middle-aged face was chubby and etched with stress, and his hair was receding, not yet enough to make him look distinguished, but enough to make him look untidy. "Welcome to GCHQ, Professor Tremaine - can I call you George?" (Back in my old academic comfort zone, people had called each other by their surnames, but those days are sadly gone...) "I'm Phil Bowen, supervisor of this project, BH9"

"Hi Phil, it's good to be here," I replied automatically, shaking his hand, "and I'm intrigued to know why GCHQ needs a modern historian - my guess is you want advice on middle-eastern groups?"

"Actually, it's more than that, George," he said, gesturing me to sit. "Yes, the Middle East Intelligence Group here will certainly value your input, and that's what outside people will assume, so essentially that will be your cover story - not that you are allowed to say anything about it of course. But it will all become clearer as we explain the details of the project to you." He proceeded to tell me that although there were a number of projects in this building, the personnel of each were not allowed to discuss their work with the teams on other projects. Each team had a code name rather than a description, and our particular project was simply called BH9. Apparently, there were only three other people on this project apart from him and myself. For the first time, I began to have doubts - it sounded very insular, with minimal colleagues to relate to - but this would not be an easy place to back out of. I carried on listening, and he unexpectedly startled me by saying that this project was literally at the highest priority of top secret, both because of the potential capabilities which had been discovered, and because the ownership of those capabilities in the 'wrong hands' would have massive implications. I was getting uncomfortable now because, although I am familiar with weaponry, having talked at length to so many participants in the Middle East conflicts, I have never wanted, or even considered, taking any responsibility myself, for owning, or using a weapon. He had gestured the quote marks around the 'wrong hands', and smiled, indicating that he perhaps understood the shades of grey in trying to define the good and bad, - it wasn't just simply them and us. I caught myself stroking the tweed on my jacket cuff - it was something I noticed that I did when I got nervous.

I asked him if his background was military.

"No, not at all, " he laughed, "I am an Ethicist by trade. I did undergraduate Politics, Philosophy and Ethics at Kings College London, and then did an MA in Ethics. The big issues, back then, were thought to be in medicine and genetics, but I ended up here managing projects. Actually, mostly what I do is listen hard to the technical people and ask lots of questions, so that I can report upstairs," (he gestured again) "to the people who interface to the politicians and military. They are generally not technical, or at least not technically adept in the *wide* range of things that they are presented with here." He cocked his head slightly to one side thoughtfully. "Actually, this is the first project I have been on which kind of needs some serious ethical input. I guess that's why they put me on it, rather than one of the other managers. But…. I must say…" He tailed off as a slightly troubled expression darkened his face. "Anyway," he took a deep breath, "I look after another couple of projects, both of them not in this building, so you'll only see me in on occasional days. As a matter of fact, after today I shall be out the next two days, back on Thursday."

"What are your other projects then?" I asked, testing the response.

"Can't tell you. We just can't talk about them *at all*. You'll get used to it." He raised both hands in an empty gesture and smiled, clearly not minding my probing of etiquette. "So it will be much better if I get in Alex to explain to you the details of this project. He's a physicist, very gifted, I would say, and actually very easy to get along with." He stood. "I'll show you your office as well." We walked out of his office and a few paces down the corridor to a door on the other side marked BH9/b. He touched his finger briefly to a fingerprint reader which flashed green, and opened the door. "Alex, sorry to disturb you, could you come and explain the state of play to our new team member, Professor Tremaine, please. But give us a couple of minutes first - I just want to show him his office." I glanced into the lab over Phil Bowen's shoulder and saw the woman whom I had seen earlier at the main door, sitting at a workbench, focussed on keying fluently into a computer with three large screens facing her. She did not look up.

My office turned out to be next door to Phil Bowen's, the label on the door again cryptically stating BH9/c, rather than my name. It was very comfortable compared with the offices in academia - a lovely large desk and sumptuous chair, and state-of-the-art PC with a large screen. The top drawer already contained all the pens and pencils and assorted extras that make office life so much easier - stapler, hole-punch etc. I sat in the swivel chair for a moment, breathing in the comparative luxury, the emptiness of the bookshelves unnerving me slightly. This could be home, I felt, as I took out of my bag the three books which I had brought in with me, and placed them on a bookshelf. I closed the bag and left it by the side of the desk. I gathered up a blank notepad, decided to use my own favourite old pen, which was always in the breast pocket of my tweed jacket, and walked back into Phil Bowen's office. I was feeling more comfortable now. My office next door would make a great hideaway for me to author those two academic books I had in mind, even if the 'project' turned out to be a pain.

There was now coffee on the small table in Phil Bowen's office, and he gestured to me to help myself. A few moments later Alex entered. Phil introduced him to me as Alex Zakarian, though I could detect no trace of a foreign accent as he welcomed me and started talking. He was tall, dark and striking with a very convincing and reassuring air. Apparently, he had formerly been a professor of physics, researching into exotic matter, they didn't say where. He had approached GCHQ himself, when, eighteen months ago, he had realised that his theories were leading to places he felt dangerous to publicise in the open environment of academia. He had been rapidly brought onboard with his co-workers Betty, a mathematician, and Mike, an engineer. Since then they had been gradually designing, building and modifying the equipment to test and apply the theories, and had just recently managed to have some verifiable success.

"I'm still looking for ways to explain the basis in non-technical terms, so please forgive me if I get too simple or too complicated," started Alex. "There is still a lot of room for conjecture in quantum and particle physics, and many of us play around with *'what-if'* particles, using the maths of the theory - exotic relatives of pions, muons, neutrinos etc. You've probably heard of tachyons for example. They have, or would have, a very interesting property of negative mass, which essentially means that they would always travel faster than light. The theory is fine, but the existence of a tachyon has never been demonstrated, and most physicists believe they could not exist, or if they do, that they would not interact with ordinary matter at all. So, as far as we are concerned, they might as well not exist. But then again, the theory around the tachyon *is* mathematically consistent, and obeys all the physical laws.

"So, particles have several properties - mass, spin, charge and so on - that's how *types* of particles differ from each other. Anyway, I became fascinated by the possible existence of a particle related to ..., well I won't be too specific for obvious security reasons. This particular exotic particle could theoretically be produced as a result of the disintegration of a parent particle, and it would, surprisingly, have an electrical charge of 'i' - that's the square root of minus one. Now, I need to go off the track a bit here - I don't know whether you remember 'i' from your maths at school? I think they drop it into A-levels as a teaser?" I shook my head - I had certainly never got as far as A-level *maths* at school, my head was already seduced by historical stories at that time.

"It's easiest to think of it as the square root of minus one. Of course, when you multiply two positive numbers together, you get a *positive* number, and if you multiply two negative numbers together, you also get a *positive* number, so that means multiplying an ordinary number by itself, you could *never* get a negative answer. So how can you get a negative number as the square answer? - that's where 'i' comes in. It's sometimes called an imaginary number, though that doesn't sound very helpful, but it does give rise to the whole set of what are called complex numbers. It just really gives us an extra dimension of numbers, at right angles to the ordinary positive/negative number set. And, this is no hypothetical curiosity, it is extremely useful in different guises all through mathematics and theoretical physics.

"So I spent a lot of effort looking at ways to generate this particular particle, because I was desperate to experimentally find out which way it travelled when you put it in an electric field. You see, if a particle has a positive charge, then it will be attracted toward the *negative* end of the electric field, whereas if the particle has a negative charge, then it will be attracted toward the *positive* end of the electric field. But if it's charge was i, where would it go? - Certainly not towards the positive or negative ends of the electric field. I assumed it would probably go sideways or up. But then, the problem is that if the electric field is simply left to right, then the remaining directions - up, down and sideways are all equivalent - so how would that particle choose a *particular* direction to go in? That's the sort of question that motivates a physicist, or gives him or her sleepless nights, if you like. Anyway, to cut a very long story short, we did finally manage to generate these particles, thanks to a lot of expensive equipment and Mike's labouring. But disappointingly, every time I tried the electric field experiment on the particles, to see which way they would move, they seemed to be too unstable and we couldn't observe them.

"By then, we had Betty on board - she is a remarkable mathematician and very capable with computer code, and had soon got to grips with the theoretical equations and was exploring them with simulations of the particle. We were all getting very frustrated with, what appeared to be, the instability of the particles - the particles seemed to be easily observable when they were prepared, but as soon as I switched on an electric field, they were gone. We had improved several of the generating steps, and the corralling of the particles - we now hold them in an extremely cold state as a BEC condensate - but I was, frankly, running out of ideas. The other strange issue was that normally, when some particle is unstable and so decays, it *always* leaves some traces behind - a pair of lesser particles, or radiation - but in our case, we were able to detect *absolutely nothing* at all. I was actually beginning to write-up the research into a paper thinking we had pushed it as far as we could. Then Betty was one day trying to combine the theoretical equations into another set of vector-space-time relativity equations - quantum equations don't easily mix with relativity equations - when she suddenly let out a sort of squeal of delight, I looked round, I remember it so well, her eyes were absolutely lit up and her mouth was open."

I noticed Bowen tense a bit and shift in his seat.

"Betty looked over and said to me 'You know Alex, I don't think the particles are *unstable*, I think that when you switch on the electric field they *do* move, but in the *time* dimension. They are pushed into the future or the past, depending on whether their charge is plus i or minus i! And *that's* why we no longer detect them!' It was one of those legendary eureka moments for us; I'll never forget the feeling. It immediately sounded right as she said it, and I rushed over to her screen to see the nature of the equations she had linked, and, sure enough, that's what they were implying - that the particle would move in time."

I was now sitting bolt upright in my seat - Alex's statement had galvanised my attention, and a shiver ran up my spine.

"The next couple of days were frantic," he carried on. "We had no way of proving that this was happening to the particles, until we could control the period of time-shift - how far into the future they would be pushed. Betty could calculate the exact electric field strengths required from the equations to give us a shift of hours or days, which we needed for testing. But those calculated results were way out of line with the comparatively large, *gross*, field we had been using, which was probably sending the particles thousands of years into the future. So we had to wait until Mike could devise a more subtle, highly-calibrated, electric field generator."

"Hang on a moment," I proffered, "isn't it a big deal that the particles would be emerging in the future - aren't they going to be creating havoc there?"

"Not really," laughed Alex - he had his reassuring smile. "There are cosmic rays bombarding the upper atmosphere all the time, creating small numbers of all sorts of particles, including ours, shunted god knows where, so you could say it's a natural phenomenon. And with the relatively small number of particles we are using, there is so little energy involved that they could all land and decay inside your brain and you would probably not notice anything."

"Ah, I see…" I nodded.

"So anyway, meanwhile, we had realised that the process of moving the particles in time, because of the nature of the dimensional change, it is not exactly pushing the particles there, rather, it is reallocating their position, not only in time, but the equations allowed for reallocation in space as well."

"Hang on, I don't get that either," I protested.

"Well, if you were to push a particle along on the table," he demonstrated with his finger and a pencil. "That is, push it through *space*, it would occupy successive different positions *as time progresses*. But you can't push a particle through *time, as time progresses*, it doesn't really make any sense. What the push would actually be doing is reallocating its position in the timeline, according to the strength of the push, rather than pushing it there *through* the intermediate instants of time. Or, looking at it another way, imagine if I could send this pencil ahead one hour in time, you would expect it to disappear and then reappear in an hour's time. You wouldn't expect it to be there, in every instant, until the hour was up, whilst it was travelling to that one hour ahead time, - that would just be what the pencil is doing *anyway*, in normal conditions. So, the acceleration in *time*, bumps it to another moment in time. Does that help?"

"Yes, that kind of makes sense," I concurred.

"So, I had already discussed with Betty that we should keep the work to ourselves for the moment. Indeed I had started to realise that, although back then, we had very limited capability, the on-going developments that we could imagine from this work, could result in a very dangerous device. So, after thinking it through, I decided to approach GCHQ as soon as we had real proof. That came about a week later. We attempted to push a set of particles one hour into the future, and we sat down with a cup of coffee watching the detectors on the computer screen and waiting. But as the one hour mark came and passed, nothing happened - I was gutted. But then, at about 85 minutes, the screens lit up, and there they were, the particles had been detected - that was an emotional roller-coaster hour and a half that I will never forget. It turned out that Betty had omitted a square-root of 2, when she translated the coordinates to the calibration, one of the very rare occasions I have known her to make a mistake. So, the calibration was out - hence 85 minutes instead of an hour. If you ever want to wind Betty up, which is a hard thing to do, just mention *'root 2'*. Actually, don't, - she'll kill me if she knows I told you. And... thinking back on it, I am not sure she did make a mistake, she might have very well known *exactly* when the result was due, and was just winding me up. Betty is great fun, but you can't always tell when she is pranking - she has a very good poker-face."

Again, I noticed Bowen shuffle in his seat uneasily.

"Sorry if I am going on about the development in so much detail - the truth is I don't usually get any opportunity to talk about it, so it's a bit of a release for me... We are certainly looking forward to having someone else in the office whom we can actually talk to, and bounce ideas off."

"And it's good for George here too," added Bowen, "otherwise, as an intelligent man, he will be consumed with curiosity. It's good for *all* the team to know the *whole* story."

"So," Alex continued, "GCHQ moved very quickly getting us all down here. They even created a cover story for us - that we were being employed by a company making security equipment a few miles away from here, so we are still able to visit old colleagues at the university, or have them stay down here, we just tell them the work is mundane but well-paid. The equipment I had back at the university was appropriated quickly on the pretence that it was being bought by another physics department, and GCHQ has not hesitated in paying for any further equipment we needed. We have a pretty open brief in exploring the science behind this, although GCHQ is primarily interested in its possible use in intelligence gathering."

"Actually," interjected Bowen, "the *politicians* 'upstairs' are the ones angling for that capability. More sensibly, the *military's* priority is that it doesn't fall into anyone else's hands, hence the very small team. Alex has told me many times that if we got more researchers in, we would be able to push the science ahead faster, but at present the imperative for secrecy trumps that."

"But we *have* been able to make progress," went on Alex, "We are able to generate batches of those particles, and super-cool them, in which state they are fairly stable and easy to manipulate. Actually, we prepare them as two clouds of particles, which we entangle - have you heard of quantum entanglement? It's standard physics these days - it just means that when something happens to one cloud, you can detect it with the other, even if the first cloud has been sent to a different place, or, as in this case, a different time, as well. So, the cloud of particles that we send, is not stable, out of the laboratory environment - it is impacted by what is present there. Specifically, the particles of the sent cloud are immediately impacted by those photons of light which hit them roughly parallel, and the cloud decoheres, the entanglement collapses. But we can read back the impacts of the photons from the entangled cloud, that remained in the lab, and we can use that data to reconstruct an image - at present a very grainy picture, of what was in front of the cloud, after it was projected somewhere else, and indeed sometime else. It's not really like a camera, as we have to process the data heavily to generate an image - about an hour on the GCHQ supercomputer. Betty is working on optimising the algorithm to make it quicker. Fortunately..."

"You mean," I interrupted, leaning forward in my seat as the enormity of the explanation began to hit home to me, "you can take a photo of *any* place, at *any* time, in the past or future?"

"Well, possibly," Alex tempered my naïve generalisation. "Right now we can only get a grainy black and white shot, a bit like the 1950s TV pictures, and we have only been trying it out in the lab on short time shifts. So for example, we have put a recognisable object - a pyramid shape or something, in the lab - then take it away, and try to get an image of when it *was* there. At the moment we are working on improving the resolution of the image - in fact, we are waiting on some major upgrades to the equipment, so we can use a larger particle cloud and more energy; hopefully, that will help." He paused and downed the last mouthfuls of his coffee, looking over at me for further reaction.

I managed a subdued "Wow," as thoughts flashed by me faster than I could formulate them into questions. It sounded like a historian's dream, but entrapped in a cage owned and secreted by the military.

It was Bowen, who then picked up the conversation. "So, at the moment, this project is not even nearly mature enough to be a strategic intelligence gathering device. But as it becomes so, the management here may be looking to you, as an expert in modern history and particularly the Middle East mess, for guidance and advice on surveillance targets, not only names and places, but the '*whens*'. We don't know how long the development will take, and to be fair to Alex, indeed *if* it will be possible to gain good enough resolution for surveillance. But in the meantime, you can help bring some *independence* to the experiments, and suggest good scenarios for the first field trials - that is the experiments where they try viewing *outside* the lab. So far all the trials have been within the lab. Of course, meanwhile, you can progress the books you are writing - you'll probably have plenty of time for that, but it was thought better to have you on board *before* the project becomes mature."

Now it was Bowen, who reached for his coffee and looked expectantly at me for a reaction.

For the first time I can remember in my life, I understood the meaning of the often-used phrase 'lost for words', as I struggled to harness some of the thoughts that were darting through my brain. "It's massively exciting," I started. "It's hard to believe - that is, I don't mean I don't believe what you're saying, it's just difficult to take in." They both laughed understandingly.

"Yes, I still have trouble getting my head around it," said Bowen smoothing his hair, "and I have trouble explaining it *upstairs*", that hand gesture again, "well, perhaps because they are not getting it from Alex directly, not being exposed to his credibility. I must say there is a lot of scepticism - probably as a defence against the problem of trying to take on the concept. They certainly want to give anything that's needed to nurture the project, indeed they couldn't say no to such a revolutionary proposal, but they are itching for a demonstration, a proof. And that's another of the reasons they want someone independently credible, like yourself George, brought in, to devise experiments. After all, a historian is the closest we can get to an expert in *time*, and they were particularly impressed by your theorising on cause and effect in that book you wrote about modern conflicts and politics - I can't remember the exact title, I admit I haven't read it myself," he laughed. "Are we painting an image of how we see you fitting in here?"

"Yes," gradually I *was* seeing it, "this is helping - I was feeling a bit like a fish out of water at first."

"Of course," he continued "you might find it very frustrating that you can't do the one thing that a 'Historian' would want to do," he emphasised the word strangely, " - get hard evidence from the past and write about it!"

We all laughed. There was some human bonding going on, we were warming to each other, despite the enormity and strangeness of the innovation we were discussing

"Who knows," added Alex, "in the fullness of time maybe the tool *will* be available to historians to play with too…"

"Not if the Ministry of Defence has anything to do with it," Bowen cut in rather too sharply, somewhat killing the good feeling that had been developing, and I saw again that tense shifting in his seat, and the cloud of stress that briefly passed across his face. "Anyway," he sighed, "I think we've covered all the basics now, George. I suggest you spend some time doing other things for a while - give it all time to sink in. Feel free to go for a walk, write your book or whatever, perhaps I could see you briefly before you go home this evening though?"

"Sure," I nodded.

"Tell you what," suggested Alex, "come and have lunch with us in the lab later, you can meet Betty and we'll show you some of the equipment? About 12:30?"

"Sure," I nodded again. Actually, that did sound good. Alex had such an easy and reassuring manner, even though it was from his mouth that I was hearing all these strange unnerving statements. However, I felt a twang of apprehension about meeting Betty for real, after seeing her in action at the entrance earlier, and remembering what Alex had said about her wind-ups, and also noting Bowen's unease when she had been mentioned.

Anyway, I needed some time to myself, so went back into my new office and sat down in the well-padded desk chair, and leaned back to think. Yesterday I had been a regular academic Historian, entrenched in my boring comfort zone, my only excitement the occasional meeting with journalists back from dangerous trips in the middle east, or leaders of militia or political groups from there, (which reminded me I had an appointment with Al Faqhhidi on Thursday in London). Today I was sworn to secrecy in the most unlikely, and fantastic, of emerging espionage techniques. Was I betraying my independence as a historian if I also advised on espionage? How had I got into this without thinking about the ramifications? - well, obviously because they couldn't explain it to me beforehand. Did I owe it to my country? - No, I don't have those kinds of feelings - I wondered if Alex is patriotic? - Difficult to imagine - but he did approach GCHQ of his own accord. Perhaps he just wanted someone else to take the responsibility? Then I remembered that Bowen had said there was scepticism amongst the management, and they wanted someone independent to look at the experiments. In fact, maybe it was all a huge pretence by Alex and Betty - but Alex seemed so genuine. I logged on the computer on my desk and googled 'physicist Alex Zakarian' - sure enough, there were references to his previous academic work: *"In this talk I explore the physical meaning of the statement 'probability amplitudes are complex' by comparing ordinary complex-vector-space quantum theory with the real-vector-space theory having the same basic structure. Specifically, I discuss whether multipartite states are locally accessible, and whether entanglement is 'monogamous'?"* I had no idea what it meant, but it was undoubtedly impressive. There was still an hour to go before lunch so I decided to read one of the books I had brought in - I think Bowen had been right, I needed to take my mind off the project for a while.

# Chapter 2
There is no word or action but has its echo in Eternity.
*Pythagoras*

I found it hard to concentrate on reading - the strangeness of the whole situation had been distracting me. When it got to lunch-time, I put down the book, crossed the corridor to Alex's lab, and doubtfully tested my finger on the fingerprint reader on their door lock. It worked, flashing green, so I entered. The woman, whom I now knew must be Betty, was sitting at one of the desks, but there was no sign of Alex.

"Ah, the History-man," she greeted me. "So what does history tell us about those who climb down from their ivory towers to mix it with the technocrats? Do they thrive?" It was a challenging opening line, but delivered with an inviting smile.

"Well," I began, "history would probably hesitate to generalise that far, but I assure you there is more ivory here than where I came from. These offices are a step up for me."

She laughed, "But I think the ivory tower refers more to the disconnect from practicalities, than to the sumptuousness of the offices?"

"Actually," I countered, "I think it comes originally from the Song of Solomon in the Bible, which is quite a steamy love poem - Solomon says *'Your neck is like an ivory tower'*. But you are, of course, right about the modern usage, which starts, as I remember, in the 19th Century, when a French literary critic uses *'la tour d'ivoire'* to compare the socially disengaged De Vigny, with Victor Hugo."

"Excellent," she laughed again appreciatively, though I realised it had been a factual, rather than witty, repartee, on my part - I was always slow with the wit.

There was a pause, during which she kept looking at me. "So," I asked, in an attempt to further the conversation, "what have you been working on this morning?"

"Oh, I wrote a letter to my mother."

I assumed that was a joke, so made a small chuckle.

"No, really," she said. "You see we have basically exhausted what we can do with the current equipment - we are waiting on some serious upgrades, and we are mostly prepared for those too, so just at the moment I have plenty of free time. I wrote to my mother, and then read a lot of computer-generated random sentences."

"Random sentences?" I queried, not understanding.

"Yes, just what you imagine - grammatically correct, varying structures, but the nouns, verbs, adjectives etc., are randomly supplied by the computer. Our minds are capable of constructing a consistent scenario to encompass almost any random sentence. It only takes a few seconds, without effort, for that scenario to form. And iteratively working through lots of sentences feels like a very healthy creative brain exercise. In fact, some of the sentences need only a little work to become elements of poetry, listen! She looked back to her computer screen…*How doth the lone heart stagger, calling on candidates from the wound warehouse to fill its aching void.* Mmm… I guess it still needs a bit of sculpting."

It all sounded plausible… but rather unlikely. I was lost for a reply.

Fortunately, at that moment the inner door opened and Alex appeared. "Hi George, ah… so you've met Betty then?"

"Sort of," I replied, feeling deprived of a proper introduction.

"Well, this is Betty Gosmore, mathematician extraordinaire, and general life and soul of the party. George Tremaine, Professor of modern history, and new member of the team." She offered her hand from her reclined position - it was warm and firm.

She whispered, "I guess you've had a boring morning with Mr Security and Mr Ethicist?"

"Well, anything *but* boring, actually, a bit overwhelming," I countered.

"Ah, they explained the i-vector then?" guessed Betty

"I got the layman's introduction from Alex," I confirmed.

"We've got a few sandwiches here George, we tend to bring them in for lunch and eat '*al desko*', as it's a bit of a hassle going out and in again through security," explained Alex. "Pastrami or Chicken salad?"

"I should go for the pastrami, they tend to overdo the mayonnaise on the salad," advised Betty, still in her reclined position feeding herself the remains of a sandwich.

Normally I would have opted for the chicken salad, but it seemed like a good strategic move not to reject Betty's advice. She leaned further back and switched on a Lavazza coffee machine that was behind her.

"There is a *communal* coffee machine down the end of the corridor," Alex explained, "but it's a bit dire because, apart from the very average coffee, we're not allowed to discuss anything about the project in an open area, or indeed anything personal about ourselves, so it gets a bit awkward when others are around."

"I asked one of those tense lads from BF5 what his favourite colour is, and he took me seriously," laughed Betty. "He said he liked yellow and orange and asked me what my favourite was. I said I preferred radiation from other parts of the electromagnetic spectrum, especially hard X-rays." We all laughed.

"So, do you guys live locally?" I asked.

"Ooh, we can't tell you that," stonewalled Betty.

"Give him a break," countered Alex. "Forgive Betty, she was once Hedda Gabler in a production, and never managed to get out of character afterwards."

Betty's eyes widened. "That's not completely true, Alex, I did play Hedda, but her character is not really consistent - Ibsen wrote fun stories, but his character construction was very arbitrary, he certainly didn't understand women. Anyway, my interpretation of Hedda was somewhere between psychopath and obsessive, that's nothing like me. If I rattle people's cages it's just to loosen them up, it's well-intentioned, people are so hung-up and tense most of the time."

This insight certainly broke the ice, and helped me warm to Betty - it was a pleasant surprise to find that the scientists I would be mixing with were enthusiastic and knowledgeable about the humanities, just as were my more usual peers back at the university. We chatted for a long time, through two rounds of excellent coffee, and then they showed me the rest of the lab. The area we had been lunching in was essentially their office, with computers and an equipment control screen. A door at the back opened into an area containing several racks and cabinets of equipment humming gently, and a table on which stood some simple geometrical shapes painted in black - the pot of paint and brush still sitting on the floor - these were the objects they had been trying to visualise, against the white wall, in the experiments. A further door at the back of this area led into another space housing more equipment - I could recognise pumps and refrigeration, but most of it was beyond my familiarity, and Alex did not seem to think it appropriate to go into too much detail.

There were some grainy prints pinned up on their office wall, which were the celebrated images of the geometric shapes, as had been described to me. I gathered from Alex that they were waiting on major equipment upgrades at the moment, due in a couple of days, that would enable working with much larger clouds of particles, and higher energies, which they anticipated would lead to much better resolution images.

\*　　　\*　　　\*

I popped in to see Bowen later in the afternoon, before I left, as he had requested. He just wanted to re-iterate the importance of me not talking to anyone about the project - fair enough, I was not used to this secrecy stuff. He made it clear that he wanted me to come up with proposals for experiments, as the project progressed, to independently verify the capabilities of the equipment. At this stage that meant giving blind coordinates to Alex and Betty - scenes that they did not know - and staying with them until the print came through to check that there was no 'cheating'. He also reminded me that I could call security on my phone anytime I felt concerned, or was approached unusually, and that I should notify security of all my travelling plans. This I had forgotten, so I popped into the security office on the way out, and told them I would be travelling home to Oxford each weekend, and that I was going down to London on Thursday to meet with a Lebanese journalist, Al Faqhhidi. This latter name raised some interest, and I was asked the purpose of the meeting, and whether I had met him before. I guessed they were going to do some background checks on him after I left the office.

No problem, I meet these characters all the time, that's my job, to understand the changing political scene in the middle east. At least that *was* my job; I had a new one as well now, maybe advising on temporal espionage. So on the half-hour walk back to the accommodation that had been provided for me, I set to thinking about just that. What surveillance would help resolve the conflicts in the middle east, or perhaps I should say 'would further British interests in the region'? And would those interests be different from resolving the conflict? Knowing what one party in the conflict intended to do, seemed of little value - any attempt to thwart one faction just made another stronger - it was such an interconnected mess. I hadn't found any clear ideas by the time I arrived home.

\*   \*   \*

The next couple of days were fairly uneventful, I went into the office, worked hard on the modern history book. It was going well, I had written about three quarters of the material, though I would still need to go back over it improving the text when it was finished. However, I was reasonably confident, now, that I could finish that one, and write the other book I had in mind, within my sabbatical, if I kept at it.

I made a point of popping in to see Alex and Betty each day - they were busy, and getting excited about the impending delivery of their new equipment, which actually arrived on the Wednesday afternoon. I gave them a hand carrying some boxes in from the front door and watched as some heavier items were trollied in. Security had obviously decided that it was pointless scanning the equipment with their metal detector, since it was mostly metal-cased, so one of their number stationed himself in Alex's office to witness the unpacking. An urgent phone call summoned Mike, an electrical engineer. He was the one other person who had been poached from Alex's university, and was in on the secrets of BH9. He was an older man, probably in his early sixties, with thick grey hair, and he carried with him an impressive array of tools in a large black case. He also enthusiastically revealed some electronic interfaces that he had been making. I didn't get to speak much with him, because there was fervour among all three of them to get the equipment unpacked, installed, connected and calibrated, which I gathered was going to take a few days. He did tell me though that he had spent most of his working life putting together physics equipment, and that he worked in a general GCHQ workshop, when he wasn't needed in Alex's lab. Alex and Betty's elation reminded me of children unwrapping presents on Christmas day. I left them to it.

*       *       *

## *THURSDAY 17th November*

The next morning I caught the 8:47 to Paddington to meet up with Al Faqhhidi. I decided to spend the train journey thinking again about the possibilities of intervening in the Middle East conflict using espionage or surveillance. In just a few days I had begun to see my old role of historian, simply documenting what had happened, as rather passive, perhaps even cowardly - I didn't personally even travel much to the troubled parts. Al Faqhhidi and his reporter peers were the brave ones, going into dangerous areas to appraise the conditions, and trying to talk to militia leaders, some of whom were barely civilised, or had strong beliefs, far removed from the accord that we usually rely on for our comfort and safety when meeting others. But then again, it was their region. They spoke the language, understood the customs, and presumably cared passionately about the devastation being wrought throughout the region - displaced citizens, in refugee camps, or trying to migrate out of the area altogether, once-vibrant cities reduced to piles of rubble, no longer able to house, or support the refugees, even if they wanted to return. But try as I might, I could think of no way in which espionage or surveillance could help the situation. Rather the problem seemed to be with the mindsets of the protagonists, each side oppressing the other in alternate countries, and the oppressors supporting those insurgents who aligned with them in other countries where *they* were oppressed. The conflict rendered perpetual by ethnic and religious indoctrination of the children.

My mind drifted back to essay titles I had set, when undergraduates had occasionally, and valiantly, attempted to identify a simplistic potential solution to the troubles. Often politically-incorrect in at least one of its two senses, most often both.

But here was not an answer that I was compelled to find - I had never suggested that I could advise on surveillance. History, my expertise, is the recording and interpretation of events; it does not pretend to identify intervention strategies.

I decided that if, and when, I was asked for advice about Middle Eastern targets for surveillance, I would just have to level with GCHQ, and tell them I could not think of any way in which it would help. If they then no longer wanted to pay for my services, then so be it. I had a little trepidation that my knowledge about their secret new technique might complicate my being able to leave their employ, but it did not worry me enough to stop me sleeping for the rest of the journey.

\*     \*     \*

The meeting with Al Faqhhidi gave me no new insights. I left with a list of which areas the regimes had gained and lost, which insurgent groups had split, or fallen out with other groups. I did gain a little more understanding of why the external powers disagreed over which insurgent groups they regarded as terrorists and thus bombing targets, and which insurgents they thought were moderate and legitimate, and should be given arms. But it all seemed depressingly intractable.

\*     \*     \*

## *FRIDAY 18th November*

The next day I went into the office early intending to spend a full day writing up my notes from the meeting, before the weekend. First, I looked in on Alex and Betty who were still very enthusiastic and apparently making good progress with the new equipment. I had just sat down to start writing when Bowen came and told me I had been asked to attend a meeting with their other Middle East intelligence staff to inform them on what I had learned from Al Faqhhidi. This I was very happy to do, as it made me feel that I was at least doing something legitimate to earn my salary. Bowen, himself, drove me over to the main complex, and helped me find the room, reminding me that I must not indicate anything about the details of the particular project that I was now personally involved in. There were six others in the meeting, one of whom I remembered from a conference a few years earlier, and several were familiar with my own work. I briefed them as requested and there then ensued a long discussion about the general Middle East situation. It was a rare pleasure to be able to discuss freely with other experts in the field, and we agreed that it would be useful to get together again on a monthly basis to keep each other up to date. I actually picked up quite a few facts, angles and ideas that I knew would be useful to my own authoring. And one of the other attendees, who clearly *also* had some academic background, actually offered to proofread my book when I had finished the writing, an offer which I gratefully accepted.

\*     \*     \*

I got back to the office after lunch and finally set to work on the keyboard, feeling quite fulfilled - it had been an eventful week. I had found both a comfort zone of like-minded individuals, with whom I could talk modern Middle Eastern history, and a couple of delightfully interesting scientists, with whom I would be collaborating on a project which was, more than novel, bordering on fantastic. I left the office very happy.

On the hour and a half drive home to Oxford, I pondered again, whether I should perhaps be commuting daily to GCHQ in Cheltenham, rather than staying in digs there. I had considered it when the arrangements were first being made, but it had seemed an attractive idea to have an excuse to be away from Marianne for a while. Since our youngest son had gone away to university, we had found ourselves back as a couple, but no longer a young couple with sparks flying, and with not a lot of common interests to bind us. Before we had had children, she had been a bright young researcher in bio-technology, but as she rightly reminded me now, biological sciences had moved on massively since then, there was no chance of her getting a job in that now, and no, it wasn't just a case of reading-up the advances. She was going to find a calling in something else, she said, she just hadn't been able to find it yet. I felt some remorse that I had been able to maintain a career through our child-raising years, whilst she had lost hers. It wasn't that we argued, just that we didn't have a lot to say to each other. With a touch of guilt I also realised that the attraction I had toward the company of Alex and Betty was stronger than the attraction pulling me home to Oxford.

*       *       *

## <u>MONDAY 21st November</u>

Monday morning was cold but sunny. I arrived bundled up in a coat and scarf which made the security process at the front door all the more tedious as I pulled off layers for them to check. I got into the office and hung up my coat and scarf. Betty burst into my office beaming.

"Come, see what we have got, George, " she entreated, linking her arm through mine and pulling me along and into their office. Her arm was warm and insistent, and I felt the contact bringing a smile to my face. Alex looked very tired, he and Betty had been working many hours through the weekend, I was told, but Betty's enthusiasm masked her *own* tiredness.

"We have a *massive* improvement in resolution," she waved a couple of sheets of printed paper in front of my face. The first was the same subject composition as last week's - an array of geometrical objects, but now starkly clear against the white background. The second was of Betty herself, next to the objects, giving a V-sign, sticking out her tongue and holding a newspaper. The clarity was remarkable, though not sufficient to read other than the headlines on the newspaper. But the prints also exhibited a dramatic quality because of the strange, almost silvery tone of their greyscale. There is always something special about black and white prints in these days of a surfeit of colour, something wondrous about seeing early Victorian photos, rare views of times long past. But these prints had something else - a kind of weirdness in the texture, which is alien to the photography with which we are familiar. I found myself shaking my head with amazement, and looking at all the different parts of the print. Alex explained that the strange texture arises because the image is not focussed through a lens, as is everything we normally look at, including with our own eyes. Instead, the image is synthesised on the computer, by extrapolating from the entire data set, recording how photons of light have impacted on each particle, and all its neighbouring particles in the cloud, that was projected in order to record the image. As the number of particles in the cloud is increased, the time taken to do this massive computation rises exponentially; apparently, these prints had taken about 4 hours each on the GCHQ supercomputer during Sunday.

"So we have been a bit restrained," continued Alex, "not constrained, but restrained, holding back, on the density of the cloud, the number of particles - because otherwise the prints would be taking all day on the super-computer, and there are limits to what we can reasonably ask for from the IT department."

"So how much better do you think you can get the resolution?" I asked.

"Well, we don't really know at the moment," put in Betty. "On the one hand, we can use more particles, but there must be some upper limit when they start crowding out and disturbing each other, so messing up the picture. Also the algorithm can be tweaked to take account of more and more neighbouring particles, but again there will be a limit we reach which gives no significant improvement."

"Or we can expand the *size* of the cloud so that we can get more particles into the image without them being so close that they interfere, though we can't do that with this version of the equipment unfortunately," added Alex.

"But I have a lot more optimisation work to do on the computer code as well," went on Betty, "so that then we can take finer pictures without over-staying our welcome on the GCHQ supercomputer."

We all laughed at the quirky metaphor Betty had come out with.

"Yes, we need to do a lot more experimentation before we know the limits, and the best use of this new equipment, but I think we've got a good working medium with these two prints," mused Alex, raking through his hair wearily.

"Yes, this is a stunning leap forward," I was stating the obvious, but it needed to be said. "Have you told Bowen yet?" I realised I had used his surname in the old academic way, but hoped it hadn't sounded disrespectful.

"No, I don't think he's in yet," said Alex. "Actually, he was saying last week, he wanted you to choose an external target - somewhere to image - a sort of independent verification?"

"Yes, he wants me to give you the coordinates of somewhere you don't know, and don't research about, just to be sure you're not faking it!" Again, I hoped I had not offended.

"The bastard," quipped Betty.

Alex laughed. "We can do that, but you know what, I'm going home to bed for a few hours while it computes - I was here half the night, not to mention Friday and Saturday nights. Have you already got some coordinates in mind?"

I thought quickly. "Yes, OK, give me a minute." I went back to my office and pulled up google maps on the screen. Embarrassingly, it took me another 20 minutes to find what I was looking for, and note down the coordinates.

I went back into Alex and Betty's office. Betty turned from her computer screen. "Alex has gone home," she said. "He was dead on his feet. We are going to meet up this evening, though, for a celebration on getting such brilliant pictures - it would be great if you can make it too?"

"Oh, sure, I'd like that. So we're not going to do the coordinates, then?" I asked, embarrassed to hear a little disappointment colouring my voice.

"*Yes* we are, we don't need Alex here, I'll program the shoot - the particle cloud preparation is almost ready, where do you want to target?"

I read from the piece of paper in my hand "52.05242 degrees North, 2.71666 degrees West."

"Ooh, I'm impressed, we'll make a scientist out of you yet," she beamed. "I was expecting you to say something like half way up the A927, 100 yards past the petrol station!"

We laughed.

"So it's not too far is it?" asked Betty. "We don't know how good our spatial calibration is yet, at long distances. If we are, say, 0.01% out at 1000 kilometres, that would be 100 metres off target."

"No, it's only 40 or 50 kilometres away."

"Great, and how high is it, what height above sea level," asked Betty.

"Oh, sorry, I hadn't thought of that, I'll just go and check." I felt stupid, and Betty chuckled as I went out the door again. It took me another 10 minutes to find the information. I returned to their lab again. Betty was sitting facing the door and cocked her head, raising an eyebrow as I re-entered. "61 metres above sea level," I played along as if the conversation had been continuous.

"Good," Betty continued. "I set up this input procedure to the equipment a couple of weeks ago. We had to get a Geographer in, actually a *Geodesist*, and not tell him *why* we were asking all the questions - there are all sorts of issues like 'does sea level mean low tide or high tide?' and we have to take into account the curvature of the earth, and the slightly flattened spherical shape of the planet. Then, if we are dealing with a time in the past, we would have to take into account continental drift and so on, and no doubt there are other things we haven't thought of yet which will bite us in the ass when we do the experiments. So give me the coordinates again."

"52.05242 degrees North, 2.71666 degrees West." She started keying into the computer. But then I suddenly realised I had compromised the blind nature of the experiment by leaving the room. She could have memorised the coordinates, looked on google maps and copied a picture.

"And the height above sea level?" she asked. She looked round when I didn't answer. "What's the matter, George, what is that look on your face?"

I dejectedly explained my failure to secure the blind nature of the experiment.

"Oh for goodness' sake George, do you seriously think I go around memorising blocks of what, 14 digits, so I can cheat on something I don't need to cheat on. All right then, let's start again, go and find another target."

"No, no, I trust you, let's carry on," I protested.

"Right. Height?" she demanded shortly.

"61 metres."

"OK, I'll add two metres to give an eye height view. Now, I don't know what this place or thing is, do you want us to back away a metre or two, and in which direction do you want us to look?"

"Back off two metres south, and look north," I answered as concisely and efficiently as I could.

"OK. And I'll program zero time shift, as it's bound to be daytime there now, if it's only 50 kilometres away," she added, pressing a few more keys. "Right, I'm sorry I barked at you George, I know you're only trying to get it right." She smiled disarmingly. "Do you want to press the 'GO' button?" She rose from the chair in front of the computer screen and gestured for me to sit there. "So, next door," she nodded toward the inner room where the equipment was installed, "the two entangled clouds of particles have already been prepared, and chilled to ultra-cold temperature. I can see from the control console over on this side, that they are ready to be activated."

As I sat down, I could see, on the screen, the window where all the coordinate parameters had been entered. Her mention of zero time-shift had reminded me again of the extraordinary nature of this equipment, although we were not using a time-shift on this occasion. I scanned through the computer window with interest. Bottom right of the window was a button outlined in green, and labelled 'Activate'. "This one?" I double-checked, looking up at her. She nodded. I centred the mouse on the button, took a deep breath and clicked. I was half-expecting something dramatic to happen, some decisive sound from the equipment next-door maybe, though I had no idea what. The button greyed out, and for a couple of seconds nothing obvious happened, then a whole stream of statistical data spewed up onto the screen. Betty looked over my shoulder.

"Hmm...," Betty sounded concerned. "Can I have the chair again, please?" She sat and scrolled the data up and down, studying it in silence.

"Did it not work?" I asked quietly at length.

"Well," she tipped the chair back, "we seem to have mostly a 'white-out'. This is the first time we have tried out in the open air. The lighting in the room next door, where we did all the previous tests, is comparatively mild compared to sunlight, so… If it were a camera, we would shorten the exposure… Here… well, we need to reduce the energy of the particle cloud even further - chill them down a bit more. So I'll have to run it again…" She leaned over to another screen, and keyed into it for a few seconds. "It will take about 30 minutes to generate a new batch of particles, and chill them down far enough." She sighed. "Actually, it's a good job you asked to look north, otherwise we might be looking directly toward the sun - I hadn't thought of that." She made a note on the pad beside her. "Tell you what, why don't you grab a book and read it in here, then you can keep an eye on me to make sure I don't research the coordinates to cheat! But honestly, George, if I'd wanted to cheat I would have written computer code that looked up the coordinates that were keyed in, and found a photo to match automatically - it wouldn't be too difficult. As a controlled blind experiment, this is far from watertight. Just so you understand?"

She was right, of course. I had not fully thought through the necessary steps for a blind controlled trial, to give proper independent verification of the process, for the management of the organisation. But this was a start anyway - I was more than eager to see the result for myself, and it was clearly throwing up some glitches that Alex and Betty hadn't worked through yet, so it wasn't wasting their time. Still, I felt a bit inadequate.

"You've got that look on your face again Georgie," she said mockingly, but affectionately, putting a hand on my shoulder. "Go and get that book." It had been a very long time since anyone had called me Georgie.

It didn't take long to get a book, as there *were* only three on my bookshelf, and I was back in her office. Not long enough to cheat, I mused, then felt a pang of guilt for even thinking that, after all the hours of work they had put in over the weekend. She had actually spent the few moments putting the coffee machine on, and sorting out some mugs.

I tried to settle down to the book, but found it hard to concentrate. Not so much because of the excitement around the experiment, I realised, but because Betty was in the same room. I was finding it hard not to watch her.

"By the way," I started, as she handed me a coffee, "are you able to angle the view a bit up or a bit down? - You didn't ask me to specify that earlier when we put in the coordinates."

"That's a good question," she began, sipping her own coffee, "we actually can't, per se, because we have to project the whole cloud as one object - we can't get the upper particles to move forward without the lower particles, so to speak. But if we wanted to angle the picture, and I suppose it's inevitable that we will eventually, then we would have to mount the piece of equipment which holds the cloud - it's shaped like a wheel about a metre in diameter and a few centimetres thick - we would have to mount that on a gimbal. So then, we could tilt the cloud, within its container, before projecting it. In fact, thinking about it, if the cloud were being projected any distance, the curvature of the earth would result in it being tilted naturally with respect to the earth anyway, so we would have to take that into account, and adjust for it. Damn, I wish I had thought about that before we specified the equipment, it's much more difficult to retrofit something like that. The container for the particle condensates is probably a bit too heavy to hold in a tilted position by hand, and I suspect the vacuum and refrigeration feed-pipes are rigidly attached anyway." She again wrote a note on the pad beside her.

"Another question," I was pleased that I was managing to be constructive, or was I pleased to sound intelligent in front of Betty? "On the activation screen, as well as the Time-shift, which you had keyed-in as zero, there was a mention of Time-delay, what is that about?"

"Ah, well," she answered, "yes, that comes from the equations. We can define what time we want to project the particles *to*, but we can also define how *long* before we want them to be there. So, if I set the time-shift to plus 24 hours, we could view an image from tomorrow morning, but I can also state how long before I want that image to be taken. So if I put in a time-delay of 1 hour, we wouldn't get the image data back for an hour after pressing the button."

"So you mean the machine doesn't send the particles for an hour, after you press the button?" I queried.

"No, no, the machine sends the particles straight away, but they don't get there for an hour. From our point of view they exist in a sort of temporal limbo until then," she corrected.

"So…, what use would that be?" I asked.

"None at all really," she shook her head. "I suppose if you wanted two pictures taken simultaneously for some reason, we could send one particle cloud with a delay, then prepare another batch of particles and send the second batch with a shorter delay, so that the second batch arrived at the same time as the first batch. Not that we have the equipment to handle two pictures' data simultaneously. But the ability to define that delay arises, not because it is useful, but because it is in the equations. We use the term 'prime' in mathematics to denote a variant of something. So we have 't' meaning *our* time now when we action the image, t-prime meaning the target time, and t-double-prime meaning the limbo time between our action and t-prime. We jokingly call it double prime time!"

I laughed at the joke, wondering what double prime time TV would be like. I wasn't sure I understood the explanation completely, but I determined to think about it again later. I tried to settle to the book again.

"So this evening," she interrupted, "we are meeting at my place around 7 for a drink, then probably going out to eat. Here's my address." She handed me a yellow sticky note.

"Actually," she added, "I need to go to the toilet now. Do you want to come with me, George, to make sure I don't do any 'cheaty' coordinate-googling on my smartphone while I'm there?" She managed to deliver the line in such a deadpan way that it sounded as if she meant it.

"No, just give me your phone to hold while you go." At last I had managed a fast repartee. She laughed and handed over her phone with a slight curtsey.

She pointed her finger at me, "Don't phone my mother while I am gone," and she flounced out of the room.

Her phone cover was rose gold, embossed with the elegant black silhouette of a ballerina, whose dress was composed of tiny crimson butterflies, some with a minute encrusted jewel to the centre. I looked at it for several moments, entranced by its simple beauty. I drew it closer to examine the minute jewels and noticed the subtle perfume, that I had not consciously noticed before, but that was immediately reminiscent of Betty's presence. I put the phone down on the desk before she returned, as it felt that I was intruding into something personal, even just holding it.

When she returned, she was obviously deep in thought and she immediately started writing more notes on her pad.

*    *    *

It took a full 50 minutes before Betty announced that the particle batch was sufficiently cooled to re-run the test. During that time, I had tried very hard to concentrate on my book. But I enjoyed Betty's presence so much that I couldn't help watching her as she keyed into her computer, or pondered with her hand on chin, or leaned back, or ran her fingers through her long hair, then keyed again. A couple of times she caught me looking at her, but she just smiled. Every movement she made seemed to be a performance, but entirely natural at the same time. I started wondering if she had a boyfriend. She was very easy with Alex, I wondered if perhaps the two of them were an item. She was wearing a thick tweed skirt today, not unlike the material of my jacket, though more colourful, and she occasionally shifted a little to adjust her sitting position. She caught me looking at her again. This time her eyes narrowed a little.

"Are you looking at my butt, George?" she questioned, and she wagged a finger at me, before resuming her work.

I might have felt very embarrassed, but she clearly was unoffended, so I mumbled "sorry," and lowered my eyes back into my book. Indeed, her ability to take seemingly everything in her stride, with good humour, was part of the attraction.

So, it was some relief to me when she finally indicated that the interminable wait was over. "Sorry it took so long George, that extra cooling was a slower process than I expected. Here we go then." She pressed the 'activate' button without ceremony this time, and a few seconds later the stream of data flowed onto the screen as before. She scrolled it up and down a couple of times, looking closely at the numbers. "Yes, that looks much better. There is a good range of greyscale, this time, so I'll throw the data over to the supercomputer..." She made a few more keystrokes, "and we are getting an estimate of 3 hours processing time back, so... I think I will also head home for a bit of a rest, and a tidy-up before this evening - you will be coming won't you?" I nodded and smiled. "So," she continued, "I will come back in, late this afternoon, to see what kind of picture the supercomputer has fashioned for us, and I'll see you again then?" She slipped into the long boots which she had kicked off under the desk, wound a maroon chenille scarf twice round her neck, and took a stylish winter coat off the hooks behind the door, slipping into it as she opened the office door and ushered me out, back to my own office.

\*       \*       \*

It was about 4 in the afternoon when I heard their office door being opened. I had spent the middle of the day rather restlessly, finding it very hard to concentrate on my history, whilst thoughts of the impending picture, currently being calculated and stitched together by the supercomputer, kept intruding. Would it really show what I had intended? It was already obvious that the system was fallible and immature at the moment, as evidenced by the failure of the first try this morning. And a remote viewing would be so much more remarkable than those earlier pictures that were located in the same room that housed the equipment. I was really hoping that it would work. And then there were thoughts of Betty that kept intruding - her smile, her fast wit…

I decided to go to her, rather than wait for her invitation. She had not bothered to take her coat off, and looked up from the computer screen and smiled as her fingers danced briefly on the keyboard. I could see from her eyes that she was excited too. "On the screen, yes? I'll print it later," she said "Are you ready?" She drew a deep breath and tapped the return key, her lips pressed together tightly. There was the briefest of delays before the screen filled with the landscape picture. I was stunned. I had forgotten in the anticipation, just how beautiful a river scene, this spot was, of itself. The top of the image was threaded and shaded with branches from a nearby tree. The outlines of willow and poplar were clearly visible on the far bank, a gothic style house with long chimneys. The water of the river had a shimmer to it, and reflections of the foliage on the far side were apparent upon the water. A bench was facing the river, with a single, perhaps old man, wearing a flat cap, sitting with his back to us. Who was he, to be portrayed in such an epic moment? Of course, he had no idea. And it was all tinted in that rather eerie silvery alien texture that had so struck me when seeing those prints this morning. The strange beauty, combined with the shock and realisation of the reality of what this all meant, made me feel momentarily weak, and I staggered slightly before regaining my balance. Betty meanwhile, had her palms to her cheeks, clearly also awed. She rose and flung her arms around me. We hugged in silence for a few seconds.

"Oh, George," she looked back at the screen. "It's very *beautiful*, but is it *right?*" she pleaded. I had forgotten, for the moment, that she had not been *in* on the 'secret' of the coordinates. For her, the process had worked brilliantly, but she didn't know whether we had hit the right spot, my chosen target.

I had to clear my throat before I could speak. "Yes, you see that darkish shape over to the bottom right of the picture?" I pointed.

"Ye... es, it looks like a dark statue of an animal, a lion maybe?"

"It's actually a wooden statue of a bulldog called Dan, who fell in the river at that point, when he was being walked by Edward Elgar," I stated. "Anyway, that was the *actual* test target. We are about 6 or 7 metres too far west, and maybe a couple of metres south, I would say, assuming of course that the coordinates quoted on the internet were accurate."

She took two or three quick breaths. "This is fantastic... just fantastic," she repeated excitedly. Her hands were in the air and she was jumping about. "I must phone Alex." She picked up her phone from the desk where I had placed it earlier and focussed on it, pacing about.

I felt a tinge of jealousy. It had been so good sharing this day, and particularly these latest few minutes with Betty. But of *course* she had to let Alex know - it was their baby.

"Damn, he must be still asleep," she concluded after there was obviously no answer. "Well, he'll have to wait until this evening - I'll have to smuggle out a print for him."

I wasn't sure whether that was a joke or not, the rules about what could be taken out of GCHQ were fairly tight.

\*   \*   \*

It was a cold evening, but we would clearly be having celebratory drinks, so I decided to leave the car at home and walk to Betty's. I had checked Betty's yellow sticky against the ubiquitous google maps, and it was about 30 minutes walk away, in an area with the delightful name of Charlton Kings. I had not yet seen much of the Cheltenham streets, so it was a pleasure to walk, especially as it was that time in autumn when many of the pavements are covered with dry leaves of various hues, and stepping through them makes that delicious scrunching sound. I flashed back to scrunching through virgin snow on Oxford pavements the previous winter. I turned right down Bafford Lane, after the Local Sainsburys, just as the map indicated, and started counting off the numbers as I walked. It was a varied, narrow leafy lane, and difficult to predict what type of housing would come next. When I eventually reached her number, I was surprised to find, secluded behind the trees, an ultra-modern, detached, architect-designed house. In the spacious drive was parked a midnight blue Mercedes Cabriolet. My first feeling was one of aesthetic delight, and then I quickly was wondering what this meant about Betty. Was she married? To a rich banker maybe? - Scientists do not usually earn the sort of money that this indicated. With a little apprehension, I pressed the doorbell, enjoying the authentic sound of a pair of real tubular bells that resonated deep and long, until the front door was opened by a radiant Betty.

"Hi George, welcome, come on in." She put an arm on my shoulder and kissed my cheek. She looked stunning, in a long flowing black and white cocktail dress, with earrings and necklace to match, very different from her simple, utilitarian work look. I hung up my coat and scarf, and followed her up the stairs - the first floor was an open plan living area, with a black grand piano at one end, and she pointed out views across to the Cotswold escarpment at the other end. The décor was contemporary and expensive, in very good taste. I looked around rather awestruck.

"So how…," I started, gesturing around.

"Oh, yes, well my family is well off, and they don't mind me using money, after all, a house isn't consumed, it's still as valuable when you move out. I hope you don't disapprove, some people are resentful of wealth? I absolutely love this house, it's so beautiful, it was designed by an architect friend of my mother, and I was really lucky that it happened to be on the market when we moved down here. There are a couple of special paintings over there." She pointed across to the other wall. At that moment the deep, sonorous ring of the tubular bells cut in. "That must be Alex, make yourself at home." She went down the stairs to open the front door. I went over to look at the paintings - they were contemporary, interesting, but I knew nothing about that area of art. The artist's signature was present, but illegible. Meanwhile I could hear Alex being welcomed enthusiastically, and they were ascending the stairs, so I walked over to greet him. He looked well and rested, completely recovered from his haggard but happy appearance from this morning. We shook hands warmly and he gave me a quick man-hug.

"So how did George's undisclosed target experiment go this morning?" He beamed, looking from one to the other of us.

"Wait," said Betty, "I want to set the mood first. Alex, can you fix the drinks - there's Prosecco chilling in the fridge." She walked over to the piano, sat, and settled herself without hurrying, whilst Alex retrieved the bottle from the fridge, shrouded it with a tea towel and eased the cork out. At the very moment the cork popped out, notes began bubbling from the piano, and I realised that not only had she managed a perfect piece of choreography, but also that her music was profound. Alex brought the glasses and bottle over, and set them down soundlessly, onto a small table in front of the sofa. He handed me a full glass, and motioned me to sit, gesturing 'cheers'. He set another full glass on the piano top, within reach of Betty, but she did not pause or react. I sipped and listened, and watched Betty deftly carving out full and intricate figures in the music. It was beautiful to watch. It was beautiful to listen to. Alex had settled back on the sofa smiling broadly. It was already apparent that this was no 5-minute wonder; Betty had embarked on a major work, romantic period, Chopin or Liszt I guessed.

As she reached the end of the first movement, there was the precious stillness as the notes died away, during which, with her foot still on the sustain pedal, she delicately took her glass, downed half of it, replaced it, and was poised to begin the second movement. Her face was lit by light from a solitary candle on the piano top. In all, the piece lasted for perhaps half an hour. After the final chords we all sat in silence for a while, savouring the moment - it would have been churlish to clap. Alex finally rose and walked over to the piano. "Brava Betty," he whispered, hugged her briefly, then led her back to the sofa, refilling her glass and mine. "So, *now* tell me about the experiment?"

She took a deep breath. "OK, so the first time I ran it, we got about 90% photon bleaching - it was targeted outside in the sunshine, hence quite different from our runs in the lab. So, for a second try, I chilled the condensate a further point three degrees below the critical temperature, which took an extra half an hour or more, by the way, and then ran it again. And *this* is what we got." She leaned over and pulled out the print that had been lying face down under a magazine on the small table. She passed it to Alex beaming.

"Wow, beautiful, that's got really good definition, and what is the target?" enquired Alex

"That little statue in the corner - we are a few metres out, but we hit it." Betty pointed out the statue.

"And where is this - it looks like England still?" Alex looked up.

"Yes, it's on the bank of the River Wye about 40 kilometres away," I put in, wanting to share in the conversation.

"That's great, but Betty, you shouldn't have brought this print *out* of the office - you know it's against the rules, and this is very sensitive." Alex sounded concerned.

"Oh, I just hid it in the lining of my coat, they are never very thorough on the door," Betty countered.

"That's not the point," Alex was insistent and seemed angry, "if they find out, the consequences are dire, it's stupid to take the risk. You could easily have waited until tomorrow morning to show me. It was a silly thing to do."

"I wanted you to see it *tonight* - I thought you'd be *happy* to see it." There were tears in Betty's eyes. She grabbed the print back out of Alex's hand, marched over to the piano, and briefly held the sheet of paper in the candle flame. As it burned, she walked back to the kitchen area and dropped it in a bowl to finish burning. "There, now it never happened."

"Nonsense, for all you know this room is bugged," retorted Alex.

Betty marched back to the piano, sat, and started thumping out angry chords. I recognised Busoni, usually large and grandiose, but this was loud and angry. Alex put his head in his hands.

I had very mixed feelings about what was happening. This was the first time I had witnessed any tension between these two, of whom I had grown very fond rather quickly. I could not see a good way to intervene - I understood little of the layers of dynamic between them, or the nuances of the rules of GCHQ. And I was actually rather enjoying the bizarre interpretation of Busoni. I doubted whether she could keep it up, but made a mental note to ask her to record it in that fashion another time, for posterity. The room was filled with the smell of burnt paper. The candle flame quivered visibly to the thump of the chords. Finally, Alex rose, crossed the room and knelt beside her, putting his arms round her. This restricted her arms and caused some distorted, twisted chords as she initially resisted, finally giving up with her fists on the keyboard.

"OK, I'm sorry, I'm sorry," he sounded very sincere, "I understand you wanted to show me the image and share the moment. And I'm just being boring and anxious. But I worry about you. And it would be awful to lose you, I can't do this without you, you know that. And we need to keep GCHQ sweet."

She took a couple of unsteady breaths. "Don't you *ever* call me *silly*," she hissed. There was a brief pause, then they both laughed, and she hugged him. "Oh, But George knows what I did, he can blackmail me into doing all sorts of favours for him!" She was back in fun mode with that convincing deadpan voice.

"George is a true gentleman, he would never stoop that low," countered Alex joining in the pretence. He dragged her back to the sofa.

"I'm not so sure," Betty persisted, "I caught him looking at my butt this morning."

Now it was me with my head in my hands. She jumped on me with a giggle and hugged my head. "I'm sorry George, you must think we are mad scientists."

"I like you both enormously," I said, my eyes slightly misty.

\* \* \*

We chatted and finished the Prosecco in good humour, celebrating the success of the latest round of BH9 equipment and experiments. Betty decided she wanted to be waited on this evening, so rather than ordering in food, we phoned for a taxi to go out to eat. I could understand that their life was rather insular because of the security restrictions at work, and it was something of a relief for them to get out and be surrounded by other people enjoying themselves.

Whilst we were getting ready to leave, Betty got a call on her phone. I glanced at Alex wondering if he was nervous, following the concerns he had expressed earlier, but he seemed relaxed and smiling now. It turned out to be Betty's sister. The orchestra she played in was to perform in Bristol on Saturday night, and she wanted to stay over at Betty's and bring her daughter to be babysat. Betty seemed delighted. I hadn't imagined her as an auntie, but she was soon planning games and a little present.

As the taxi arrived, Alex reminded us not to say anything more about GCHQ or the experiments whilst we were in public. Betty amicably told him to stop fussing, but I was grateful for the reminder - I was still not used to the security regime, and we had drunk enough alcohol to loosen our tongues somewhat.

At the restaurant, it was actually good to leave the project behind, and talk about our lives and ourselves - they still knew almost nothing about *me*, and I had an incomplete image of *them*. It turned out that Alex had a wife, Petra, and two small kids at home, whom he was happy to have consume his life outside of physics. Betty on the contrary, had the time to have a wide range of interests, and often had friends or family visiting at the weekend - she seemed to prefer to host, rather than to visit. Her family seemed endlessly talented, her mother a psychotherapist, and her father had been a hospital consultant, before he had died young. Alex and Betty were both very interested to hear about my past at Oxford. Betty was relieved to hear that I was not a stuffy historian studying, as she joked, 'Laudian and Royalist polemic in 17th Century England', and they both zeroed in on my knowledge of the Middle Eastern situation with many questions. We concluded that history was a little like science, in that I was trying to establish cause and effect, but on a broader, more complex front, than science, which relies on reductionist experiments. Betty questioned me at length about my marriage, why I said it no longer had magic. I was only now getting some distance from Marianne, and coming to accept the reality, and I was happy to think it through with them. I told them about Al Faqhhidi, and his work, and we ended the evening discussing the difference between journalism and modern history. As we left, I looked round the restaurant wondering if there were any security people keeping an eye on us, or indeed foreign agents waiting on loose words, but the other dining parties all looked very ordinary.

## Chapter 3
## Perhaps that suspicion of fraud enhances the flavour.
*C.S. Forester*

### *TUESDAY 22nd November*

The next morning, Alex spent a long time in Bowen's office briefing him on the latest results. I had been surprised at his words "*we need to keep GCHQ sweet*" the previous night - presumably GCHQ would be eating out of his hands after seeing the latest pictures, which must have more than justified the expenditure on the latest equipment, though I had no idea how expensive that had been. I spent a little while with Betty in her office, but she was clearly concerned about the length of time the pictures were taking to process on the super-computer, given that they were not yet even using the full resolution that was theoretically possible with the new equipment. She was rather pre-occupied about working on the software, and phoned Mike to ask him to come over as I left her...

In the middle of the afternoon, Bowen summoned us all into his office. He announced that the top military brass had become very interested in what we had done, and that they had set us a test, so that they could verify the capability for themselves. He had an official-looking envelope on his desk, and held a sheet of notepaper in his hand, which had only typed coordinates and times on it.

"They have given us the coordinates of somewhere on a military base, and want us to take remote, timed, pictures, one as of yesterday (Monday) 18:00, one tomorrow (Wednesday) 18:00 and one for Friday 18:00, all to be delivered to them by Thursday 18:00," he announced. "I trust that will all be OK? I really don't want to have to make excuses to them." He shuffled uneasily as he said the final sentence. Clearly, he felt his credibility was on the line. He looked at Alex, who had leaned forward with his hand on his chin, clearly pondering the request.

"Well, we can try," Alex started, "but let me add a few caveats. As I said to you this morning, we are still at the beginning stages with the experiments, each attempt brings new issues to solve - like yesterday Betty had to make a substantial change to compensate for the brightness of sunshine that we had not experienced before, and we still have to refine the calibration - we were several metres out yesterday. Also, we haven't even tried serious time calibration yet - we will have to do a dummy timed run first, to establish the calibration. You are pushing us ahead rather faster than is comfortable. It's possible that we will fail for some reason or another, but I am happy to try the first two requests. I'm not prepared to do the *future* test though," he finished firmly.

"But why's that?" Bowen sounded disappointed.

"Well," explained Alex, "suppose we do an image and show them there is going to be a machine gun, or whatever, at that coordinate on Friday. Then what if they decide to be perversely clever, and not put the machine gun there?" Betty was looking at Alex intently.

Bowen opened his mouth to say something, and then closed it again. There were a few moments silence. "So how does it work?" I put in. "Can you *change* the future by bringing *information* from the *future* into the *present*, or is there a single future which is pre-determined and fixed?"

"Good question," said Alex coolly. "We haven't done the experiments to establish the answers to that yet, or indeed to see *if* we can get information from the future at all. All we have done so far is to project a cloud of particles into the future. Whether we can maintain that cloud entangled with a cloud in the present, so as to get pictures, is another thing entirely. I know what my educated guess would be, but potentially it opens the way to paradoxes in physical theory. We could go on philosophising about the possibilities, but the point here and now is, if the military decided to be clever, and to *not* put the machine-gun there, then we would have been *wrong*. So, Phil, that's not a chance we should, or need, to take."

"I can see what you're saying," said Bowen, "but couldn't we do the military's future-test as your first experiment, so as to keep them happy."

"No, really," Alex was standing firm. "It's not as if we have briefed them that we can do future pictures. It's not a capability that we claim to have, yet, unless you have overstated our position, Phil? They'll have to wait, otherwise they'll be asking for next week's winning lottery ticket numbers, and god knows what next. I'm not sure it's a valid capability for the military anyway."

"But suppose, as an example," Bowen persisted "if they could have an image of the Russian front-line tank division, for every month for the next couple of years. If the tank lines hadn't moved, then the country could save billions on defence because we know the border won't need to be defended."

"Unless they found out what we were doing" interjected Betty.

"Is that a threat?" asked Bowen.

"No, of course not," snapped Betty. "Listen. If the Russians *found out* that we thought we knew the future, and that we had therefore run down our defences, then there would be nothing to stop the Russians changing their minds, thus changing the future, and we'd be sitting ducks. The whole principle of successful deterrence rests on a level of transparency… "

"Well, yes, obviously," Bowen defended himself, "that was just an example."

"Maybe, perhaps, it's all supposition right now…" Alex wanted to close down the conversation. "The whole idea of getting information from the future opens up a Pandora's bag of worms - we need to approach it very carefully and methodically. We need to experiment properly and understand before we plough ahead. I'm not saying we can't do these things *ever*, Phil, I'm saying that (a) we don't know *if* we can do them, and (b) we are not *yet* ready to do them. Surely, an image from inside a secure military base will be enough to satisfy the top brass, let alone an image from *yesterday* inside a secure military base? Good grief? Surely they will already think all their Christmases have come at once!"

That seemed to satisfy Bowen, Alex had a very convincing tone, though it sounded likely that Bowen had bragged a little too far to the military, or perhaps made it sound too easy to them. "OK," said Bowen "I'll tell them that the future-picture mission has to go on ice for the time being, please make the other two pictures your top priority though."

"I have a couple of caveats too," piped-up Betty. Bowen audibly sighed. "Firstly the lights have to be on."

"What are you talking about?" snapped Bowen.

"At 18:00, this time of year, it's dark. If the target is outside it needs to be floodlit, if it's inside, the lights need to be on. In fact, they need to be on *yesterday*!" Everyone laughed except Bowen, who scribbled a note on his pad.

"Good point Betty," added Alex, "you see, it's like a camera, Phil, but we have no flash."

Bowen nodded. "OK, I'll check."

Betty leant forward and gestured to be given the sheet of paper with the coordinates typed on. Bowen ignored the gesture and put the sheet of paper back in its envelope.

"And secondly, I need to borrow a military-grade GPS receiver," said Betty.

"I can't get you *that*," protested Bowen.

"You must," insisted Alex. "We have to measure the position of our test targets with maximum accuracy, so that we can calibrate our equipment. It would be no use us taking an image of a sandbag a few metres away from the military's target, that won't impress them at all."

"Just for one night," persisted Betty in a mock-pleading voice.

"Oh… Um…. Well, OK… I'll see what I can do," said Bowen fidgeting uncomfortably.

"Tonight preferably," added Betty abruptly. I didn't know whether she was winding him up, or whether she really wanted to get the calibration done so soon. Actually, it would *have* to be done very soon if we were going to meet the military's schedule, I realised.

"OK, OK, Let me make a phone call," grunted Bowen as he rather brusquely waved us out of his office, pointedly handing the envelope containing the mission coordinates to Alex, instead of Betty. Alex slipped the envelope down Betty's jumper as we left the office, eliciting a giggle from her. I could see that Alex was trying to reassure Betty after Bowen's snub.

"He thinks the GPS is a top-secret device," laughed Betty as she closed the door back in their own office, "because I said military-grade! Every Tom, Dick and Harry in the military has one."

She extracted the envelope with a flourish from inside her jumper and opened it. "And the winning coordinates are:…" she announced. There was a pause as she sat down at a computer, brought up google maps and keyed in the coordinates. "It's inside the Ministry of Defence Bovington Camp in Dorset." She switched to the aerial view. "Looks like a single story building, judging by the shadow length, but it doesn't matter - they've given us the height above sea level."

She turned to face me. "George, dear, we're going to have a hell of a time breaking in to an army camp to fake this - you will help us, won't you, perhaps drive the getaway van or something?" She had me with the deadpan for a couple of seconds. Alex grinned.

"Only if we can use your Cabriolet," I parried.

"Oh, you want a ride in that - well actually I was going to ask you if you wanted to come on a journey with me tonight - you can do a bit of the driving if you like? But it's too cold to put the top down, of course."

This sounded too intriguing to say no to.

"Shall we try the first run now?" suggested Betty. Alex nodded and opened the inner door to go through and turn on the equipment. "It will be half an hour or so before the particle clouds are prepared and chilled, let's have a coffee." She leaned back languidly and switched on the coffee machine.

\* \* \*

About half an hour later, Bowen appeared at the office door with a small khaki-coloured bag, looking rather pleased with himself. "I got you a military-grade GPS," he announced to Alex with a slightly triumphal tone. "For god's sake, don't lose it. They didn't seem to think you needed an escort, but you'd better keep it hidden in a bag. Do you know how to use it? - They said it was fairly simple." He handed the bag to Alex, who pointedly handed it to Betty. Never one to miss a joke, Betty handed it to me, then took it back at the last second as I reached for it.

Bowen did not look pleased. "Don't drop it for god's sake."

"Don't I get a set of khakis to wear with it?" quipped Betty in her best deadpan.

Bowen sighed, "Look... No.... I've cleared it with security at the front door by the way, they know you'll be taking it out."

"That's a relief," Betty continued her deadpan. "I was thinking I would have to conceal it up my... um... jumper."

"I'll expect it back in the morning, then," concluded Bowen, "in one piece." He turned and went out the door. Betty saluted - I'm not sure whether he noticed.

"You are wicked to him," laughed Alex, shaking his head.

I was slightly uncomfortable with the way Betty scorned him, but I also remembered her explaining she only did such things in a well-intentioned way to loosen people up. I was not at all sure that would work on Bowen though - he seemed rather highly-strung. I determined to ask Betty about it again some other time.

"We can do a run now," declared Betty reading the temperature from a control screen to Alex. "This target is 133 kilometres pretty much due south from here. Whereas yesterday's target was North-West, so we're going to have to guess at the calibration correction from how far out we were in yesterday's run, and hope that the correction is the same to both the X and Y vectors; sorry George, in the East-West and North-South directions," she added for my benefit. They both looked at a print from yesterday's run at the bank of the

River Wye and debated how far west and south they were from dead-centre of the statue. I watched as Betty scribbled numbers on a pad and double-checked with a calculator before keying into that window with the 'Activate' button at the bottom. This time she was also keying in a time-shift, 22:47:00, which she had clearly calculated with respect to a stopwatch that she had started on another screen. The stopwatch counted down to zero, the button was pressed and the cloud of particles was silently projected back 22 hours and 47 minutes into yesterday, into an unseen single-story building in a military complex, near the Dorset coast; or so we all hoped. After a few seconds, the expected stream of data flowed onto the screen. I watched Alex's face as he leaned over Betty's shoulder. She was studying the numbers hard, scrolling up and down several times. "So there is a section from about here to here," she highlighted the section for Alex, "which looks fairly normal, but the rest seems to be mostly under-bleached. There is another bit of variation there." She pointed.

"I think it's interesting enough to be worth processing the picture," said Alex. "I can't see any point in trying to shift a metre or two to improve it, we don't know what the under-bleaching is, or which way to move to avoid it. Let's process it, have a good look at it tomorrow morning, and then when we've got the proper calibrations tomorrow, we can re-run it properly."

Betty sent the data to the super-computer. Then she stood and picked up the khaki bag containing the GPS receiver. "Go grab your coat, George - we have got a date. See you tomorrow Alex."

Betty concealed the khaki bag inside her coat, and strode toward the front door with me following. "Goodnight Fred," she smiled as she passed through the security area.

"Have a good evening Miss," he replied. He did not search her at all, but then, he had been told she was taking out equipment - maybe he realised it was beneath her coat, maybe not. The two of them seemed to have a certain rapport.

When we set off in her midnight-blue Cabriolet, I was not sure which of two presumed destinations she would head toward. I half-expected her to turn south, and head for the Ministry of Defence camp in Dorset. Although I could not think of a good reason for that, it was difficult to rule anything out with

Betty. It would have been a very long drive there and back. But in fact, she headed northwest toward the River Wye statue, presumably to measure its exact coordinates, and thus refine the calibration. Although she had not spelled this out to me - she probably thought it was obvious. I was also a little apprehensive whether she might be a crazy driver, matching the freer part of her personality, but in fact, she drove meticulously on both the motorway and then across the Wye valley. I knew this as a beautiful drive in daylight, and though it was dark by that time, the moon and stars helped mellow the domination of the headlights. After a comfortable hour's drive, we parked up in a small car park near Hereford town centre, by the river. She slung the khaki bag, with the GPS in it, over her shoulder, and linked arms with me. We began the walk along the towpath and it was only 3 or 4 minutes until we reached the statue.

She turned the GPS receiver on and placed it on the centre of the statue. She pulled a tiny notepad out of her skirt pocket and noted down the numbers, then she repeated the procedure with the GPS on the ground next to the statue. With the aid of a compass app on her smart phone, she checked the North-South direction, and then made me take photos with her smart phone, in a series of positions forward, backward and sideways, to try to duplicate the exact position which the experimental image had been taken from. At each position, she placed the GPS receiver next to the smart phone and copied the numbers into her notepad. She explained this would give her sufficient data to calibrate the laboratory equipment accurately. She replaced the GPS receiver in its khaki bag, and her notepad in her pocket. Job done, we sat down on the bench.

There had been only a couple of passers-by whilst this strange ritual had been going on, and neither had seemed to pay us much attention. Now a middle-aged woman was approaching. Betty accosted her politely, and asked her if she would take a photo of us, sitting on the bench. Betty took some time explaining the exact position she wanted the woman to stand in, and the exact direction she wanted the photo taken. We sat together on the bench, she pulled my arm around her, and our photographer recorded the moment. It was a nice touch - a replica of the original, with us instead of the old man in the cap. Although it was dark instead of daytime, the flash on the camera would have ameliorated some of that difference. We sat there, for a while more, in silence, taking in the calmness of the water, the gentle rustle of the breeze in the trees, the Cathedral spires just visible above a thicket on the opposite bank.

"So tell me the story of the statue, George?" Betty whispered.

"OK, well, the dog was called Dan," I recounted. "He was a bulldog who belonged to George Sinclair, the organist of the Cathedral over there, and Sinclair happened to be a great friend of Edward Elgar, the celebrated composer. Elgar himself was a great dog-lover, but whilst he was married, his wife would not let him own a dog, so he used to walk Dan occasionally, or accompany his friend with the dog. One day in 1898, the two of them were walking the dog, or who knows, maybe even sitting just here, when the dog slipped on the edge, just at this spot, and fell down the bank into the water. The dog paddled upstream strongly to find a landing place, then made a 'rejoicing bark' on landing, and shook itself dry. Sinclair suggested to Elgar that he set that little episode to music, and he did so - it's the initial part of Variation XI of the Enigma variations. The statue came much later of course - it is carved wood."

"How do you remember all the details, George," asked Betty. "Is that what historians do?"

"Yes, I think historians do remember lots of little threads, to some extent anyway, joining things up. But this story I knew as a child. My parents brought me here, I can't remember why, and showed me this, and the statue of Elgar on the other side."

"You remember the statue," pursued Betty, "but you don't remember why you came here?"

"Well, my father was a historian too. He was always taking us to interesting places, where he was rooting around for scraps of history. I expect it was one of his excursions. But to be fair to him, he always managed to make it interesting for us too."

"So you didn't rebel then?" queried Betty.

"No," I admitted, "I am very conscious I followed in his footsteps, and I still find memories of him very comforting - his tweed jackets, the smell of his pipe - not that I have ever got into smoking. I carry round his old battered leather briefcase."

Betty sighed thoughtfully and shifted her position on the seat.

"Hey," I said. "I'm getting cold. Shall we go and find somewhere to eat?"

"No, we have to stay here for…," Betty looked at the time on her phone, "another 3 minutes 41 seconds."

"What. Why?"

"Because when you were all out of the office this morning, I programmed the equipment to take a future image of here at 19:00."

"Oh, What… and you want us in it?"

"No, I saw the picture. We *were* in it. I mean, we *will be* in it. And we have to be careful not to change the future - you remember what Alex said this afternoon, otherwise paradoxes will break loose and the world may end."

"What, that's not exactly what Alex said."

"No, but I did it before Alex warned about it, so I want to make sure the future is exactly as it was in the picture, then nothing can go wrong. OK?"

"Well, I suppose so." I was confused, not sure whether she was winding me up or not.

"Oh, and George, there is one other thing. In the image we were kissing."

I was still confused, but now *I didn't care* whether she was winding me up or not. That had stopped me thinking about it. I didn't need asking twice. The kiss was amazing. I felt like I was floating. Certainly, the desire had been growing inside me, but I had not yet openly acknowledged it to her or me. Now very suddenly everything felt good. As our lips gently parted, I was aware of footsteps close by. As I glanced up, there was the old man in the flat cap giving me a very strange knowing look. I was startled, the whole scene seemed too weird, and my heart started racing. Betty gave a sort of stifled scream. The man walked off.

"It was the man from the original picture," I gasped out.

"It must be just a coincidence," Betty shook her head. "He probably walks this way twice a day, we've been here half an hour, that's a one in 24 chance of bumping into him. Actually, there are probably half a dozen men in flat caps walk down here, that's a one in three chance, it's not that big a coincidence really."

But her statistical rationale did not sound very convincing to me, and certainly not reassuring. Why had he looked at me like that? A shiver went up my spine, and confusion, a feeling unfamiliar to me, filled my head. The last couple of days had been so full of events, unlikely events, it was hard to put them all together consistently, in the way I was used to, as a historian, cause and effect. Now I felt more like I was in a dream, and trembling.

"George, George... what's the matter?" Betty had cupped my head with her hands.

"I just feel so confused."

"Don't worry about it now. Tomorrow night is going to be really exciting, the Ministry of Defence complex is only surrounded by a wire fence. We'll take cutters, I know which building to run over to, a quick photo through the window, and out again. You keep the car running. It will be amazing fun. We only have to keep the hoax going for another few days. I've got a future image of next Saturday's winning lottery numbers. Then we can all jet off to somewhere and relax."

"But... is it real or... what are you telling me?... I can't... I'm just so confused," I was trembling profusely.

"Lie back on the bench George," now she was speaking tenderly, "close your eyes, relax, that's it, go back to when you were a child and felt that feeling. Go back. You are clutching at your coat sleeve, what is that? When you were a child... Tell me, say it..."

"It's... It's my father's tweed jacket sleeve," I whispered as I saw it, "he always told me the truth, he is always clear... But this can't be true, what he's saying, what he's saying about my mother, no it isn't true, but he always tells me the truth. It's so confusing... it's too confusing... I don't want to hear it."

"What is he saying about your mother, George, what is he saying?"

"He says that my mother has died... No... she can't be gone... she is always here when I need her... she mustn't be gone... it can't be true... He told me my mother had died, but... ," then resignation, "... OK, it's true, my mother has died." The crying came now, and the sobs, deep from inside, buried for three decades, the confusion broken, the truth finally accepted. I cried and sobbed for a few minutes, lying there, Betty's hand on my chest giving encouragement, and a little comfort. Finally, I felt calmness and I cleared my throat. Betty handed me some much-needed tissues, and I cleaned up my face, then sat up gently and took a couple of deep breaths. Despite the preceding drama, I now felt rather content.

I turned to face Betty. "What just happened?" I looked into her face for answers, but I felt no confusion now.

"That," started Betty "was a catharsis. I am afraid you may be cross with me when I explain… So, to begin with, I was just winding you up - I hadn't taken a future picture, of course. But you have such an organised mind, always trying to sort out cause and effect, pigeon-holing the truth. I had noticed that when something happens which challenges that order, and introduces confusion, you look worried and do that thing where you rub your sleeve. And it seemed such fun to make that up that tale about a future-picture. And earlier in the day, I had the idea about the man in the cap. I have connections in amateur dramatics you see, and it was really quite easy to find an actor to do that little cameo part, for a small fee - to walk past here at the time I had pre-planned, and give a quizzical look. But it seemed to hit you *much* harder than I thought it would, it kind of, went beyond a joke. So when I saw you were very confused in a distressed emotional way, and so close to getting in touch with that big feeling, I thought it was an opportunity that might not come again for you, so I dug up, and said, all the most confusing things I could think of, to push you deeper into confusion. By rights, I shouldn't have done it, but I took the risk and sure enough, you were so close to the core feeling, that I could guide you straight into the catharsis. You are safe with me, I learnt well from my mother. I'm sure you will feel easier now about things that don't immediately make sense, you will probably still experience confusion occasionally, but not as a general tension anymore, it won't be that unpleasant feeling. You have every right to be cross with me for pranking you with the story about the future-picture, and the actor in the flat cap, though to be honest I still think that's hilarious." She threw her head back and laughed briefly. "But pushing you further when you got distressed, with all that deliberately contradictory nonsense about adventures and hoaxes and lottery tickets; well, I had no right to do it without your permission. But then, to ask your permission would probably have broken the opportunity. And because we are working on a project that stretches credibility, the opportunity for confusion is magnified. So, I hope you'll forgive me, I meant well for you. I really do hope you'll forgive me, George, because I really am very fond of you?"

I was actually feeling quite serene now, listening to Betty's explanation. "And the kiss?" I finally said, "Was that real or a wind-up?"

"That was real," she whispered, sounding sincere. "I wanted it, and thought that would be an amusing way to get to it?… So are you angry with me?"

I smiled at her without saying anything. "Well, you really are most thoroughly exciting to be with, Miss Betty Gosmore, never a dull moment, I just hope I can keep up with you. I suppose I should really think of some inventive way to wind you up, in return, but right now, my head is feeling just pleasantly empty. So, no, I'm not cross with you. Here." I drew her close and we kissed again.

"This time it's *me* that's getting cold," said Betty at length, "shall we go, find somewhere to eat? But no wine, if you want to drive the Cabriolet back."

"OK," I concurred, "and on the way, I'll walk you past the bronze statue of Elgar, on the other side of the river, by the Cathedral. He's leaning back on his bicycle, admiring the Cathedral - its one of the most inspired statues I know."

# Chapter 4
## Of boots, guns, clocks and sparks

### *WEDNESDAY 23 NOV*

The next morning I made sure I got in early, I did not want to miss the unveiling of yesterday afternoon's attempted retrospective image of the military's target. Bowen was in early too, and when he saw me, he asked whether we had made any progress on the military's request yet. I told him that we had completed the GPS coordinate measurements last night, so we would be able to do accurate calibration today, though I told him none of the details of that remarkable evening. I added that Alex and Betty had done a trial-run image yesterday, before the accurate calibration, so they might have missed the actual target, and that indeed it had sounded to me from their discussion when they were looking at the preliminary data, that only parts of the image were present. Bowen was clearly itching for results and said he would pop in to their office later. I wasn't sure whether it was right for me to be briefing him on what Alex and Betty were doing, but I didn't think I had said very much of significance.

Betty was in before Alex. The coffee machine went on first. Then the computer screen. I stood behind her chair and gently put my hands on her shoulders as she studied the screen. "Not in the *office*, George," was the only response. I withdrew my hands, and looked over her shoulder. The image seemed strange to me - the bottom centimetre or so was completely black, and most of the right of the image was blacked out, delineated by stark vertical lines. The bulk of the rest of the image was a fairly monotone grey, with a grid laid out, in perspective, on it. But following Betty's pointed finger I could make out what looked very much like a military boot towards the top left corner. That clue made it easy for Betty to interpret.

"First of all we are looking from about ground level. The bottom centimetre of the image is actually within the ground - the height above sea level they gave us must have been literally ground level. This large blacked out area on the right is a wall - the particle cloud got positioned partly *in* the wall, and partly viewing the room. That other vertical black stripe may be a chair or desk leg, and the floor is tiled giving that grid pattern. But we got a good booted-foot!"

At that point, Bowen came in the office door. I wondered if the image would be enough to satisfy him. To my surprise, Betty welcomed him in, calling him Phil, and sat him down in the chair in front of the computer screen, going through the interpretation in detail again with him. She explained that now they had a more accurate calibration available, which should adjust the positioning by a few metres, and of course then raising the viewing height by a couple of metres, should enable them to visualise the correct target.

"And you'll have time to do all that?" queried Bowen.

"Sure," Betty replied, "and while you're here, Phil, there is something you can help us with." Betty was not as convincing as Alex, but it was difficult to resist her enthusiasm. I waited to find out what she was after.

"As you know, Phil, it is taking a long time on the GCHQ supercomputer to process these pictures, even though we are still not trying to use our full resolution capability yet, which would take exponentially longer - so for example, if I doubled the resolution it would take about 4 times as long. Although the IT department has been very generous to us so far, I know we are putting pressure on their scheduling, and if we ask for lots more processing they may not be able to accommodate us. Most of the problem is that their computer is not really suitable for processing these pictures - what we really need is a SIMD computer - that stands for Single-Instruction-Multiple-Data. It's a sort of graphics processor that performs each instruction, not for each pixel of the screen *in turn*, but on a large number of pixels all *simultaneously*. I've already talked to Mike about it, and he said that if you could buy in say, a hundred GPUs for us - GPU stands for Graphical Processor Unit - then he could easily rack them up for us, and I could re-write the algorithm to process the pictures much faster on our own custom-built computer."

"A *hundred*?" Bowen started.

"Oh, they're not expensive," countered Betty, "look, I've costed it up with the details of the equipment on this sheet. If you check with the IT department, I'm sure they will confirm that it will save them more money in the long run, since we won't be taking so much time on their machine. And it means we can get our own pictures processed much more quickly, so if we have to take a series of pictures we can get them done same day, and not have to wait a week."

"So how many pictures could we do each day with this," asked Bowen.

"Well, we are limited by the speed of cooling a cloud of particles - that's the slowest part of the process, so perhaps 8 outdoor pictures or 12 indoor pictures a day, and that GPU array would enable us to keep up with that many.... Oh, here is your military GPS unit by the way, thanks for the loan." She handed over the khaki bag. I silently wondered if she had replaced the GPS with something like a stone, as a prank. But perhaps today she was about getting something from Bowen rather than winding him up.

"OK," Bowen rose from the chair. "I'll talk to the IT department and check with Alex later. Let me know when you get the next image through."

After he left, Betty shook her head, "*I'll check with Alex later,*" she mimicked his voice. "He just can't take women seriously, have you noticed? Or is it just me, am I not convincing enough?"

I laughed. "It may just be that Alex is *very* convincing, so Bowen naturally gravitates toward Alex's opinion. But I agree Bowen doesn't treat you respectfully. I don't know the full history of your conversations with him though. Maybe he doesn't take to your jokes?"

"Mmm... Well, I need to get on and do those calibration calculations, ready for Alex to double-check." I took the hint and went back to my own office.

\*     \*     \*

The next picture, again of last Monday, but taken after the re-calibration, was something of an anti-climax, when I was invited into Alex and Betty's office to see it during the afternoon. There was a table, and on the table was a gun, probably not standard issue, I thought, looking at it briefly, though I was no expert. They both seemed satisfied that the image was now of the correct location, although that could only be actually verified by the military. The equipment was being readied to take today's, Wednesday 18:00 picture. Apparently, Betty had suggested trying to take it ahead of time - as a trial image from the future, but Alex still felt that accessing the future should be tested by simple experiments first.

"Actually, George," started Alex, "do you have one of those alarm clocks which shows the date, as well as the time - it would be ideal for tests - but neither of *us* have one?"

"No, I haven't either," I replied, "but if you like I'll go down to the shopping centre and get one now. You two are busy and the least I can do is be a 'gofer'!"

"Thanks," Alex smiled, "that would be great, just give the receipt to Bowen and he'll reimburse you in due course - unfortunately the admin wheels grind rather slowly here. Get one with a nice big display, then we can run at a lower resolution to save computer time."

"So what do you think, George," chipped in Betty, "shall we drive down to Dorset tonight, break into the Ministry of Defence place, and check whether we got the right picture?"

We both laughed, but Alex just grinned, not being party to the profundity of the joke. "You'd better add wire-cutters to the shopping list then, George," he added.

\*     \*     \*

I was hoping to find a clock shop to hunt around in - that would have been the romantic way to do it, but I had to settle for scouring department stores, and most of the clocks just gave the date as an afterthought, generally in very small letters. I did finally find one that looked the part, proudly announcing the day of the week at the top in large letters, with morning, afternoon, evening or night on the second line. I found out from the shop assistant that it was intended for people with dementia, who, I knew from personal experience with my own father in his final days, have trouble with timekeeping. She assured me that it made no mention of dementia or Alzheimer's in the instruction booklet or packaging, which did seem thoughtful toward the intended users, even though irrelevant to us. The clock seemed very expensive for what it was, but I rather liked the juxtaposition of using a clock that was intended for dementia sufferers, in the world's most advanced scientific experiment. I had been rather lazy cooking for myself since arriving in Gloucester, so I decided to make a proper meal that night, and, carrying on shopping, bought Barnsley chops and vegetables.

\*     \*     \*

The last two nights had been very exciting, so after eating my hearty homemade meal, I found myself restless and rather at a loss for what to do. Then came a knock at the door. I was very surprised to see Alex.

"Hi Alex, I didn't know you knew where I lived," I started.

"Hi George," he mysteriously put his finger to his lips, "Betty told me your address - she knew from dropping you off the other night. I wondered if you fancied a pint or two this evening?"

"Oh sure," I said, "That would be great, I was feeling at a loose end."

I put on my coat, and we went out the main door. Again, Alex insistently put his finger to his lips. I had no idea why, but I obediently said nothing as we walked out, and I saw Betty sitting in the Cabriolet. The boot opened and Alex gestured for me to put my coat in there - I noticed that their coats were in the boot too.

We drove off and they made polite conversation asking whether I had seen the beautiful countryside near Cheltenham, and indeed that seemed to be where we were heading, although it was dark by now. Despite the clandestine atmosphere, I trusted these two completely, so I felt intrigue and excitement, but no fear. Alex kept me occupied with aimless chat about this and that, and I was fairly sure he didn't want me to say anything of import, so I played along. After about 20 minutes drive, we parked by a gate on a narrow lane, and got out of the car. Alex gestured to me to take one of the blankets, which were stacked on the back seat, took one for himself, and put another round Betty's shoulders, then they led me off across a field, and up a hill. The moon was to the West, which gave a little light, though the copses and hedges were only really visible as dark shapes. Looking back, there was a vast stretch of city lights shimmering, the beauty of which can only be appreciated when looking down from a distance. We all stopped near the top of the hill huddled in our blankets, looking back, enjoying the contrast of the empty countryside to the buzz of the city in the distance.

Betty was standing between us, and she closed the silence by putting an arm around each of us and saying, "Brethren, we are gathered here together to…umm… Alex, why *are* we gathered here together?"

"I apologise for dragging you both out here," started Alex, "I needed for us to have a private conversation, private from GCHQ. And I have no idea how much surveillance we are under - the office is probably bugged, maybe our homes and the cars, and although I am no expert on surveillance I imagine overcoats are fairly easy to put bugging devices into, since they are thick - hence the blankets, George." I nodded and smiled. "But I am fairly sure we are private up here, out of range of anything I can imagine, and we can see any vehicle approaching from a long way off. That may all sound a bit paranoid, but imagine yourselves in GCHQ management's shoes, a revolutionary surveillance device in the offing, you would want to be sure the staff on the project were totally loyal. If the surveillance isn't in place yet, my guess is it will be as soon as the military see the results of their 'test'. We'll drive back in a while for an 'alibi' drink somewhere, to allay any possible suspicions."

"So are we *not* totally loyal?" Betty asked softly, and the same question was on my tongue.

"Well, when we first discovered the i-vector, Betty, we knew it had massive consequences, and that's why we agreed it would be safer in GCHQ's hands than in academia, or any other option we could think of. And I think that's still true, at least as regards the remote surveillance, and surveillance of the past. But I am seriously concerned about putting surveillance of the *future* into the hands of GCHQ. We haven't done the experiments yet, so let's first think about the possible outcomes:

"Firstly, it's possible that when we try to take an image of the future that there is nothing there - no image - the particle cloud may be projected into the future, but there is nothing there yet for the cloud to interact with, hence no picture. If that's the case, I will give a sigh of relief, (though I might be a little disappointed inside,) and can carry on telling GCHQ the truth. And indeed this meeting would not have been necessary.

"Secondly, it's possible that we *do* get an image from the future. Then comes the question of whether we can intervene in the future. If we deliberately decide to change what would be in the picture, put a different vase of flowers there, so to speak, then clearly that changes the future. Presumably the original image would stay the same, so we are dealing with different strands of the future, the original image would represent a particular strand of the future which never actually came to exist, never came to fruition.

"But thirdly the image might change, in our hand, to show the new vase of flowers. So maybe we could switch the vases over and over, and watch the image changing as we do it. Or maybe we could just think about changing the vase, and the intention itself would be enough to change the image in our hand. It would be a bit like choosing which version of the multiverse we wanted to run with. Or perhaps we would be unaware of the image changing - it would be as if it had *always* shown the second vase, and we would not be consciously aware that we had changed our mind, and therefore changed the future, because our brains would only know the current version of the future. In fact, that's a bit like the way we operate in the *ordinary* world, we decide what we want to do, based on what we *think* the future would be like as a consequence of what we do.

"And fourthly, some physicists believe that the future is already predetermined, so that, try as we might, there is no way we could actually change the vase of flowers to a different one. But I can't, myself, see how that is compatible with getting a picture, that is *information*, from the future - there would always be the impulse to use that information from the future, to change it, to a subjectively better future.

"But, most amazing of all, we can work out which of these possibilities is correct, by doing a few simple experiments, in a couple of days, with a clock and two vases of flowers. For me as a physicist it will be the most amazing couple of days of my life.

"However, I think it will take longer than that to determine if it is a safe option to let GCHQ have access to see the future, so that they could maybe change that future. What does it do to democracy, if they can see the election result before it happens? If they know the winner of every bet? Are they going to repeatedly change the future until they get what they want? What does that do to the free will of the rest of us? So I really want to hear from you guys whether you think the ability to see the future, and secondly, to change the future, is a capability that should be passed on to GCHQ, if it turns out to be possible?"

"Woo," cooed Betty. "But how could we not pass on the capability to GCHQ if the results show it. If you walked away, they would just get in more physicists; if you blow the equipment up, they'll just get it re-built…"

"I'm suggesting," replied Alex, "that we tell them it's not possible to get an image from the future - give them a couple of blank pictures to 'prove' it, act disappointed, whether the experiments actually show positive, or negative results."

"Uh, um," countered Betty, "but when they expand the team, any new physicists will be bound to try it - you'd have to be a very uncurious scientist not to try it, even if you believed Alex's results."

"Well, yes," admitted Alex, "but we can delay any expansion of the team by giving the management everything else they ask for - it should buy a lot of time."

We all laughed as we heard the unintended pun.

"What do you think George?" asked Betty. "You've got a special viewpoint on this, knowing so much about history."

"Well," I started slowly, "knowledge of the future, and using it to change that future, is something completely outside of the familiarity of a historian - I feel very unprepared for the question. But within history, there are cases where special powers are available to the few, and it usually doesn't work out well. I think you are right, Alex, that giving a power like that to a few within GCHQ, and the elite military and politicians who run it, would be a magnet for corruption, the misuse of it would be irresistible, or so history suggests to us. On the other hand, it doesn't sound like the sort of technology that could be made available to everyone, although that's what was thought about computers in the early days, and look where we are now. And if it were widely available, as you intimated, it would radically change our experience of life. Indeed, it would change the meaning of life itself. I have the same feeling as you - the curious part of me hopes that the experiments will give a positive result, but the wiser part thinks it probably would be an anathema to human life experience. I really feel the need to think about the question for a few days. Maybe your delaying tactic at least enables us to think it all through. The other thing I would say now is that you can't *un-invent* things. Even if you were to abandon or hide the project now, there would be other physicists who would discover the process at some point, months, years, or decades ahead, and then the same questions arise - are they going to publicise it, or will it end up in the hands of some arbitrary elite. At some point it *will* be used, it *has* to be a part of the future of humanity."

Betty interjected "Hmmm... that makes our problem sound as if it's intractable. Our only way out would be to pass the buck to someone else."

"Really," I said, "we are into the realm of ethics - talking of which, Bowen is an ethicist by trade, but I don't suppose you think he would be any help with this?"

Betty snorted.

Alex shook his head. "He is part of the management of GCHQ - his main concern is always to look good to his seniors, he would never withhold anything from them - he has no interest in acting ethically, *independently* of them. We absolutely must not give him wind of this. He would shop us without batting an eyelid."

Betty nodded. "He is actually not very bright either, undergraduate ethics course, no help there."

"It also matters," I added, "which one of the options that Alex outlined, turns out to be the way the physics actually works. Some of the options are more innocuous than others. It's a bit difficult working out what is the best course of action, without knowing *precisely* what we are dealing with."

"OK, then," Alex seemed to want to draw the conversation to a conclusion. "So I intend to tell GCHQ that the experiments on future-pictures indicate that it's not possible, whether the results are positive or negative. You will both have to play along with that in the lab, in fact everywhere, except up here. George, I don't want to pull you into a compromising situation, so if you don't want to be involved in any further private discussions like this, just say so now, and we'll forget this evening ever happened."

"No," I said, "on the contrary, I feel very engaged with this, please include me in any private meetings, I really want to know what is happening, and to help if I can, even if it's only being someone to bounce ideas off."

"Thanks," responded Alex. "That's good to know. Of course, if the results of the experiments are negative, then we will probably never need another private meeting. But if we do, then I'll use that phrase *'a pint or two'* and you'll know I'm coming. Betty and I already have a code word that we set up before coming here. If anyone should ask, we just came up here for a breath of fresh air and to admire the view before going to the pub, OK?"

"OK," I replied

"*Roger*," said Betty using military slang.

And we trudged off back down the grassy slope, three figures in the dark, draped in blankets, with the weight of the future on our minds, off to the pub for a *real* 'pint or two', with Betty breathily singing 'Somewhere only we know'.

\*   \*   \*

## THURSDAY 24th November

I woke rather later than usual, having been troubled by some strange dreams in the night, which I couldn't quite recall. It was again cold, but, carrying a bag with the clock in it, I walked the half-hour from my accommodation to the office, hoping the chill of the air would clear my head.

"I'm afraid you can't bring that in, sir," the door security guard said blankly. "But I was specifically asked to buy a clock, and bring it in, by Alex and Betty in BH9," I responded, "You can check with them."

"I'm afraid neither of them have the authority to allow it sir."

"What about Phil Bowen?" I tried.

"Yes, but he's not in this morning, sir, as of yet, I think he said he would be in at lunchtime today."

"Well, look, it's still boxed, unopened, the shrink-wrap is still intact, it hasn't been tampered with?" He shook his head.

"Well can I leave it here until Mr Bowen gets in?" I tried.

"I'm afraid not, sir, leaving things here unattended is definitely not allowed."

"Well, what do you suggest I do with it then?" I tried to make it his problem.

"You could leave it in your car until Mr Bowen gets in?"

"No, I walked in, I don't have the car with me," I countered.

"You've all got smart phones, so why do you need a clock anyway, sir?" His suspicion was actually well founded.

"I'm afraid," I replied, "that I'm not at liberty to discuss *why* we need it." I slightly felt I was getting my own back with that.

He opened both his palms in a gesture that said, 'Your problem mate.' Though to be fair to him, he had been polite throughout, and was obviously following rules, not of his own making. It was indeed *my* problem, my frustration. I turned and walked back out with the clock. I was in no hurry. I would walk back home and leave it there. Then I could decide whether to walk back in again or drive in.

As I walked, I idly wondered if I could have avoided this problem if I could see the future. No, because it was not a specific event that I would have chosen to examine by picturing it. Indeed, an image of me talking to security would not, in any case, reveal what was being said. I suppose if I had worried whether I could get the clock through security, then I could have tried to image me and the clock just after going through security, but that presupposes that I thought there might be a problem, in which case I could have done something about it anyway. The situation was not *foreseen*, in both senses of the word - the old sense, in which our brains extrapolate to predict the future as best they can, and the new supra-modern literal sense, which only those, party to BH9, knew about.

I continued to walk and think. So maybe the future would not be *so* different if we *could* choose to see it. How often would we choose or bother to look? Only for the important things may be, so all the little surprises, trials and tribulations of life would still be there. Just the important things would be guaranteed. Or would they? I carried on systematically examining the possibilities as I walked. Some pictured events would be fairly definite, like scheduled public events, and not very easily, or likely, changed by an arbitrary individual; Other pictured events would be more ephemeral, like *where* a specific individual was standing or which way he was facing, and obviously the attendance of an individual at an event could be altered at his or her discretion. Accidents maybe could still intervene before a pictured event - an accident usually requires a combination of coincidences, each unlikely in its own right.

But no betting of course, the bookmakers would be out of a job in one stroke. And investment would no longer be a speculation; the markets would know where they were going. Although we would not know which new ventures *might* have succeeded had they been funded - there would still be opportunity for skill-based risk and reward there. And no competitive sport? What would be the point in playing or watching if you knew the result? We would be like actors, acting out the plot, in a movie that we had already seen.

But, on the other hand, maybe people would deliberately abstain from getting pictures from their future, so that they could, all the more, *enjoy* the experience of living. If you don't know the result of the football match you are playing in, then it's fun again, and you are motivated to try hard. After all, people have a fair idea of the future by extrapolating anyway; It's part of what we do to hone our decision-making.

And what about those legendary winning lottery numbers? The process of ball selection is chaotic - as the mathematicians would tell us. The slightest difference in vibration or gesture or timing when the balls are being loaded, a microscopic difference in timing when the selection is triggered, maybe even the vibration of footsteps around the machine would ensure a completely different result. So, maybe a prediction of something chaotic, by picturing the future, would not work definitively.

Maybe you'd know when you were going to die - that's a strange one. So, you could take more risks before then? But then you would certainly be more likely to change the future by taking more risks.

By the time I reached home, or at least the minimalist apartment that served for home at the moment, I was tending to the view that the ability to occasionally image a future, which could anyway be changed by choosing to act differently, would not be too radical an adjustment to the life of the man in the street. And it was perhaps unlikely to radically disrupt the current nature of everyday existence.

I was cold by now and the priority was to have a mug of hot chocolate before setting off again. As I gradually warmed with the soothing drink, I began to wonder about what Alex had said about our homes maybe being bugged. This apartment had been provided for me by GCHQ anyway, so it would have been very easy for them to 'plumb' in a device. In the old days, a bug would have been put in the phone, but no one bothers with a landline these days. I wandered slowly round the apartment with my hands encompassing the warm mug, taking comforting sips, and aimlessly and fruitlessly looking for signs of a device. Then I ran my thumb and fingers along the seams of my overcoat to see if I could feel a telltale bulge. I found nothing. But I also felt rather unconcerned whether I was bugged or not - in the rare event that Alex, Betty and I wanted to have a private conversation, we had a meeting place for that. Otherwise, I had nothing to hide or be ashamed of. I had always valued openness rather than privacy anyway.

It was beginning to feel like the extra walking and thinking time was paying dividends. My head was clearing as I thought through the questions raised by the private conversation yesterday evening. I was reasonably sure that the future pictures would not be overly disruptive to the man in the street if he ever gained access to that capability. I was unconcerned about the possibility of being under surveillance, and I had dismissed thinking about the possibility of a *fixed* future - it didn't seem to make sense. I therefore decided, as I walked back into the office again, to focus on thinking about that more difficult, and thorny, problem where a novel capability is kept secret, and is only in the hands of the elite.

I started with the issues around democracy. The elite of a ruling party might visualise the election result. That gave them the opportunity to stick with their message, or try something else and re-visualise the result. However, importantly, they could not undo any part of their message so far, or anything they had added to it. Nor could they undo their record in office. And it might be difficult for a political party to make big changes to its message without justifying it to the rest of their party, when, of course, they couldn't reveal the reason that they were proposing changes - that they had looked at the future. I came to the opinion that the advantage was very marginal - considering that the parties already have access to opinion polls and sophisticated voting intention analysis, which give much the same guidance.

There would also be the temptation, to the elite, in control of foresight, to make money by gambling or investing in assured futures. However, there always have been ways in which the elite can, and sometimes do, break with ethical practice, to make money. The foresight technology would no doubt be surrounded with safeguards against selfish use.

If a government had the ability to read the front page of the newspaper printed any day in the future, then it would probably be able to better govern, because it would have forewarning of disasters, problems, economic trends etc. Major crimes could be foreseen and prevented. Whilst being able to get pictures from the *past* would help in solving the less salient crimes that would still happen.

Then the issues to do with military use. It would be possible to foresee unexpected military movements, or first strikes, and thus deter them. It would be possible to see adversaries' novel weapons, and more effectively defend against them. It would be possible to foresee the effects of an intervention, and therefore make better-informed judgements about intervening. If the ability to image the future were in the hands of an adversary, our own technological advancements would be countered and plagiarised. But overall, the capability to image the future would favour balance of power, eliminating surprises, increasing transparency. It might tend to discourage an arms race, as powers would be disincentivised to try for novel technological weaponry, knowing that their adversaries would inevitably foresee their technology.

However, I could see a new strand of absurdity here. If a technologist from the future laid out his plans and designs in a methodical way, so that his past self could image those future technological designs, then the technological development could be telescoped, could be accelerated massively; inventions could be facilitated before their time was due. Had Alex thought about that? - If he laid out the results of his week's work on a particular table every Monday morning, then his past self could view that future work, and get to design advanced systems much more quickly - maybe moving ahead, improving black and white still pictures, getting to full motion colour video with audio? There must be something illogical here - how could technology continuously benefit from written experimental results, when the experiments to produce those results had not actually been done. But I suppose those experiments *had* been done, but in a different version of the timeline. It's just that passing knowledge of those results back to someone in the past, had made doing the experiments unnecessary, in *their* current timeline. I supposed it is not very different from the everyday situation of a scientist, reading results from experiments done by someone else, and using those results to inform his own new experiments. However, this potential massive acceleration of technological advance was perhaps the most troubling strand of my thinking so far.

The area around where we worked seemed to be devoid of cafes, but I had noted a pleasant one, about half way, on the route walking from home, so I decided to break the walk, and have an early lunch there. I sat at a table by the window and watched the traffic flowing by, punctuated by traffic lights and right-turns; people walking by, stopping to cross the road, occasionally disappearing into doorways. Although every instant was different in its particular arrangement of vehicles and pedestrians, the overall pattern was tediously the same, offering no real interest, and no outstanding event to differentiate one moment from any other, or make any one moment more important than any other. Indeed, I was just another customer, they must have hundreds each day, some of whom sat in this seat, some on the others, eating their way through a parade of very similar and unremarkable sandwiches. Nothing worth picturing here, I thought, maybe ever. Maybe this is the nature of time, most of it just flows by, unremarkable and unexceptional, but there also exist rare moments and places of import, worth picturing, able to be learned from. However, I supposed a 25th Century historian might value this image from a coffee shop window, showing the tedious detail of life in the 21st century, as indeed I might value an image of humdrum life in the iron-age. So, out of context, even monotonous moments could be informative.

I picked up a couple of extra sandwiches, avoiding mayonnaise, for Betty and Alex - they had been more than generous to me with their lunches, and set off on the final walking leg. It was the same security guy when I arrived at the door.

"Did you sort the clock, sir? Mr Bowen is in now if you need him to authorise it." He waved the handheld metal detector over the sandwiches lazily and smiled. Clearly, I had not sorted it - I could have carried it back in, anticipating Bowen's arrival, or I could have *driven* back in, and stored it in the car, but my mind had not been on the clock problem. I felt as if I had spent the last two hours judiciously thinking about bigger issues, and was satisfied with the result.

I walked into Alex and Betty's office. Betty was busy keying into her computer. "How did the second military image look then?" I asked.

"Same table, different gun," she said indolently, and faked a yawn without looking up. I put the sandwiches with their others on the side table. The inner door was open, so I went through assuming Alex was there.

He was pinning up a couple of pages of a broadsheet newspaper to the wall.

"Hi Alex, I gather the second military image wasn't very interesting?"

He smiled and ran his fingers through his black hair. "Well, it was a good picture, clear as a bell, we got the cooling temperature just right for the ambient light, but it was very similar to their other picture in content. Bowen was pleased, though. He rang his military brass boss who came straight over. A loud guy, didn't meet him, but you could hear him through the door. Apparently he was amazed with the proofs, took them with him back to HQ. Then Bowen came in a little while ago and said they were fast-tracking Betty's new graphics super-computer, and would we now prioritise finding out how far we can increase the resolution."

"That surprises me," I said, "surely the pictures are pretty clear as they are?"

"Oh, I think they are after being able to read documents on desks, so the more resolution the better," he explained.

"Oh, I see... and hence the newspapers?

"Exactly." He stood back and looked at the print on the wall. "So it's actually an interesting set of experiments. We can try using more and more particles in the clouds, and we can also try varying the energy we give the particles, or more precisely the amount of cooling we do before projecting them. But the more densely packed the particles are, the more quickly they will go unstable by interacting with close-by air molecules, or each other. If I was back at the university I would try to work out the theoretical density/resolution function first, so we could predict the 'sweet spot', but it's probably going to be just as quick to do a series of pictures at different densities and energies to deduce it."

"Right... Oh, I got a really stylish clock for the time experiments by the way, but I couldn't get it past the security guys at the door."

Alex laughed. "Yes, sorry, I should have thought of that and warned you - if you have a word with Bowen, he'll OK it for you. Where is it now?"

"At home," I informed him.

"Oh well, not to worry," sighed Alex, "the time experiments have to take back seat to the resolution experiments at the moment anyway, orders from the military."

"I did a lot of thinking about the impact that the future pictures might have, while I was walking," I continued.

Alex raised an eyebrow and gave me a quick, intense look, clearly worried that I might say something untoward, in the possibly bugged environment of the lab. "Go on."

I smiled to reassure him that I was aware of the limitations on what I should say. "Well, have you realised that if you make a rule that you will write out your week's experimental results, and leave them on the same place on your desk on the same day every week… "

"Then the *future* me can feed back details of advanced science to the *present* me, enabling me to win a Nobel Prize!" interjected Alex laughing.

"Yes, but the process means that technological advancement is enormously accelerated because the results of experiments can be learned without the experiments needing to be done in the current timeline," I added excitedly.

"Which is just the sort of paradox," insisted Alex, "which makes me very dubious about whether *actual* physics would *actually* allow pictures from the future. The idea of transferring information from future to present, probably violates thermodynamic and entropy laws."

"Right," continued Alex in a tone that clearly drew a line under that conversation, "would you like to be *in* this picture, George? It's time we made you famous. Just stand *next* to the news pages… A bit more to the left. We've ramped up an extra dense pair of particle clouds, and they should be sufficiently cooled by now to have a go. I'll go back next door and key in the coordinates, and give you a shout when to smile."

He left me alone in the room with the whirring and humming of equipment. I had never liked posing for photos, and now I felt that same awkwardness. I wondered how long Alex would be. I remembered that the last photo I had been in, was the one Betty had engineered of us, sitting together on the bench with my arm round her. I had not seen that photo yet; I must remember to ask her to show it to me... Still no Alex. If it had been Betty, I would have expected a wind up - her leaving me here for ages waiting for nothing. But not Alex surely? I might not be able to hear him call from the other room anyway, it was fairly noisy with all the equipment in here. Perhaps he had already done it... His head appeared round the door at last.

"OK, I'm going to activate now, George, smile!" I was not going to smile. I would look serious and distinguished. I stood very still, though I had no reason to believe these pictures would blur with movement. Of course, I knew there would be no shutter sound, but maybe there would be an extra whirr or hum or something.

There was a spark. But it wasn't on or in the equipment, it was in midair, in front of me, or had I imagined it? It had made a sparky sound too. A little high-pitched crack. I had not expected that.

Alex's head appeared round the door again. "All done George, do you want a coffee?" I followed him back into the office.

"There was a spark," I said blankly.

"What? A spark?" repeated Alex, "Surely not, where?"

"In the air in front of me," I reported.

Betty abruptly stopped her keying, and looked round at Alex, whose brow had furrowed.

"In the ai.." Alex swallowed the last word. "Show me exactly where."

We all trooped back into the equipment room, and I attempted to recreate the direction where I thought I had seen the spark fly.

"OK, well, the position," agreed Alex, "does suggest the spark came from the projected cloud. I hadn't expected that, because the amount of energy in the actual cloud is still fairly minimal, even though we have ramped up the number of particles. But when we project the cloud of particles into air, there must be a chance that some particles, will be so close to some air molecules, that there is a massive repulsion. In a sense, we are creating surplus kinetic energy by putting the two collections together without them having equilibrated together. And there might be some nuclear reaction when one particle slams into another, or more likely an air molecule - that's an area we haven't explored yet. Either way we must be getting some particles energised sufficiently to cause some molecular ionisation - to rip electrons off the molecules, and hence a spark.

"So Betty, we had better observe each activation we do in here, best with the lights out, and score each spark subjectively, if there is one, so that we can get some idea what densities and energies are causing it. But what worries me most at the moment is whether the ordinary pictures, that we have already done, are creating a spark. Because, if they are, we need to inform the military straight away. It wouldn't be very subtle espionage if there were sparks flying in the Kremlin every time they do a picture."

It sounded funny, but we did not laugh because Alex was clearly concerned.

"Right," said Betty, "if we prepare and run a batch every 50 minutes, then we have got enough time left today to duplicate, in here, the settings for each of those military pictures 3 times - that should give us a pretty reliable indication whether there is sparking at those lower particle densities. We don't need to process all those pictures on the computer of course, we just need to witness each activation to look for sparking."

"Excellent," replied Alex, "if you organise that, Betty, I'll see Bowen and request urgent use of a spectrophotometer, so we can analyse the spectra that precedes the sparks. That will give us a good idea what molecules are involved in the reaction, George," he added by way of explanation for me. "Actually, I'll also see if I can get use of a hi-speed video camera - we might just get clues from that - it would be entertaining to watch anyway. Then I'll calculate the numbers in the thermodynamics equations - see if that helps predict when the problem might occur."

"I'll man the coffee machine." I joked, sensitive that I was not able to contribute much of substance. They laughed. "No, seriously, I'll do anything I can to help - do you want me to sit in the equipment room and watch for sparks when you activate?"

"It's OK," stated Betty, "I can activate with a time-delay so I can walk into the equipment room in time to observe. Oh... but you want to be with me in the dark!"

I smiled, but said nothing.

"You are supposed to deny that, George," she said in mock rebuke.

She had been scrolling through the data from the last activation, the one which had caused the spark. "We have got no image from that activation, by the way, Alex. It looks as if the cloud is too unstable at that density and temperature. But I guess we'll have to wait until next week to try some more variations. Let's prepare another batch and get on with the spark tests." She leaned over to the control screen and made a few keystrokes.

\*     \*     \*

And so it was, about 45 minutes later, that I found myself again standing next to the news pages, this time in the dark, for greater visual clarity of any sparks, waiting for an activation to occur. Betty had amended the computer software now, to count down from ten seconds to the activation, in a loud synthetic speech voice, which was still just audible in the equipment room with the door shut. Betty made it in with about 5 seconds to go, shut the door behind her, and came over to stand next to me, her warm hand finding mine... two... one... zero. Nothing, no spark.

"I didn't see anything," said Betty quietly. "Did you?"

"No," I agreed.

"You are *sure* there was a spark last time?" queried Betty.

"Um... yes, I am pretty sure," I replied.

"OK," said Betty, "well, I guess no spark is good news for the military. I'll go check the data is good, and start another batch. If we can do another 5 runs, paralleling the parameters of those military pictures, without any sparks, then Alex will sleep easier tonight." She slipped her hand out of mine and returned to the office.

And so it continued through the afternoon, 4 more runs without sparks. I gathered from Betty that science was often like this. The negative results were just as important as the exciting ones, important as controls, and in completing the scientific story. "Never mind," Betty reassured me, "next week we can try with higher particle densities, and see if we can get you some really big sparks!"

Then Bowen came into the office with news. Apparently, the military wanted to get started straight away using the equipment for surveillance. They wanted to build a duplicate of the particle generator and projection equipment for their own use. Alex suggested that it would be sensible to wait for a few days until he had finished the experiments on resolution, so that then they could build with the optimum design. Betty reminded Bowen that they would also need a duplicate of the proposed new graphics super-computer, and that they would need to incorporate gimbal mountings to enable the cloud to be projected from any orientation.

Then Bowen dropped the big surprise; that they also wanted to run a night-shift on *this* machine until their own equipment was ready, starting next week, and would Betty make a version of the software that was easy enough to be operated by a military technician, and train the operator on the equipment early next week. A night shift should not, he assured Alex and Betty, disrupt their development in any way.

I watched Alex and Betty's faces - I wondered if they might feel some resistance to this idea, since it was their 'baby' and their 'territory', but their faces only registered the expected surprise at the rapidity of the response from the top brass, and Betty agreed to modify the software first thing next week, ready for training.

I think it was actually myself, who felt the invasion more deeply - I had got fond of working with Betty and Alex, and it felt like the cosy environment would be disrupted by an outsider, even though, if the outsider were working at night, I supposed I would never meet them. I had also begun to realise I was on a 'cushy number' here, doing very little of worth, and if the organisation moved so fast, would they soon realise the irrelevance of my presence, and just discard me at some stage? That idea flooded me with sadness, I was so enjoying the time here, I felt my throat tighten.

The final test that afternoon also produced no spark, so Alex was happy to conclude that when the equipment was operated at the densities and energies normally used to get pictures, there was no telltale sparking. That meant it was OK for the military to use it operationally, at least on the validated settings checked so far. Next week should show if we could ramp up the resolution further.

# Chapter 5
## An unwelcome weapon

### *Friday 25th November*

When I got in on Friday morning there was a great deal of activity in their office. Betty was busy modifying the control software to be suitable for use by the military operative. Alex was still working on the theoretical basis of the projection, trying to understand what values of density and energy would give good pictures, and which would be unstable. I noticed that they already had a batch of particles in preparation - I had got quite used to the meaning of the indicators on the control screen, during the last week. There was crosstalk going on between Alex and Betty informing each other's tasks. I heard Alex reminding Betty that the time-shift should only be allowed to be zero or negative (i.e. present or past) for the military operations software, he was clearly still keeping a tight rein on that, until he had done the preliminary experiments on future shift. And on top of this, Mike was in again, working his way through a pile of cardboard boxes, extracting the graphics processors and installing them into a tall frame in the equipment room, leaving a mound of packing materials on the office floor. Clearly, when the management here talked about expediting an order, they really meant business.

There seemed to be an on-going debate between Alex, who was favouring mean free path calculations, and Betty, who was arguing that those measurements had little relevance to the sparking problem, and that statistical expression of proximity was the way to go. I asked what the terms meant - they always seemed happy to interpret for me, presumably because otherwise, secrecy forced their discussions to be very insular.

Alex explained that the 'mean free path' described the average distance that a particle or molecule could travel before it collided with another.

"So," he continued, "just after the particle cloud is projected into air, this distance would be very reduced because of crowding. And, although this would cause an increase in pressure, which has to relieve itself, and effectively means that the particles would be stable for a shorter time, it probably wouldn't account for enough energy to cause sparking.

"On the other hand, the more particles there are in the projected cloud, the more likely that particles will land almost on top of existing molecules in the air. The repulsive forces between any particle and molecule, rises exponentially, by the sixth power, as they get very close together. So that probably means a steep sudden rise in excess kinetic energy as the number of particles in the cloud is increased, and hence, perhaps, the sparking.

"Then there is another possibility, that if a particle happens to be projected to appear actually within the radius of an atom itself, within the electron cloud, or between the bulk of the electrons and the nucleus, then there would definitely be some *very high energy event*, but we've no idea what, because that's never been done in physics before. All the atom smashing that goes on in orthodox physics, is done by *colliding* things with each other. This is the first time in the exploration of physics, that things could be projected *inside* of other things, so to speak. So we have no way of calculating the consequence, as of yet.

"So," concluded Alex, "it means we will just have to do a large number of activations at different particle densities, and different energies, to find out where the dividing line between spark, and no spark, is. And whether that line is a clear, or fuzzy line. I mean whether it is clearly predictable."

"Best then," Betty cut in now, "to do a series of pilot activations with different particle densities, but all at *high* energy, because that involves *minimum* cooling time, and therefore we can get a lot done each day. Then we can try stepping back the energy by more cooling, which is time consuming, *only* on those results, which *do* cause sparking, but are close to densities that *don't*. That way we should be able to get to the line fairly quickly."

"Sounds like a plan," confirmed Alex. "How is the current cloud preparation coming on?"

"We're up to 80% max density, moderate cooling. Shall we lay down a marker?" asked Betty in reply, rubbing her hands together in anticipation. "We were at 60% yesterday, George, so we should definitely get a spark off this."

I remembered that I was the only one to have witnessed a spark so far, hence Betty's enthusiasm. She was already hustling Mike, in the equipment room, to move the half-finished rack towards the wall, so that we could all fit in to watch the spectacle. She explained briefly to Mike what we were looking for, as he walked the rack aside, and then she retreated back into the office to prepare the activation, switching off the equipment room lights as she went.

Mike, Alex and I lined up against the wall. Then we heard the synthetic voice start counting down from ten, and Betty rushed back into the equipment room, closing the door behind her, and lining up with us, with a bit of a squash, in the relative darkness. Three… Two… One…

A very bright flash, blue with a tinge of purple, accompanied by an ear-splitting crack, but it was gone again in an instant. We had all instinctively ducked aside. Unfortunately, Alex and Mike had ducked in towards each other, and had banged heads. A strange mixture of profanities, gasps of awe and a whoop from Betty filled the aftermath, as we all groped towards the door. Ever the scientist, Alex urgently mumbled, "Smell." Mike seemed to have come off worse with the shock compounding the head bang, so Alex sat him down in a chair. I sat on the edge of one of the desks. Nobody spoke for a moment, but there were several deep breaths, headshakes and stretches.

"Did anyone smell anything?" asked Alex at length.

Mike, who usually spoke very little, half-whispered, "NOx and ozone - what do you expect from a discharge?" whilst rubbing his forehead. Alex looked at us questioningly. I shook my head, as I had not noticed any smell.

"Maybe ozone," added Betty.

I pushed the equipment room door back open and sniffed again, to show willing, but I could detect nothing. I was not even sure what ozone smelled like, though I seemed to remember it was something to do with the seaside.

"And colour?" queried Alex looking round.

"Kingfisher blue, touch of purple," proffered Betty. There were nods.

"Are you OK Mike?" asked Betty, looking at him with some concern.

"Yeah, I'll be OK in a minute, love, I could do with a coffee, please?" he replied ruefully. Betty reached back to the coffee machine switch.

"Well," said Alex, "there was way *more* energy in that zap than we put into the cloud!"

"No, son," objected Mike, "not if you take into account all the energy you spent on generating and cooling the particles for half an hour. Don't kid yourself you've invented an energy generator. You haven't. You've created a nasty weapon, and I'm the first victim." He was still nursing his forehead. Alex's head must have caught him awkwardly.

"No, you're just collateral damage," joked Betty.

"Shit!" said Alex decisively, sitting back and raking his hands through his hair.

I do not know whether Alex and Betty had already realised the potential. I had not thought about it until Mike mentioned the word weapon. The zap or explosion or discharge, or whatever it was, had happened a couple of metres in front of us. If it was targeted to happen *in* something, or someone, it seemed it might do them a lot of harm. And the equipment was capable of generating an even denser cloud. Maybe here was the potential to assassinate anyone, anywhere, perhaps *anytime*, assuming you could locate them. Alex had been fretting about getting *information* from the future. Now he had to be worried about *changing the past*. Indeed, from the looks on their faces, it did not seem as if Betty or Alex were happy about creating a weapon, whereas they had been reasonably comfortable with creating an espionage tool.

No one spoke for a few minutes - we were all lost in thoughts about the implications. Betty handed round coffees. She knelt in front of Mike, her hands on his knees. "Are you OK, Mike? Let's have a look." She examined his brow, which had a slight raised bruise.

"Yes, love, it was the shock more than anything. I could do without excitement like that at my age. I'll be OK. But you two have got to deal with a monster. I don't envy you that."

"The equipment all looks as if it is still working OK," Betty stated, having made some studied keystrokes, "No emf pulse damage."

"Mmm, good, right," Alex started in a decisive tone, "so the cloud goes unstable at higher densities. We need to establish the line between better resolution and instability. No more observing in the equipment room, for safety reasons. Until we get the video camera in there, we can check whether an activation has worked, by whether we get an image or not. Lets try further activations gently pushing upward to higher densities from where we know the pictures work well. Mike, we'll make sure we ask you to come out of the equipment room before we do any activation."

But Alex's tone, and the way he looked at us, sent a compatible, but different, message. '*No more mention of weapons, lets put our attention back on to resolution, and forget the weapon issue ever came up.*'

"I think we may need a couple of pints this evening, would you like to join us Mike?" added Alex.

"Oh, OK, son, so long as it's not too late," responded Mike.

I was not sure whether Mike was in on the codes, but the surreptitious words had stung me to attention, and I agreed with enthusiasm. I was not that surprised - this new issue was potentially more problematic than the previous issue on which Alex had sought to find consensus suppression.

\*      \*      \*

We were up on the top of the hill, in the countryside outside Cheltenham again, this time with Mike as well. Alex was explaining to Mike the reason for the efforts toward privacy, but Mike did not seem pleased to be dragged into this. "So," Alex was saying, "we have got a by-product of the i-vector project, which to me, at least, is unwelcome. And the ramifications are not obvious yet - we would need to do experiments to determine whether those energy bursts can be sent back in time or even forward, and how big the bursts can be. But I can see no reason why they shouldn't be projected back in time, except that of course, it opens up the possibility of paradoxes."

The city lights were twinkling in the distance again, but it seemed quite a lot colder this evening, and the blanket was not keeping me warm, so I was hoping we would not be out here too long.

"So," he continued, "I am proposing that we say nothing to Bowen about the zap, or its possibilities at the moment, to give us time to do the experiments to know what the capabilities are. Then we can decide what to do."

"What?" commented Mike. "You're proposing to keep it secret from GCHQ? But they pay your wages. It belongs to them doesn't it?"

"Well, yes," replied Alex, "sort of."

"Anyway," continued Mike, "I might have mentioned it to Bowen already."

"What do you mean, *'might'*," asked Alex.

"Well, I had a conversation with him this afternoon, bumped into him. He asked how I was getting on. Just chatted. I can't remember exactly what was said."

"Well, did you mention the blast?" asked Alex directly.

"Um, well, I said we had a shock from a discharge, I think. I don't know exactly. I'm not sure what he would have twigged. *I* didn't know you were planning this. Look, I'm not happy about being dragged into any subterfuge, son, I've got my pension coming up in a few months, I can't afford any trouble. Look, I won't volunteer any details to him - as far as I'm concerned, I don't understand what physics you're doing. But let's just forget this conversation ever happened, OK?" And he walked back towards the car.

"Oh dear," said Alex softly - I had the impression he was more sorry about upsetting Mike, than about Mike potentially spilling the beans. "It's all getting too complicated, science was never supposed to be like this." He looked weary and was raking his hair.

Betty moved in. She took both his hands. "It's OK Alex. We'll all just play dumb for the moment - the cloud gets unstable at high densities - period. Sparks and stuff. It should give us enough time to do the experiments to find out the details. Then we can decide." I nodded accord.

"But," Alex was still distressed, "we've still got all the experiments to do on future pictures, and optimising the resolution, and the graphics supercomputer, and the army operative… It's all too much… its piling up too fast."

Betty squeezed his hands tight and lifted them. "No, it's all right Alex, *really*. We'll just work through it all methodically, at our own pace. Once the military operative gets working, all their attention will be on their own pictures. We'll sort out all the complex details and issues slowly." Alex took a very deep breath. Betty was very soothing. I recognised the Betty from our evening on the banks of the River Wye, though there had been no prank from her tonight. "Let's get back to Mike," she suggested, tugging him in the direction of the car.

"Just one question," I interjected as we walked. Betty looked at me scornfully, her gaze telling me that now was not an appropriate time. But I carried on anyway. "How could sending a blast back in time cause a paradox?"

"OK," said Alex. He actually seemed happier when focussing on some science. "Well, suppose your coffee mug is sitting on the table, and suddenly it is engulfed by a blast and it cracks. And I think, great, that's me in 10 minutes time sending back a blast. But now I could decide to be perverse and not send back a blast in 10 minutes time. It's the same problem as before. We are allegedly getting information from the future, but we have the choice *not* to act in a compatible or compliant way. Or alternatively, if your coffee cup is sitting on the table and I decide to send a blast back 10 minutes to crack it. But if your coffee cup is not already cracked *now*, that contradicts my ability to send back an act to crack it 10 minutes ago?"

"Thanks Alex." I acknowledged his crisp explanation, delivered in the only 20 seconds available to us, to do so. It would certainly give me lots of grist to think over at my leisure.

We were nearly back at the car now, and Betty shifted her reassuring attention back to Mike. She linked one arm through his, and put her other arm on his shoulder, but, giving him a warm smile, she found no need to say anything to him.

Then, back in the driver seat, Betty announced, "Right, I'm cold, I think we could all do with a drink now." And she drove us to a pleasant bar that was warm, with soft seats and green marble tables. The bar, I found out later, was intentionally, not too far from where Mike lived. It was, of course, Friday evening, and I think both Alex and Betty were relieved to be able to take the full weekend off, after they had worked right through the previous weekend, whilst they were getting the new equipment up and running. Indeed, it had been a very busy few days, with lots of open-ended questions remaining, but we soon slipped into the spirit of celebrating another workweek done.

Mike was actually the only one who did have a 'couple of pints' of beer, and then, when he left, he seemed happy enough, giving Betty a kiss on the cheek, and Alex a quick man-hug, before setting off on the few minutes walk to his home.

"Do you think he's OK?" said Alex.

"Yes, I do… Really, I do…," replied Betty with a reassuring smile. She went off to the bar to get us another round of drinks, came back with our two, but then she returned to the bar, where she sat on a stool, engaged in a conversation with the young barman.

As a historian I was, of course, interested to ask Alex about his Armenian roots, which I had correctly deduced from his surname. He was telling me that as far as he understood, his great-grandfather had fled persecution, and immigrated to the UK just before the First World War, but that since Alex, himself, was third generation British, he did not really identify with the diaspora, or, he admitted apologetically, have much interest in Armenian history!

I looked over to the bar a couple of times as we chatted, and felt some twinges of jealousy - was Betty interested in this barman, or did she already know him? He was certainly attractive, with an athletic body and blonde hair.

I remarked to Alex how Betty was always so energetic, supportive and fun. "Yes," replied Alex, "there is something of an Angel about her… a doomed angel."

I was puzzled at the expression, and looked at Alex quizzically, expecting him to clarify what he meant, but he shook his head as he saw Betty was returning. My jealous feelings about the barman were mocked when she came back over to our table. "Sorry guys," she apologised, "I had to teach the barman how to make a cocktail." She was carrying an elegant, layered drink in a straight glass.

"What is it?" I queried.

"It's called a 'New York Sour' - bourbon with a red wine float," she explained, taking a few sips and looking well satisfied. She offered the glass to me to try. "You need to drink the lower layer through the upper," she explained.

I declined. "Thanks, but I'll stick with my gin-and-tonics."

Alex laughed. "And you'll not get me onto complicated drinks half way through the evening."

"God," I sighed, "it's good to relax, it really does seem like it's been a long week. So much has happened."

"But remember," Alex retorted, "Betty and I were both working through last weekend, getting the new equipment on-line, while you were happily doing whatever. For us, it's been a *really* long haul. So, yes, it's good to relax. I really deserve this."

"Are you going back to Oxford this weekend, George," asked Betty, "or would you like to come and meet my niece tomorrow?"

I had forgotten that Betty was babysitting her niece this Saturday, but the invitation dovetailed very well into my mood. I wanted to enjoy as much of life here as I could while I still had the chance. The idea of driving back to Oxford held little appeal. "Oh, I'd love to, Betty, thanks. What's her name?"

"Kendall."

"That's unusual - how did she get that name?"

"Her father is American. I think it's not so unusual over there."

I found myself iterating American history through my head without finding any famous Kendalls.

"You can drop by our place, if you like," interjected Alex. "Kendall's quite a bit older than my kids isn't she? But they'll probably find a way to relate. I've got the kids all Saturday afternoon while Petra is out."


And so we found ourselves, the next day, three kids, Kendall, Charlie and

Mia, and us three grownups, eating ice-cream, playing, joking, shopping for trendy kids' clothes, and having silly races down our hill, that same hill where, a couple of evenings that week, we had had very serious private discussions. It felt healthy and liberating.

On the Sunday, I put my feet up and read a novel. It had truly been an ideal weekend.

\*      \*      \*

## *MONDAY 28th November*

The weather had turned milder and, as I walked in, I thought through the new experimental milestones that lay ahead in the next days or weeks. Alex had been asked to prioritise the resolution experiments, so presumably that would be the main activity this week. Betty would be readying the software for the military to use, and their night shifts were expected to start this week. The attempts at pictures from the future sounded very exciting, but I knew Alex was a little cautious about 'opening that box', and would, in any case, state to Bowen that it did not work. I would have to try to be around when he did the experiments if I wanted to know the actual truth. Then there was the latest finding that the equipment could possibly be used, at high particle densities, as a weapon. Did Bowen already know this from his brief conversation with Mike, or was it going to be feasible to keep the possibility hidden from him? And what about those strange paradoxes that Alex had described, which might occur if aiming the weapon into the past? If, indeed, a zap would work at all, into the past? I could not remember a Monday morning when I had been more keen to get into work.

I had some trouble opening their office door - there were cardboard boxes and packing material piled up and falling against it. Mike had been in early trying to complete the racking of the 128 graphics processor cards. "Whoops, sorry George," he apologised, "let me chuck them over this side. Did you enjoy Friday night - it's good to spend a bit of time with people outside of work isn't it?"

"Definitely," I replied. I assumed he was only referring to the bar. "Yes, we carried on drinking and chatting for quite a while, got a taxi home. I like that bar a lot - it's really comfortable."

"I prefer a traditional pub, myself," said Mike. "But it's the company that really matters."

I put the coffee machine on. Betty was not far behind me. "Wow Mike, you've nearly finished," she said, swinging her coat onto a peg. "What a star. Thank you so much."

"Yeah, now, I've run a separate ring main for the supply to the 12 volt rails, because these cards are quite power-hungry. It might mean you get a cooling problem in the equipment room. There is an air-cooler in the ceiling in there, but I'm not sure it's man enough for all this new gear as well - see how it goes. The other thing is - which PC do you want the PCIe cable run into?"

"The same one as the equipment control interfaces, Mike, please," replied Betty. "Yeah… CUDA manual here I come."

"What is CUDA?" I asked, curious about her enthusiasm.

"Oh, It's a computer architecture for parallel programming," explained Betty. "Sorry, I just love getting into new software languages."

"Oh, have you finished the version of the control software for the military then?" I asked.

"Yes," she answered, "it was a fairly trivial matter to simplify that interface. By the way, what would be helpful is if you could sit down and learn it from me. Then you can point out any aspects that are still too technical or obscure?"

"Sure," I agreed. "Do you want some help disposing of all this packaging, Mike?" He was carrying a pile out of the door. I picked up another pile and followed him to the front door where we separated the cardboard from the rest, and left two piles for the recycling and rubbish collections. Alex was coming through as we sorted it.

"Morning guys," he greeted us. "Hey Mike, can you leave behind a couple of the large empty cardboard boxes in the office for me please." We had to make a couple more trips to the front door to completely clear the office floor, apart from the two large boxes that Alex wanted to keep, and then we all sat down for coffee.

"Do you realise," Betty said to Mike, "that you're going to have to do this all over again - the Military want a duplicate of the graphics computer?"

"Well, it's light work compared with much," said Mike refusing the bait to complain.

"And a duplicate of the i-vector equipment, with gimbal mountings," Betty added.

"Yes, Bowen mentioned that to me, the gimbals will require some thought with all that wiring and piping. It might be easier to mount the whole contraption on gimbals. Anyway..."

At length Bowen came into the office. I immediately felt a bit tense as to whether he would ask awkward questions about the blast last Friday. "I just wanted a couple of words about the military operative who is coming in this week," he started. "When do you think you will be ready to give him training?"

"Tomorrow should be fine," announced Betty. "The software is all ready, I just want George to proof-trial it today."

"That's great - I'll let them know. The other thing is that although the top brass know about the *'time'* thing, they don't want any of the operatives knowing it - at least not yet. So, in the software that *they* use, can you not have any references to 'time' - as far as they are concerned, they will take all the pictures in the present, as they would normally expect to. They have been told not to ask any questions, and you will have to avoid mentioning anything about the technique when they are around. There is no reason for them to look in the equipment room either. Is that all OK?"

"Mmm, OK," Betty considered, "I'll take a couple more bits out of the software interface, and change some of the wording. So how will they have been told it works?"

"I think they will only know the capability, but nothing about the method. Some people are good at doing what they are told, and not asking questions, Betty." It was a strange response, maybe his attempt at a joke, maybe he was harking back to something between them, but before my time. I resolved to ask Betty about it later.

"I gather you've had a bit of a setback with the resolution improvements?"

Alex was in like a shot, maybe too fast, but perhaps he wanted to ensure it was himself answering. "Yes, the particle cloud goes unstable above a certain density, so there will be an upper limit to resolution. But we should be able to get some significant improvement over last week's pictures - during the next few days, we will be working on defining the line between good resolution, and instability. It may depend a bit on energy too - the best resolution we can obtain will probably be outdoors, where there is more intense light and so we cool the cloud further. But we'll show you an example, when we find the optimal resolution." Alex had cleverly focussed on the positive issue of improving resolution, implying that instability was just an undesirable nuisance. Would that do it for Bowen, or did he already know that there could be a sinister use for an unstable cloud? I watched his expression. If he knew more, it did not show on his face.

"Yes, keep me posted. I'm going to be out now until Wednesday afternoon. One other thing," he added. "The military are understandably concerned about reciprocal use of this technology - whether the other side can do it, and indeed whether there is any defence against it. They have asked if you could write a report listing the names of other physicists who were working in related or adjacent areas, and who therefore might get into, or stumble upon this technology. GCHQ have their own specialists who quietly observe scientists and their research fields, so they are already halfway there, but they would appreciate your input with names. And on the defence question, we haven't talked about that yet, is there a way of blocking the picturing, would we know if the other side was blocking our pictures? Have a think about that and tag a paragraph on the end of the report if you can. Thanks." He turned to leave.

"Oh, one other thing," I interjected, "I need to bring in a clock, and security say you need to authorise it."

"A clock?" His interrogative intonation was so exaggerated that it brought Lady Bracknell from 'The Importance of being Earnest' to mind. I found myself simultaneously trying to suppress a giggle, and feeling rather embarrassed at the inconsequence of my request compared to the preceding conversation.

Betty also caught the unintended intonal reference, but laughed without reservation. "We asked George to get a clock with *large* date lettering, so that we can run time tests at *low* resolution, but still be able to *read* it," she explained on my behalf.

"But why would you want to run at low resolution?" queried Bowen.

"Because low resolution pictures take far less computer-time?" Betty replied interrogatively, but calmly.

"Oh yes. Right I'll tell security it's OK. Presumably it's still boxed?"

"Oh… Err, no, I unpacked it to show Kendall," I admitted, feeling the conversation going downhill.

"Who's Kendall?"

"Betty's niece," I supplied in a small voice.

Bowen sighed. "Well, if it's unboxed electronics, it will have to go through the big scanner at the main building entrance. OK?"

"OK," I agreed. Bowen left. Betty looked as if she was going to fall off her chair laughing.

*Betty had brought Kendall round to my place to pick me up.*

*"Auntie Betty says you work at the same place she does."*

*"Yes, that's right."*

*"Auntie Betty is a mathematician. Are you a mathematician too?"*

*"No, I'm not."*

*"What do you do there, then?" she persisted.*

*"Well, I'm a sort of 'gofer'." I said, trying to be cute.*

*"What's a gofer?"*

*"Well, if Betty wants something, I 'go for' it, and get it." I hoped she'd find that funny, but it seemed to go over her head, and she carried on relentlessly unravelling my story.*

*"So what did you get for her?"*

*"Well, I got her a special clock." (It was actually the only thing I had got for her.)*

*"Why is it special?"*

*"Because it tells the day, as well as the time, in big letters."*

*"Can I see it?"*

*"Oh... yes... OK, here it is." I fished the box off the shelf, and handed it to her.*

*"Can we take it out of its box?" She was already picking at the cellophane. I helped her take it out of the box and remove the packing materials.*

*"It's not working, I think it needs batteries," she noted perceptively.*

*"Ah, OK..." I looked around thinking batteries, and eventually got the idea of cannibalising the TV remote, and so put those batteries into the clock.*

*"It's not working properly - it says it's Tuesday morning, and that's wrong, it's Saturday afternoon."*

*"Well, you have to tell it the time first." I should have said 'set' the time.*

*"I thought clocks were supposed to tell us the time. Did you get her anything else?"*

*"Erm.... I got her sandwiches?"...*


Betty wisely waited until Bowen was out of earshot, and then did the definitive Lady Bracknell - "A clock?"

Back in my own office, I had an email from the coordinator of the Middle East intelligence staff, whom I had talked to in the meeting the previous week, listing four names, and asking if I could supply any information about them. One of the names I was familiar with, from discussions with a Turkish correspondent some time ago, so I emailed back all that I could recall and find, glad that I had always made notes to spur my memory. I also emailed the other names to a couple of my contacts, to see if I could get any further information. I was very happy to do this sort of work as it made me feel genuinely employed at GCHQ, and less of an impostor who might be discovered at any moment and gently shown the door.

Then it was time for me to trial the software that Betty had modified for non-technical operators. I had become familiar with scraps of it over the last week, though it had been simplified even more now. The equipment was to be left powered on all the time, now that there would be a night shift working on it as well, so there were no switches to worry about. She sat me down in the chair in front of the control screen, and began the explanation from the beginning.

The procedure consisted of keying in the required density and temperature-delta before pressing the 'Prepare' button. This started the process of generating the clouds and cooling them as appropriate. The keying of density and temperature were automatically restricted to being in the range that was known to produce good pictures, (and no sparks), and there was annotation suggesting appropriate values for indoors, outdoors (sunny or dull), high and low resolution. The computer showed an estimate of the time required to produce the clouds as requested, which seemed to range from 20 minutes to an hour or so, depending mainly on the amount of cooling required. A red status light showed before preparation had started, an amber light whilst the preparation was in progress, and a green light confirmed that the cloud was ready to project, though Betty had changed this description to 'Ready to take a photo'.

Then the operator was able to key in coordinates - latitude, longitude and elevation. There was no longer any mention of time, though Betty showed me a cryptic keystroke combination to reveal the keying of time coordinates - I wasn't sure why she showed me that. Then the operator simply pressed the 'Activate' button to project the cloud and get an image. Instead of a stream of data which I had seen Betty scroll through to assess whether the image was intact, there now came a couple of lines of text declaring whether or not the image was viable, and that it had been queued to the super-computer for post-processing. Another window displayed the list of 'photos', time taken, coordinates and whether they were yet viewable, after being processed by the super-computer.

It was actually simplicity itself, with all the physics and maths hidden from the operator's view, but I felt a surge of power knowing that I could now run the complete process. Then Betty made my day by asking me to run all the activations for that day - this was the series of pilot activations with different particle densities, and minimum cooling, designed to pinpoint the line between high-resolution success, and instability. She gave me a list of the numbers to use, and went across to another screen to work on the new graphics computer that Mike had completed this morning.

The work made me again feel genuinely employed and seriously productive. It was very episodic work, however, in that after about a minute or so of keying, there was a wait of 20 or 30 minutes, before another quick bout of keying. I did find some useful little tasks to do during these waits, but I also found my mind wandering to what I might picture, if I myself could choose, given this newfound power. There were the iconic battles - Bosworth, Trafalgar; the epic moments - the Fire of London; or general views of life in periods long before the age of photography - the Iron Age, Ancient Greece; there were unsolved mysteries that could be solved - Marlowe or Shakespeare? Who shot Kennedy? The list was endless, but as a *modern* historian, these were not really the pictures that would inspire me.

By the end of the day I had completed 12 activations, without any complications, although, in the last two, I had heard a telltale zap from next door in the equipment room, which I assumed meant that we had passed the maximum density, before instability set in. The text status reports, coming back on the computer screen, seemed to confirm that; but in addition, had also called out the two activations before that, as unstable. At the end of the afternoon, Alex and Betty examined the data I had produced, and seemed content that we had established the density, above which, the instability set in. The next day's tests, they decided, would be a similar set of tests with greater cooling, to see whether that made any difference. They drew me up another list of numbers. As they were now confident to leave the equipment running overnight, we set a particle cloud preparation running with extensive cooling, so that it would be ready to activate first thing in the morning.

## *TUESDAY 29th November*

As it happened, I was the last one in the next morning, so Betty had already done the first activation and set the second to prepare. That first shot had in fact gone unstable, even with the maximal cooling, which pleased Alex because, as he put it, it ruled out a large part of the parameter space. When I asked what he meant, he explained that if *that* density went unstable, even with maximum cooling, we can rule out that *any* densities greater would produce pictures. Indeed, he had crossed some of the numbers off my to-do-list as being unnecessary now.

"Oh, and I had an email," he continued, "from Bowen, saying that we should expect a Major Hetherington in this morning for training, in preparation for the night shifts."

"Doesn't sound like an orderly, then," put in Betty. "Must be someone who chooses the targets, as well as keys in the numbers. I hope he's not going to be too disappointed with the simplicity of actually operating the equipment."

I felt slightly put down with that latter comment, since I had been rather enjoying doing that job. But of course the keying would become tedious after a few days, and was as nothing compared to the complex coding, which I caught glimpses of Betty manipulating, behind the neatly-presented windows that resulted from her work. And of course, nothing compared to the sophisticated science within the humming, anonymous, enigmatic equipment, hidden in the equipment rooms. But then I remembered the thrill was more in knowing the power that the equipment could wield at the behest of the operator.

There was a confident knock at the door. This was unusual since everyone with access rights, including myself, used the fingerprint scanner. Alex opened the door.

"Hello, I'm Harriet Hetherington from Joint Forces Intelligence - I think you're expecting me? For some training?" Alex greeted her with a handshake, and invited her in. She looked around 30, and was dressed in working uniform - the olive-green chunky-knit pullover, with shoulder straps displaying a golden crown, the rank of major. Under the jumper, she wore a shirt and tie, and she was dressed in dark-green trousers and army boots. Her blonde hair was tied back in a ponytail. In all, she was a striking figure. She looked as though she would probably get around the commando assault course, but at the same time, the creases round the sides of her eyes showed some wisdom and sensitivity. Alex took the lead and introduced her to first Betty and then me. I noticed, as she turned toward me, that she had the sort of eyes, which seem to be able to see something inside you.

"Coffee?" asked Betty. "George, why don't you bring one of the spare chairs from your office in here, then we can *all* sit?"

I did as asked quickly, as I was reluctant to miss any conversation. The extra chairs in my office were comfortable, but with four legs, unlike the swivel chairs which we generally used. I found a space for it and sat on it, as the others were already seated on the swivel chairs.

"So I hope you don't resent me crashing in on your party," Harriet was saying, "I know the military thing can get on some peoples' nerves around here. To explain, I'm embedded in GCHQ, and I also have to liaise with the other individuals who are embedded in MI5 and MI6 and the other services. So most of the people I interact with are actually non-military. I have to salute if I see one of my bosses, but if you just ignore that, and the fact that I have to wear a uniform, I can behave fairly normally."

"I think it's a cool uniform," countered Betty with a twinkle in her eye. "I'd love to try it on one day?"

Harriet laughed. "Yeah, sure, but it will have to be at home, it's against regulations otherwise."

"So," continued Harriet, "I mostly work with satellite surveillance photos, and they are superb these last few years, especially now that we have AI computer analysis of the images to alert us to the interesting bits. But, of course, we can't see inside the buildings, and there are a few that we would dearly like to see inside. So that's why I'm here, my boss said you can help me get some interior photos, I've no idea how, and I've been told not to ask about the technique…"

"Oh well," said Betty, "that's simple - we all get in a helicopter at midnight with balaclavas on, and loads of guns, and fly there, and…"

"You'll get used to Betty's sense of humour," Alex put in, but Harriet was grinning to Betty appreciatively. "Yes," he continued, "we have a technique which effectively boils down to keying in the coordinates of where you want to view, including an elevation."

"So what about windows and doors?" asked Harriet. "Because we don't always know the locations of those from satellite images."

"We don't need to know," replied Betty. "You key in the coordinates of inside, and you'll get an inside photo."

"Whoa, so you can effectively see through concrete, there's no drones or anything involved?" asked Harriet incredulously.

"Yup, that's effectively it," confirmed Alex.

"Wow, you guys have certainly cooked up something here, then," concluded Harriet.

Alex laughed. "Actually, that's something of an understatement. Maybe one day we'll be able to tell you about some of the other capabilities of the technology." I was surprised that Alex had intimated that there was more, but perhaps he was, as I think we all were, glad, and perhaps proud, that the equipment was receiving an enthusiastic response.

"One other important question," Harriet added, "- is there any indication to the personnel at the location, that a photo has been taken? - You understand it's one thing for us to get a photo of something covert, but it's quite another thing if the other side *knows* we have photographed it."

"No," Alex answered, "provided that you stick to the parameters that you are allowed in the control software, then anyone close by would have no idea that a photo has been taken."

"OK, so what would happen if we use parameters outside those permitted?" asked Harriet.

"Well then...," started Betty. But Alex put his hand up to stall her.

"You can't, because the control software won't let you," stated Alex firmly. "Otherwise, that's a question too far."

I wondered if Harriet would take offence to that, but she responded positively. "Excellent, you're being really clear with me about where the boundaries are. I appreciate that. Another question - we know of the entrance to a military complex built into a mountainside. You've said that you can effectively see through concrete walls, does that go for metres of rock as well?"

"The basic answer is yes," supplied Betty. "The photo will be taken anywhere you can supply the coordinates for. The only caveat is that with a mountainside, you are going to have to work out exactly, from where, the rock has been excavated. If the coordinates you supply are within the rock itself, then you will get a blank picture. But you could start at the entrance, and then do another photo a few metres forward and so on, kind of exploring the space. We took a few photos inside a UK military base to demonstrate the photographic capability." I noticed Harriet raise an eyebrow. "The first one landed halfway inside a wall, and indeed the floor, both of which were represented by thick black stripes on the photo, so then I just moved the coordinates a couple of metres into the room, and adjusted the elevation so as to get a good perspective."

"This is terrific, I'm getting really excited about the possibilities," said Harriet scratching her head. "But you mentioned photos inside a UK base - is there any possibility the other side also has this capability? And is there any defence against it?"

"Mmm… good questions," replied Alex. "I'm just doing a report for our superiors at the moment on that. My best guess is that the other side do not have the capability, at the moment. As for blocking the photos, I can think of no way of doing that as yet, apart from obvious precautions like shrouding anything sensitive with a tarpaulin."

"Or keeping the lights off," threw in Betty. "We haven't told you yet, Harriet, but the photos can only be taken where there is lighting, - we can't supply any light of our own, unlike the flash capability on a camera." Harriet was nodding. "So you need to think about daylight hours, and work-time hours, for your photos. By the way, Alex, I was thinking it might be possible to have a particular sort of interior lighting, maybe red and low-light, which might make it difficult for us to get a picture, and so be an effective defence."

"Oh, OK, good thought, Betty, thanks," said Alex. "We can try that." He jotted a note on his pad.

"So how long will it take for me to learn to operate this… thing… what do we call it?" asked Harriet.

"About 10 minutes," threw in Betty. "And we haven't got a name for it… yet. Maybe you can think one up for us Harriet, from an *'operations'* point-of-view? I think it's probably best if George teaches you the operating procedure - he sees it straightforwardly as he doesn't know the nuts and bolts behind it."

"Oh, you're not a physicist then, George? - What's your speciality?" asked Harriet.

I hesitated, "I think that's probably a question too far, as well." I chose caution and humour, not sure whether the connotations behind the word *'historian'* might lead to out-of-bounds areas.

"OK," accepted Harriet, apparently happy to quash her inquisitiveness.

"George keeps us on the straight and narrow!" quipped Betty. "Most of the time. When he's not looking at my butt."

Everyone laughed except me, but I think I was slightly less embarrassed than the first time Betty had used that against me.

"I would suggest, Alex," continued Betty, "that Harriet use her own coordinates for training, rather than using George's test numbers. Both because it will be more meaningful to her, and also to avoid us doing or saying anything which Harriet shouldn't want to hear."

"Cool," agreed Alex, "and we can get on with other things."

"And, regarding coordinates, Harriet," continued Betty, "we have calibrated them accurate up to about 100 kilometres, but if you are dealing with distances around the world, you may find we are a few metres out. But feed the corrections back to me and I'll refine the calibrations. Also, this prototype machine has a fixed orientation, so depending on where in the world you are looking at, the angle at which the photo is taken may be awkward. George will show you the fixed orientation - it's roughly East-West, and vertical, here at Cheltenham."

I took over and explained the basic cycle of operating the equipment. "The main issue, Harriet, is that there is a lot of waiting involved, while the equipment prepares itself for the next photo - anything from 15 minutes to an hour. So, you need to have odd jobs to do, or a book to read, to pass the time. It could be very boring if you're here on your own at night - no-one to talk to."

"Ah, but I'm rather looking forward to having the daytimes off, for myself, though," said Harriet. "There's a good wind forecast for tomorrow afternoon so I thought I'd go land kite-boarding."

That had caught Betty's attention despite her focus on her coding. "Ooh, that sounds like fun. Can I come and watch? We worked through the weekend before last, so I'm sure no-one would mind me taking an afternoon off."

"Sure," Harriet beamed, "I'll sleep through tomorrow morning, and meet you for a late lunch."

I had always thought it looked a rather unpredictable and dangerous sport, and knowing Betty wouldn't resist having a try, I felt a little concern.

"Right, so is it easier to do an outside, or inside, photo for my first try?" Harriet switched back into work-mode.

"I would go for an outside shot, then you're pretty sure to get something." I answered.

Harriet checked her watch. "OK, it's still light in the Middle East, there's an unusual heavy vehicle convoy that parked up last night, that we'd like a look at. Presumably you are on the normal GCHQ network here?" I looked over to Alex who had obviously heard since he nodded. Harriet logged herself into the computer, and spent a minute panning around online maps - presumably the military satellite equivalent of google maps. "OK, the convoy was still there at the last satellite pass." She noted down coordinates onto a notepad. I helped her adjust the coordinates slightly to anticipate a good view of the road.

The equipment had been preparing and cooling a particle cloud, all the time we had been talking, so it was not long before Harriet completed her first activation. "Oh, so I don't get to see the photo for about 4 hours," she noted disappointedly, reading the text spewed back from the computer.

"Well," said Betty, "this is a prototype machine and we are still processing the photo data via the main GCHQ super-computer, which we have to queue for, and the processing takes a long time. But we have just assembled a new graphics computer of our own to process the data, and it just so happens that I've got the software working on it successfully this morning. So, we may as well put your first photo through it now. Then, if necessary, you can adjust the coordinates and run again. Don't forget to start the equipment preparing for the next photo straight away, so that you don't lose time."

"So how long will the photo take on your new graphics computer?" asked Harriet.

"Well, the ones I ran this morning are taking about 15 minutes," said Betty. "But what I am hoping to do is get the photo displayed on screen in grainy pixelated form within the first couple of minutes, and then iteratively increase the resolution as the minutes go by. That way you can quickly scrap any photo that isn't worth processing fully, or use the grainy image to help refine your coordinates for another try. But that will take me a few more days to code up. As for the waiting time for the equipment to ready itself for the next photo, there's nothing we can do about that, on this machine. But the military do want to duplicate this equipment, and we will obviously make some changes to the design, so as to decrease the waiting time, and increase the number of photos which can be taken each day. And any feedback you can give us this week will help inform those design changes too."

So, about a quarter of an hour later, Betty called the finished photo up onto Harriet's screen, and we all crowded round eagerly to see what it was like. It wasn't the greatest of pictures - rather dark, but it had picked out a line of about 4 vehicles.

"I think," commented Betty, "that the light there was bad - probably a very overcast day. If you run it again with parameters a little closer to indoor lighting, then the photo will probably be... Oh, I've just thought, Alex, what would happen if it was raining...?" There was a concerned look between Alex and Betty, which was not continued into conversation.

"But this is amazing," stated Harriet, who was still panning around the picture. "I can tell from the shape that this is a Chinese short-range missile carrier, and it's politically surprising that it is in this particular country. We have completely missed the shipping of these. Yes, we should try to get a better photo so that the identification is easier to confirm, for the other analysts, but that has made my week already! Thank you so much."

Alex smiled gracefully, but I could see that he was more concerned by Betty's question about the rain. I was also intrigued by what Harriet was saying. "Which country is it?" I asked.

"I'd better not say." Harriet shook her head.

"Oh, I am one of the Middle East specialists here," I tried; wondering if that would make a difference.

"Oh..." She seemed surprised, but had no reason not to believe me. "Well, OK, I'll point it out on the map later. I need to make a call."

A slightly awkward tension had developed in the room. Alex and Betty had realised an issue about whether images in the rain would work, or go unstable, and which they couldn't discuss in front of Harriet, whilst Harriet didn't want to name a country in front of them, or indeed, I guessed, to make a call in front of any of us.

I was glad to be able to resolve this. "Harriet, I'll show you my office and you can use it to make private calls while the equipment is preparing for the next photo." I took her across the corridor and gave her use of my computer. "So which country was it?" I tried again. She lowered her voice to a whisper and told me and I realised why it was such an unexpected scenario. I left her alone to make her call, and returned to Alex and Betty.

The issue, which had suddenly concerned them, was whether the particle cloud would remain stable in the rain. Whereas the particle cloud might be stable in the air, in which molecules are well spread out, the much greater density of molecules in drops of rain might be a game-changer.

"But when we did the first image in the Ministry of Defence camp in Dorset, we hit the wall and floor, and we still got a picture," Betty was saying, "and that's a comparable density of matter."

"Yes, that's definitely some encouragement," replied Alex. "But we don't *know* whether there was any sort of flash or sound. That's really the urgent issue to determine, because if Harriet tries to take an image in the rain, and gets a little explosion… well, we have assured her that there is nothing to alert the people in the vicinity to the picture. We need to test this urgently - I know it's silly, but we'll have to get a watering can into the equipment room."

"No, there's a *shower* in the ladies', we can try an image in there," put in Betty.

"I'm glad it's *you* who suggested that!" quipped Alex, and everyone fell about laughing as the tension was relieved. "Oh dear, we're trying to do science at a running pace, it's meant to be methodical, if not leisurely. I still think the watering can in the equipment room is the easiest - at least we know the precise position where the particle cloud is projected to. We might need some towels or cloths to clean up the mess though."

"What about," I suggested, "if we get a couple of plastic cups from the coffee machine and prick holes in them?"

"Well, that would avoid having to get a watering can past security," Alex laughed.

"OK, I'll get some plastic cups and try them out with water in the gents," I offered, checking in my pocket to make sure I had a ballpoint pen to spear them with. I spent a frustrating few minutes trying to make holes in disposable plastic cups with the end of a ballpoint pen. The plastic was surprisingly strong and preferred to stretch, distort, and crumple in preference to yielding a small hole. I returned to the office disillusioned. Harriet had now returned and was arranging her lunch date for tomorrow with Betty.

She saw my hands full of mangled cups and looked at Betty quizzically.

"We're trying," explained Betty, "to simulate rain in the lab by making little holes in a disposable cup, and letting it drip water."

"But the pen won't make holes," I grumbled. "We need something sharper."

Harriet felt on her shoulder and removed her crown badge, then held out her hand to me for a cup. The pin pierced it easily and neatly. "OK," she said, "But I'm not lending you my pin, - I'll go and do it myself." She retreated off to the ladies'.

"Improvisation not your strong point, eh George," joshed Alex.

When Harriet returned, she carried a pair of perforated cups, each full of water, but each placed inside an intact cup, to stop them dripping.

Alex briefly lifted one of the perforated cups out of its container, and it neatly rained on the carpet, and would have done so for a full few seconds, if he had not returned it into its container. "Perfect," he concluded, "we'll try it later. Thank you, Harriet."

\* \* \*

Harriet's second image was superb - perhaps a trifle too light, this time, as we over-compensated for the gloomy weather, but her skilled changes in the coordinates had positioned the vehicles into a perfect close-up, with markings clearly visible. She was understandably enthused.

Alex suggested she did a couple of indoor photos, to get the feel of those, leading up to lunchtime, and then leave the afternoon for us to do the rain experiments. Harriet said she would like to stay to watch, but Alex said there were reasons why that was not possible. He was obviously still mindful of the possibility of sparks and explosions, and the ideas that might bring to Harriet's mind. It was agreed that Harriet would return about 6, when we were going home, or 18:00 as she put it, to carry on for as long as she wanted into the night.

*     *     *

After lunch, we planned the rain experiments. It seemed the only practical way to do it would be for one of us to stand on a chair to the side of where the cloud was projected to, and manually start the dripping with the cup. But that would be a brave assignment with the possibility of a small explosion resulting. We were beginning to wonder if the shower, in the ladies', was the more sensible option. Eventually Alex was able to find safety glasses, ear protectors, gloves and a lab coat from the workshop. We brought in two of the stable chairs from my office, to make a solid base to stand on, and Alex marked a cross on the floor below the exact midpoint of where the cloud was projected to, so there was a clear place to aim the drips at. It was eventually agreed that Betty would operate the control screen back in the office, I would stand on the chairs to deliver the simulated rain, and Alex would stand nearby to observe and rescue me if need be, though I actually felt fairly invincible wearing the full protective gear.

The first try was with normal parameters. Betty started the countdown. At two seconds to go, I started the rain, and at zero, notwithstanding our tensing, there was no obvious effect. We had to wait 15 minutes for the image to be processed - it was a fairly clear image of the news pages that had been pinned on the opposite wall, flanked by Alex himself standing there. But the image was speckled, mainly down the centre, with black splodges - evidently the water droplets obscuring any vision there.

This result was on the one hand a great relief to Alex, who had been very concerned about the alternative outcome - a crack and a flash - from a practical point of view. But it was also a frustration to him, because he had been assuming that the reason for the violent instability that we had observed with high particle-densities, was the result of crowding with air molecules. Now it seemed that his theory was wrong, because the density of molecules in the water droplets was far greater than in air, but that greater density had not caused a violent interaction.

We repeated the experiment, each time stepping the particle density up through the normal range that was allowed to the military operators, and each time we got a similar result, but with increasing resolution, exactly as we expected and hoped.

It was only sensible that we complete the experiment by using a very high particle density to see what would happen when the cloud was unstable, and Alex offered to take over the 'hazardous' role from me. But I opted to stay in place, feeling reasonably safe with the protective gear on, and perhaps lulled into a false sense of security by the previous runs. In fact, the shock was irresistible when the zap came - my hand jerked upward, splashing the ceiling with the remainder of the water in the cup, and I staggered sideways, fortunately falling against the wall rather than onto the floor. The area of the cloud zapped, as it had done before, and there were wisps of steam evident.

Alex too had ducked reflexively, but he rushed over, concerned to check that I was OK. I walked back shakily into the office and slumped down into one of the chairs. At that moment there was a knock at the door, and Harriet walked back in - she obviously now had fingerprint-reader clearance on our rooms.

"Hi guys, how did the rain checks go?" she asked breezily. Then she noticed me dressed in lab coat, glasses, gloves and ear protectors. "Wow, you guys sure worry about a little bit of water!"

Betty laughed. "Yeah, they were very successful. Look." She showed Harriet the best of the earlier pictures. "Obviously the water droplets do obscure small parts of the picture."

"Wow, but the other parts of the photo are really clear, you can actually read some of the newsprint," said Harriet admiringly, as she studied the picture. "And Alex is half in the picture… looking rather worried?" she observed.

"Right, well, we'll clear up and leave you in peace," commented Alex, fetching back the chairs from the equipment room. I noticed Harriet peering through the door after him inquisitively. "Actually, don't sit on this one Harriet, the seat's a bit wet," he added as he brought it in. I stripped off my health and safety gear and dumped it in the corner of the office. Harriet had brought a small briefcase with her, which she placed down on the desk in front of the control screen, and pulled out a notepad and a book. I immediately recognised the collage of flags on the book cover, as soon as she put it on the desk.

"I'm afraid we have only just done our last run, a few minutes ago," Betty informed Harriet, "so you'll have a half-hour wait while the equipment prepares for the next photo."

"That's OK, I've got plenty of work and a book to keep me going," replied Harriet.

"What are you reading?" asked Betty, reaching for the book. "*The Evolution of Modern State Boundaries in the Middle East,*" she read the title. "Ah, is that work or interest?... Oh!" she exclaimed as she looked at the back cover.

"Both really, it's on the recommended reading list," replied Harriet, "the writing is a bit declamatory, but it's fascinating stuff.... What?"

Betty pointed to the image of the author on the back cover and then over at me. There was a second or two of silence.

"Oh, wow, what an amazing coincidence," said Harriet. "It's really impressive, George. Maybe I can ask you some questions sometime, you seem to be implying that although it's possible to understand events unfolding in the short term, that in the long term it's all pretty arbitrary?"

I guessed she was trying to insert as many words as she could to dilute the memory of the word 'declamatory', but in truth, I was much more flattered by her reading it, than offended by her calling my writing 'declamatory'.

"Would you like him to sign it for you, Harriet?" put in Betty, always loving a pretence.

"Why not?" I said, and picked up her pen before there was any more space for misunderstanding or embarrassment.

"So, this evening, Harriet, if you have any problems at all just call me," I told her, jotting down my number on a pad at the same time. "I haven't got anything on this evening, and I like to be useful, to take the load off Alex and Betty, who are really pushed."

I had not really expected a call from Harriet, but only about an hour later, she called to say she was having trouble getting her photos processed. I drove in - rather than leave her waiting while I walked.

The office had a completely different atmosphere from the daytime. Harriet was wearing a hands-free phone system, and had all the screens displaying what I assumed were satellite surveillance photos. There were notepads in front of each. She was fielding calls, using jargon and acronyms, most of which were unintelligible to me. She acknowledged me entering the office, smiled, but continued the call she was on, whilst I fixed us both a coffee. She apologised for having to make one further short call to pass on some information up to a General. It was fascinating to observe her speed and efficiency, and the military protocol, though unfortunately I could only hear one side of the conversations.

Finally, she relaxed, took a coffee from me, and thanked me for coming in. The problem turned out to be that the pictures were still being automatically queued to the GCHQ super-computer, whereas during the afternoon Betty had been shifting them to the new graphics computer for speed. Just a bit of a misunderstanding, but a quick call to Betty enabled me to show Harriet how to divert the data files.

Then she started chatting about the content of my book. I was very used to undergraduates trying to impress me with their knowledge of the history, or trying to propose new thematics to link it all together, but her issue was rather different.

"So, as I read the first part", she was saying, "where you laid out the long history, I was just amazed how many empires, or the equivalent, had been and gone, just how much tit-for-tat conquering went on? I had always thought, in my ignorance, that the present day countries had existed for ages, with minor fluctuations to boundaries and so on. But then, having laid out all that detail of conflict, the second part of your book seems to imply that all of that was for nothing, that it's only the last hundred years or so that really matters, in considering boundaries. So what I wanted to ask, is if you really think that long-term history is just futile - I don't mean the study of it, I mean the act of it."

I took a deep breath before answering. This was not the sort of question I was asked by history students. "Yes, I'd agree that fundamentally what has happened in the last couple of thousand years, is interesting to look at, but yes, it's just a mishmash which could just as easily have been a different mishmash. I think the main input of long-term history on *modern day* conflict in the Middle East, is to inform the long-lived prejudices of tribalism.

"You said 'in the Middle East' - do you think it's different in the western democracies then?" she queried.

"Well the Middle East is my speciality, but I won't dodge the question. Yes, I think you can argue that there is something of a post-modern understanding that war is a waste of life, resources etc., in the more advanced democracies. But the bigger question is whether that is a long-lived understanding, or whether there will be a decline in those democracies, as the demographics change, or populism gains control, and then that intelligent understanding gets lost again"

"So you don't see a progression of humanity?" queried Harriet.

"If you look at history in the round, it's not evident yet," I replied. "Other than perhaps in technology."

"And what if you could go back in time," asked Harriet "and take out some of the problematic influences - Hitler for example. Would that help establish progression?"

"Well, no, because the vacuum that you create in history would be filled by other leaders and movements, some good, but some might be even worse. Also, I think that there is a pendulum swing back after a bad influence. After Hitler for example, the understanding and memory of fascism and the holocaust are very vivid, and quite long-lived, and probably serve to moderate behaviour in the medium-term."

"What about," persisted Harriet, "if Mohammed had never lived, then the endless warring between Islamic factions would disappear?"

"Yes, history would take a different course, but again, you can't control or predict what appears instead, it could be better, it could be worse, but in the end, it's *'just another mishmash'*, like we were saying at the beginning."

Harriet sighed. "So isn't that a rather nihilistic view of life - dismissive of peoples' efforts?"

"Well, no, it's simply an acceptance of the facts. What people do with their own lives is a different topic - we can certainly have fun, and make our corner of the world happier. Religious people need to see an overall purpose, and they try to obey an arbitrary set of rules, and to some extent may do good. But even when people don't have religious views, they can be very caring, helpful, generous, sensitive to other peoples' needs. The fact that you don't acknowledge an overall purpose doesn't necessarily stultify your actions - this is a theme in teachings as diverse as Krishna's on Dharma, and the philosophy of hyper-pragmatism."

"OK, but are you saying that all the historical military leaders were simply doing what they thought right at the time?"

"No, they perhaps did live in a more violent era, which might excuse their actions somewhat, but most military leaders were psychopaths - simply unable to empathise with others' feelings, and unable to feel fear. So, they did not respond to deterrence appropriately, and they would rather attack than defend. It is quite different now; in your modern UK army there are a large number of bright people involved in building decisions which are based on a lot of knowledge and intelligence. But again, if you all take orders from the man at the top, who I suppose ultimately may be a politician, there is still scope for blundering into war."

"People talk about learning from history - do you think that's valid?" asked Harriet.

"Well, I think the main lesson has to be that war is almost always wasteful of lives and resources. Gains are at other peoples' expense, and almost always short-lived. The pendulum always swings back."

"So would you never go to war?" she asked.

"Probably not," I replied. "But I would maintain armed forces - deterrence has a valid role in the modern world. So why are you asking this? - What are your life views?"

Harriet took a deep breath. "Well, I work in military intelligence, as you know. - Maybe you see that as just a game? - But I always thought that I was working toward the common good, keeping us safer from those who would do us harm. I admit I was ignorant of history, actually I think most people are - I knew the basics of the two world wars of course, but until I read your book, I had no idea that the past, before that, was such a bloody farrago of armies repeatedly conquering each others' territories. And some of the massacres and cruelty that you describe are literally sickening. I have found it quite disturbing.

How do you manage to cope with all that disturbing knowledge?"

"Well, history is just what I do, it's just a load of facts and inferences. I'm not attached to it, I don't approve of it, I don't believe in it, or proselytise it. I suppose to some extent it can be learned from. But I only do it because it's what I happen to be good at - remembering the stories, stringing them together, I don't really *care* about it. And you have to remember that this book is about borders, and therefore war features prominently. But there was plenty else going on in the Middle East at various times - art, philosophy, science and so on. I guess it is slightly different for Alex and Betty; they do seem to be involved with their science, and attached to what they do. But then again, when their efforts create an application in the military sphere, they do a certain amount of soul-searching about good and bad."

"And what about you?" she countered.

"What do you mean?" I asked.

"Well, when you give advice about the Middle East to GCHQ, does that cause you to soul-search?"

"Ah," I paused "well, no actually. Probably because I'm only supplying facts, not making decisions. But more than that because, I expect, those facts are pretty useless anyway. I have racked my brain trying to think of ways to improve the Middle East situation, and I have come up blank."

At that point another call came in. "*Yes, Captain? OK, yes… Refer that to SatCon, Captain, that track is important to us, but they will certainly want to try a reset on the satellite first. Yes… OK… Bye Captain.*"

"I guess I'd better get back to doing some work now, but it was really interesting talking with you, George. I'll have to think some more about all this. Thanks for coming in and fixing my problem, by the way."

"Oh, that was nothing; but yes, it was interesting to hear your viewpoints, we'll talk again sometime soon. Oh, have a good time kite-boarding tomorrow, and look after Betty won't you?" I said, leaving her to her late-night satellite photos and image activations.

On the way home, I pondered on what Harriet was really asking. Her questions seemed genuine enough - someone who has suddenly just discovered the brutality of violent history, wondering what it all means, especially since her role is actually within an army. Did it matter that the majority of people were ignorant of history, that it no longer occupied much of the school curriculum? Probably not, and anyway, I was the historian arguing that it was all irrelevant in the long run. Indeed, I was ignorant of *science*, though that was clearly *relevant* to life.

Then I realised I was also answering a question that I had subconsciously posed to myself, but not yet pondered at length. If the equipment here were capable of changing the past, could it be a positive step to do so? Clearly this historian tends to think not! But if it were, what specifically would it be advantageous to change? My own reasoning was clearly sceptical that any change would produce *long-term* benefit.

# Chapter 6
# Paradox lost

### *WEDNESDAY 30th November*

When I arrived the next morning, there was no trace of the operations control centre atmosphere that Harriet had created the previous evening. Betty was in early - she wanted to make sure that she finished integrating the graphics computer into the operating procedures, before she went off to meet Harriet at lunchtime. Soon after Alex got in, a technician arrived with the high-speed camera and spectrophotometer that Alex had requested a loan of, the previous week. I offered to help out, as I had a reasonable understanding of photography. The high-speed camera was indeed an impressive piece of kit boasting 25,000 frames per second at 1 mega pixel. Alex looked at it the other way round - to him it meant that there were 40 microseconds between each frame and, as he put it, the interesting physics might well be complete in a few microseconds, so he was not optimistic that we would see very much.

We tried filming a spark first and then a full-blown 'zap'. They were both done in the dark, with me triggering the camera and spectrophotometer at one second before the activations.

It was very simple to play back the videos, and what we saw was a very faint quivering, shimmering and undulating lilac pattern, like an old-fashioned plain quilt - Alex called it a standing wave - which collapsed after a couple of milliseconds (50 frames). The collapse was like a bubble bursting in slow motion, into the spark. The spark itself, in contrast, was relatively long-lived.

When we played back the 'zap', the impression of the standing wave was only very brief, and the collapse happened at a multitude of points, leading to a veritable firework display. Alex was well satisfied with the result, saying that the standing wave gave him very good data to work with. The spectrophotometer also gave data, but Alex said that it would take some time to analyse and interpret it.

*   *   *

After Betty left to meet Harriet for lunch, Alex and I chatted over sandwiches. Alex's spirits seemed buoyed by the results and he finally seemed motivated to try the 'future picture' experiment, which he had been resisting. "So, have you brought in that clock yet, George?" he asked.

I remembered that it was still sitting on my shelf at home, minus the batteries, which had been returned to the TV remote control. Bowen had told me to clear it through security at the main complex, which I had not yet got round to doing. I apologised.

"That's OK George," he said, "But if I take the image this afternoon, looking ahead one week, that's to next Wednesday, can you make sure it's here before then, so that it will be sitting on the table in the picture?"

"OK," I promised, as we both laughed at the incongruity of the request. There was also a slight anxiety in my stomach, as I wondered what would happen if I lost the clock, or did not put it in the right place on the table, to match the photo. What then? "So, do you think you *will* get an image then?" I asked him, remembering that he was already committed to telling GCHQ that trying to picture the future does *not* work.

"Well, as a scientist, I have to be open to all the options," he replied. "But personally I doubt we will get a future picture, because of all the paradoxes that could potentially be involved. Physicists have proposed several differing philosophical theories. Frankly, I'm surprised our picturing works on the *past*. The fact that it *does* work on the past rules out the 'Presentist' View, according to which only the present exists. So, it might be that the 'Growing Block Universe' theory is correct, in which both the present and the past exist, but the future doesn't. As time passes, more moments come into being, so the block universe is said to be growing. The growth of the block is supposed to happen in the present, with the continual addition of a very thin slice of space-time. Of course, in that case we couldn't get an image of the future.

"On the other hand the 'Eternalist' View could be the correct one, in which the past, present and future all exist. After all, if the dimensions of space all exist, and time is shown to be an inextricably related dimension, in Relativity, then why shouldn't all of time actually exist? Past and future are thus directions rather than states of being."

"But then, by that view," I questioned, "there would be no free-will because everything is pre-determined?"

"Yes, that's right," confirmed Alex, "but you could argue that there is no free will in any of the theoretical views, because everything, including the brain, is governed by physical laws. So, any decision you make is simply a product of your memories, and innate behavioural tendencies. Any time you choose to try to do something different, that is also just another decision, based on the same physical processes.

"There is an aspect of physics, which does mitigate against a pre-determined future though. Quantum Probability Theory implies that there is an element of randomness built into everything, so from the same starting conditions you wouldn't necessarily get the same end result. But of course, that's not free-will, it's slightly-random-will!"

"That's a good name for a cartoon character." I said grinning.

Alex was confused. "What is?"

"Slightly Random Will."

"Oh, OK," he laughed.

"But seriously," I asked, "how come there are so many theories of time? Doesn't the evidence narrow down the field of theories?"

"Well, frankly there is very little evidence, other than *our* past pictures, which are of course not public," he replied. "So most of what I have been describing are, strictly speaking, more philosophers' views than physicists' theories. There's not much in the way of equations to back up any of the views.

I guess your opinion is worth just as much, perhaps more, as you're an Historian. What is your view?"

"OK, well," I replied, "Harriet was not very happy last night with my view that the past is fairly arbitrary."

"You haven't been talking to her about past or future pictures have you?" Alex looked concerned.

"No, no, she had read my book on national boundaries, and wasn't very keen on the idea that all the warring of the last two thousand years amounts to very little. She prefers to believe in a progression of civilisation. But as to the structure of time, I don't know. I suppose I see the dates just as serial markers on a set of unfolding stories."

"Anyway," said Alex, "Maybe we'll find out some more in a few minutes, the equipment is almost ready for a low-resolution shot."

However, at that moment, the door opened and Bowen came in, asking Alex to go and discuss the specification for the duplicate equipment that the military wanted to have built.

So I was left to finish my sandwich on my own and wait for Alex to return - I certainly did not want to miss the next experiment, the result of which was going to be epic. As I relaxed, I began to wonder again about changing the past. Would it be possible to devise an experiment that changed the past in a minor, but measurable way? A test, which would not produce drastic changes to the present, but which would demonstrate the capability, and allow assessment of the knock-on cascade of changes initiated by one small change. My mind was returning to the dog statue by the River Wye. Suppose we located the real dog accurately on the day *before* he fell into the river. Suppose we then projected a blast from an unstable cloud onto the dog and killed it the day before it was fated to fall into the river. Then the incident of the dog falling into the river would never happen, and the statue would never be commissioned or crafted as a memorial to the event. Of course, there was also a piece of music which Elgar wrote, allegedly inspired by the dog falling into the river, the Variation XI of the Enigma variations, which would also not be written, at least not in the same form. But it was a minor piece of work, of no particular importance. The renowned Nimrod variation had already been written, and so had the famous Cello Concerto, by that time, so the premature death of the dog would not significantly change Elgar's legacy, even if it upset him for a time. It seemed like a small change to history - a missing statue, a missing minor piece of music. In fact I had, myself, always doubted that music composition was really very directly inspired by the events that it was supposed to portray. That was more a justification used by the early composers, who were patronised by the church, and so they had to declare that their pieces portrayed one or another biblical or spiritual scene. Perhaps the minor piece of music would not be missing, except in name? The small change to history seemed an innocent enough plan, except perhaps to dog lovers. But maybe there was some risk of a cascade of, initially-small, consequential changes following the event, which might lead to a real impact on history, and more importantly on the present? History was very fickle and arbitrary - I knew that. No, it would probably be too dangerous an experiment, justified only by idle curiosity about the nature of consequences.

\* \* \*

It was a full half-hour before Alex returned. "How did it go?" I asked.

"Good," said Alex, fixing another coffee, "they are going to increase the diameter of the new cloud containers - that will enable us to get even greater resolution without over-doing the density, and they are going to double-up on the slower parts of the process - the cooling particularly, to get a greater throughput of pictures. And of course mount the projector casing on a gimbal so as to get better image angles."

"Right," he continued, "how is the particle preparation going? Oh, wow, it's well ready - looks like we'll be getting a high resolution image instead. OK." He keyed a few numbers in. "You know, this is a huge moment, George, first image from the future,... maybe!..." His finger hovered over the Activation button.

"So why are you doing it with Betty away?" I asked.

"Uh." He took his finger away from the button and sat back. "Well, it's a fair point, Betty should be here by rights, but... You know I have been worried about the obvious paradox, where someone perversely intervenes to make sure the future is not how it was formerly pictured? I just feel Betty wouldn't be able to resist that, so... well, I figured it would be better if she just didn't know the time and date that the image comes from, then she wouldn't be tempted. I'd rather test it one step at a time. Of course, if your clock is in the picture, showing the date and time, then I won't even be able to show her the picture. Oh dear. Do you think I am being unfair to her, not including her? Do you think I am doing the wrong thing, George?"

"God, that's a difficult one, Alex. Do you remember she ran that first really good image after you had gone home to sleep, and she tried to phone you as soon as the image was processed? She was so excited that you should see it as soon as possible. Too excited, maybe, and in the end it caused an argument. I think if you said to her how anxious you are about the paradox, that she would respect that. But on the other hand, it's true that Betty finds it hard to resist a prank. Maybe you'd be doing her a favour not letting her know? Of course, there is a good chance that we won't get an image because the future does not exist yet - I think that's what you said earlier? In which case you *can* tell her. But then again, she might be put out that you didn't include her? Oh dear, it really is a knotty one. But, you know what Alex, you shouldn't have to feel anxious because you can't trust someone, it's great that you are concerned about Betty's feelings, but it's Betty's problem if she's made you feel that way, go on, press the button."

He did. The next few seconds, as we waited to see the result, were filled with a mixture of guilt and excitement.

*As a historian, it is important that I am completely truthful with my readers. The remainder of this chapter and the following three chapters are reconstructed, - they are not written directly from my memories - the reason will become clear later. The salient facts are true and correct, but for the sake of consistency of narrative, I have embellished them to read in the same way as the rest of the story.*

Eventually the stream of data came up on the screen. Alex scrolled it up and down examining the technical characteristics of the picture. He shook his head. "It's completely unbleached - there's nothing there. In fact, I don't think that quantum decoherence even occurred. The particle cloud seems to have been projected into pure nothingness. I'll get the image processed anyway for completeness' sake, but it's all black. The future does not exist yet. It looks like the 'Growing Block Theory' is right." His voice went sad with the last few words, and I thought maybe I glimpsed a tear in his eye.

"What's the matter Alex?" I asked, putting my hand on his shoulder.

"Mixed feelings," he muttered. "It's such a huge moment in science, but I can't publish it. I can't share it. And a big relief that there are no paradoxes to worry about. Although it's also a disappointment that we can't see into the future. But I should have included Betty, there was no reason not to, as it turns out. I should text her now, let her know the result." He tapped away on his phone for quite a while.

It would be difficult to believe that Alex was not completely sincere, especially with the display of emotion. But I couldn't help remembering that this was the result he had intended to report to GCHQ in any case. I did not understand the process he had activated, well enough, to be *sure* he had done what he said. He could have duped me, producing a blank picture, so that we would all believe that future pictures were not possible. But I felt the balance of probability was strongly that Alex had been straightforward. I preferred to believe that what I had just witnessed was truthful.

"So, a question Alex," I started. "Is the particle cloud kind of sitting, waiting for the present to catch up and create that slice of time?"

"Good question, George," he replied. "It might just have disappeared into nothingness, or it might, as you say, be waiting for us to catch it up. I suppose if we had left the machine on for a week, with the cloud here still entangled with that projected cloud, that it might decohere as the present meets the nascent future, and give us an image of the room then. So in other words, we would get the future picture, but not until the future arrives." He laughed. "That's quite neat! And we could test that too. If I asked for an image just a few minutes in the future, we could delay reading the data until it becomes ready at decoherence. Yes, I'll try that next." He made a few keystrokes to start the preparation of the next cloud.

A text reply came back from Betty. "*Sorry to hear we have no future ;) We are at our hill. Harriet is flying down it on her board.*"

Alex smiled. "It sounds as if Betty is preoccupied with other things."

A while later we had an image of the equipment room - the projected cloud had indeed waited the three minutes for the present to catch up, and then pictured the equipment room as requested.

"This is good," said Alex. "I'm in the mood for trying new things out now, having got those reports done for the management. Can you give me a hand with the cardboard boxes, George?"

I had wondered why Alex had retained the boxes, which had been untidily sitting in the corner of the office for a couple of days. We took them into the equipment room where he positioned one on top of the other, exactly beneath the position where we had experimented with the zap from the unstable cloud. Then he fetched his coffee mug and placed it carefully on top of the boxes so that it would be exactly within the projected cloud. Clearly he was going to see what damage could be inflicted to the mug, though I said nothing because he had subtly put his finger to his lips, intimating that we should not discuss the experiment explicitly in the laboratory, in case we were being monitored.

This time the wait was longer because the density needed was higher, although there was not so much cooling time. We activated the zap from the computer room with the inner door closed - it was not pleasant being too close to the zap of an unstable cloud. Then we went in and examined the coffee mug, which had split. The cut was not clean; there were several pieces and some small fragments. There was no sign of burning, although the top of the cardboard box, which had essentially survived structurally, bore a singed line, like toast.

"You might find this next experiment a bit gruesome," stated Alex mysteriously, delving into the carrier bag of shopping which he had brought in with him. He pulled out a supermarket sirloin steak. "But we need to know the answer," he added. I nodded with distaste. Again, there was a long wait for the cloud to be prepared.

Eventually we were able to examine the damage to the steak. It had certainly been cooked well through by the zap, but only down a fairly narrow line. It had not been ripped apart like the mug, presumably because it was pliable rather than brittle. "What do you think?" asked Alex quietly. "Is it lethal?"

"Almost certainly," I replied. "But my guess would be a very slow and painful death. It would essentially be internal burns, and I'm not sure even a pathologist or coroner would know much about those, or have any experience of their prognosis." We were silent for a minute or two whilst Alex returned the part-cooked steak to his bag, and then keyed into the computer to ready the next batch.

"What I want to try now," said Alex, beckoning me to follow him into the back room behind the equipment room, "is to see if it's possible to cancel out the unstable cloud. You see, every particle has, what is known as, its antiparticle - which is essentially the same particle but with opposite charges. When a particle encounters its antiparticle, they annihilate each other. It's easy enough to make a cloud of antiparticles - we just need to reverse polarity on a couple of the connections here." He unscrewed some cable connectors on an equipment cabinet, which I assume was associated with particle generation, and re-connected them the other way round. "It's not something we can do in the software - at least it hasn't been included yet." We walked back into the office. Alex had lowered his voice almost to a whisper now, obviously not wanting to talk about zaps loudly enough to be monitored. "So what I want to do is project a cloud of antiparticles, and then a cloud of particles, to the same point and time in the future. Then, if it works, your coffee mug will survive the zap, which we now know would, otherwise, crack it."

"*My* coffee mug?" I proffered the obvious quip.

"Oh ye of little faith!" replied Alex, making the keystrokes to prepare the antiparticle cloud. "So we have two batches to prepare, I'd better aim for an hour and a half in the future. Is Harriet coming in this evening?"

"I assume so," I said, "she didn't say otherwise."

"OK, well, we should just be able to fit it in before 6 o'clock," stated Alex.

I wanted to pursue the conversation, so I turned the coffee machine on, which produced a sort of background chugging sound, and continued in a near-whisper. "But, when a particle annihilates with its antiparticle, doesn't that produce a lot of energy anyway, so that might crack the mug?" I asked.

"Yes, the annihilation produces photons to dissipate the mass energy," replied Alex, "but our particles have so little mass that the energy produced will not be much, at least compared to the zap that we usually get. And most of the energy will be directed out of the plane of the cloud. You're right though, we should be able to pick up that radiation on the spectrophotometer."

This had reminded me of the thoughts I had been having earlier in the day. "So, Alex," I began with deliberation, "does that mean that if you projected back a cloud of antiparticles, into the past, to the moment when your mug was cracked, that the mug would retrospectively *not* crack?"

A broad smile filled Alex's face. "Yes, I suppose that's correct, *if* the test, that we are setting up now, proves to work."

"So that means," I carried on with my proposition, "that we could make a change to the past by zapping something, and then if we didn't like it, or we didn't want it to be permanent, that we could douse the original zap, and get back the original version of the past?"

Alex laughed. "Well, there's one big problem with that. After you change the past, you will be living in a different present, a present in which, you would only remember the new, altered past - you wouldn't be aware that the past had been transformed. So you wouldn't be able to make comparisons with the original past."

"Oh, ah…. that needs thinking about." My mind was spinning, but also racing. "But you could first project the dousing antiparticle cloud, with a *delay*, and then send the zap. So the zap would change the past, and then the delayed quench could arrive say ten minutes later, and cancel out the change, automatically reverting the past back to its original version again."

Alex's eyebrows rose. "Wow. That's creative!"

"Let me give a specific example that I have been thinking through," I said. "A particular dog fell into a river in the past, and the event gave rise to a statue at that spot. We could zap the dog the day before the fall, so that the fall couldn't happen, and check whether the statue disappears. Then the zap would be automatically doused by an anti-zap so that the dog is fine again, and the original past is restored."

"Right," said Alex slowly, "but again the problem is being aware of what you want to test. Once you have made the change to the past, as far as you *then* know, I mean as far as your brain *then* remembers, the statue never existed, so you wouldn't be aware of the test you had set up. And once the past has been restored to its original state, you would have no way of knowing whether the statue was there, or not, during those few minutes that the past was in its *altered* state."

"Ah doh, of course!" I put my palm to my forehead. "So the problem really is getting information from one version of the present to another? Would there be no way of doing that?"

Alex was thoughtful and said nothing for a full minute. "I can't answer that right now, George. Let me think about it. We'd need extra experiments to explore some more possibilities. I have some embryonic ideas, but I'm not sure any of it would work. And when you talk about changing the past, you are really talking about life and death. In alternative timelines, some people will die, some extra people will be born, you and I might never meet, it's *heavy* stuff. I realise you are talking about always reverting the past back to its original, but do we have the right to say that those extra people born in the alternative timeline should not have a life?"

"Sure, I appreciate that," I replied. "That's why an ideal test of changing the past should be absolutely minimal, historically almost insignificant, producing ideally just one clear effect, of little impact, with no unintended consequences. That's why I was proposing the dog and statue example."

Alex nodded. "Absolutely," he agreed.

The anathemic particle and antiparticle clouds had been timed to collide with my coffee mug at five minutes to six. We stood at the door of the equipment room in anticipation. Harriet arrived early.

"What are you two guys looking at?" she said as she walked in and saw us poised to witness.

"Oh, Nothing," I said with mock nonchalance.

"Hopefully nothing!" Alex added meaningfully.

Harriet joined us at the door, looked in and saw the mug sitting on top of the cardboard boxes. "Well, you guys sure do some strange experiments!" she observed, shaking her head. "But you've progressed from paper cups to mugs. Now, that's impressive!... Don't worry, I won't ask!"

We waited a few more seconds, Alex checked the time again on his phone, smiled and nodded. There had been no visible sign of a conflagration, and my mug was still sitting there intact. "OK Harriet, it's all yours. I'll check the spectrophotometer data tomorrow morning, George."

"Thanks," said Harriet. "By the way, Betty has hurt her ankle, but she says she will come in tomorrow. She came off the board awkwardly."

"Oh dear," Alex sounded concerned. "Does she need anything? Should I go over to her place?"

"I don't think so," replied Harriet. "I took her home. She said she would just rest up. She was quite upset about it - I don't think she'll be in the best of moods. Although we had a great time until then."

"It's OK, I'll give her a ring and pop over," I said. "You need to get back to your kids, Alex." And turning to Harriet, "If you get any problems Harriet, just ring, like last night." Actually, I was feeling a bit cross with Harriet, it seemed so predictable that Betty would hurt herself, even though I was sure Harriet would have instructed her well.

I phoned Betty, she sounded grateful, and asked me to bring over a take-away curry and a bottle of wine, which I did. She had left the front door on the latch for me so that she did not have to keep walking up and down the stairs.

"I really admired the way Harriet jumped and shifted her weight around," Betty was saying, "she made it look so easy. I really thought I could do it. Then, when I hurt my ankle, I felt so silly cutting her afternoon short. She says I need to learn how to fall safely - go to martial arts or parachuting classes. Anyway, I got some really good video of her on the board, look." We sat on the sofa, viewing the video on Betty's phone. Betty had positioned herself halfway down the hill and filmed Harriet flying and boarding almost over the camera and on down the hill. I had to agree with her that it was impressive, and I admitted I would have wanted to have a go as well.

"The worst thing is I can't express myself - I can't use the piano's sustain pedal with my ankle like this," Betty was saying, pointing at her ankle. She was actually able to limp around the house, although she was most comfortable sprawled on the sofa, with her foot raised on it's arm.

"Perhaps," I suggested, "you could play some really ancient pieces that pre-date the invention of the sustain pedal?"

Betty puckered her nose. "No, the whole piano was built completely differently then, it sounds horrible keeping the sustain pedal permanently on or off, on a modern piano. But yes, I suppose maybe I could try some Bach," she added somewhat grudgingly.

"OK," she said, between mouthfuls of curry, "so tell me what experiments you did this afternoon - Alex said you tried the future image but it didn't work?"

"That's right, the future image came out blank."

"What, black blank or white blank?" she asked.

"Oh, *black* blank - Sorry, I forgot, the difference is significant for you scientists isn't it?"

"That's right. So if it was black, it means there is no light there at all. The future is dark." We both laughed.

"Oh, and Alex said it hadn't even decohered," I added, not understanding exactly what that meant, but finding the word impressive.

"Really," Betty seemed surprised, "so there was no air or light, not anything to disturb the cloud - that's weird to conceptualise."

"But then he tried an image just a few minutes into the future. And the cloud waited in the future limbo, until the present caught up, and then gave us an image of the present."

"Oh, so the entanglement held for a full few minutes?" mused Betty. "That suggests that there are not even any vacuum quantum fluctuations in the future limbo - as you called it - curiouser and curiouser!"

"Then we tried a zap on Alex's mug and destroyed it," I continued. Betty tried to laugh through a mouthful of curry, which resulted in a short coughing fit.

"Oh, not that nice mug with the thick indigo glazing," she protested. I shall miss that one."

"Well, it's possible it could be retrospectively reprieved," I said intriguingly.

"What do you mean? He's not going to super-glue it?" she asked.

"No, he did this trick of projecting a cloud of *anti*particles, with a delay, so that they hit at the same time as a zap, on my mug. So, the cloud of antiparticles quenched the cloud of particles, and prevented the zap. And my mug survived."

"He saved the wrong mug, then," she put in. "Your one used to be the spare - it's cheap and ugly. But what did you mean by a retrospective reprieve? - He's not thinking of projecting antiparticles back to when his mug was zapped, and saving it, is he? That's just the sort of paradox which Alex is usually afraid of."

"Well, no," I admitted, "he didn't mention anything like that, it just occurred to me as we were talking."

"It sounds like you guys had a fun afternoon as well, and got away with just a busted mug, instead of a turned ankle," said Betty ruefully.

"Yes, I think Alex was in the mood for breaking ground today, though he was a bit reluctant to do it without you there to relish it as well."

"Yeah, now we have the military up and running, and he's got that report out of the way, I think Alex is feeling a bit more on top of things, and freer to experiment. It's nice. So on the subject of antiparticles did Alex tell you about the disagreements we had over choosing a name for the particles?"

"No, go on." I asked eagerly.

"Well, so, physicists mostly give particles names ending in '*on*', like *meson*, *muon* etc. Some have a Greek letter prefix like *muon*, others have a quality as a prefix - for example, the *tachyon* is so-called because '*tachy*' means *rapid* in Ancient Greek. So since Alex's particle is special in that it has a charge of '*i*', it would have been perfect to call it the '*ion*'. Except, of course, that '*ion*' is already the name for an atom stripped of one or more electrons. So then I suggested that since the Latin for time is '*tempus*', that we should call the particle the *tempon*, but Alex hated it because it was so close to the word *tampon*. I did point out to him that some physicists do have a bit of fun in naming, for example the *quark* which comes from *'Finnegan's Wake'*. And in fact, there is another particle called the *wino*, which I think is hilarious," she said, supping ostentatiously from her glass to make the point. "It took me days, then, to come up with another idea - the well known Latin phrase *'tempus fugit'* means time flies, and, since the particles do indeed fly through time, it seemed very appropriate, to call them *fugons*. But when I later suggested the antiparticles could be called *fugoffs*, he wouldn't hear of that either. Then he rejected *Khronon* - *Khronos* means 'time' in Greek - as being too like something in 'Star Wars', and the Greek word for 'fly' was too long and unpronounceable. Physicists seem to be quite serious with their naming, unlike geneticists who call discovered genes things like '*sonic hedgehog*' for no logical reason. In fact, many of their genes are characterised by taking them *out* of an organism, to see what you get. Then they name them after the result, so the name becomes actually the opposite of what the gene actually *does*. So for example, the gene *headless* causes the head to form, and the gene *eyeless* causes the eye to form. There's even a gene called *twin of eyeless*. Good grief, I could never work in a contrarian science like that. I suppose naming doesn't come into History much, does it?"

"Well, no," I considered. "I suppose, rarely, someone has the privilege of coming up with a term like The Dark Ages, Renaissance, Medieval or Cold War, a term which catches on. But mostly, the period-names derive from leaders, or regal names, like Jacobean, Victorian and so on."

"So, I suppose," mused Betty, "that we will end up naming the particles after one of the still-available Greek letters. Oh, yes *gammon* - that's another name I suggested, which he didn't think was funny! It doesn't really matter because Alex will never be able to publish the research anyway - it's quite frustrating for him, not being able to discuss the work with other physicists. But I think he accepts the reason why."

Despite what Harriet had said, I had found Betty in good spirits. I reasoned that she had probably been dejected in front of Harriet because she had felt embarrassed at hurting her ankle. However, when I suggested that her ankle would heal in a few days, a dark shadow seemed to cross her face. Other than that, she did explain that not being able to express herself on the piano, made her feel a little grumpy and pent up.

# Chapter 7
# But within the mathematical formalism of quantum theory, ambiguity about causation emerges in a perfectly logical and consistent way - paradox regained

## *THURSDAY 1st December*

Betty had asked me to collect her, the next morning, so that she did not have to walk or drive. I pulled into her gravel drive around 9, and parked next to the Cabriolet. I had seen her wave from the upstairs window, so I waited in the car rather than knock on the door. It was a windy day and I watched the leafless boughs of the trees bending and swinging around. She was a few minutes getting to the front door, and I went over to offer an arm so she could keep the weight off her ankle.

"Actually it's quite a bit better this morning," she stated. "I managed to practice on the piano before breakfast, and the ankle wasn't too distracting. What's this?" she asked noting the box on the passenger seat. "Oh, the clock!"

I had decided to bring the clock again, to see if I could get it cleared by security. "We'll have to detour via the main complex to put it through their scanner," I said. "Actually we'll have to detour via a shop as well, I need to get some batteries for it."

"That's OK, no rush," she responded. "But I thought the future experiment had come up blank so we won't need it?" she added.

"Well..., yes," I admitted. "It's a bit late, but we could still use it for experiments on the *past*?" I added hopefully, realising that it was a weak reason.

"Actually I am a bit attached to the clock, because it is designed for people with dementia. It reminds me of the problems my father had, before he died.

"He kind of lost track of day and night - sometimes used to sit up all night thinking it was day, complaining how dark the days had become. It was no use explaining it to him; he was past taking in any new explanations. I remember once hearing him in the middle of the night, and went into his bedroom to see if he needed help. He was half-dressed, struggling with his trousers. I asked him if he was getting dressed or undressed, as I wasn't sure. He looked at me and said he didn't know either. It was a kind of seminal moment between us, when I fully realised the state of mind he was in. That the man who had brought me up, my mentor, was now incapable of looking after himself. He needed me, not so much to help him with the little things, but to run his life for him - to move him into a care home, actually. Not that he would have wanted that, if he had understood…" My voice cracked slightly and my eyes misted.

"Anyway, this clock is designed for people in that condition. It has the day of the week, and the *part* of the day - morning, lunchtime, afternoon, evening, night - and all in large print so it's easy to read, even without glasses."

Betty smiled and nodded. I continued driving in silence for a minute or two. I popped into the Sainsburys at the end of the road for a pack of batteries, and then we drove on to the main GCHQ complex. I left Betty listening to music in the car, whilst I walked to the main entrance with the clock. I had been expecting difficulties with the security people, but immediately I told them I worked in an annexe, they understood what I wanted, scanned it and put it in a plastic bag, with their own security seal. We drove on back to our own building, and Betty limped in, supported on my arm. It was the usual security guy, on his own.

"Oh dear, Miss Gosmore, what happened to you then?" he opened.

"Good morning Fred, I sat on the toilet too long and my leg went to sleep."

I chuckled to myself, but Fred did not seem too certain that it was a joke and kept his head occupied looking through her bag contents.

"You know, Fred," she continued, "there's an old Irish saying: *'May those who love us, love us; And those who don't love us, may God turn their hearts; And if He doesn't turn their hearts, may he turn their ankles, so we'll know them by their limping.'"*

"Indeed Miss, OK Miss." He turned to me. "Oh, the clock again, sir. I'm afraid Mr Bowen isn't in today to authorise it."

I explained that it had been vetted at the main building, but he did not seem familiar with any such procedure. Betty was watching, amused, from a few paces in front. I knew I was on firm ground this time so I persisted. He still denied knowledge of any vetting procedure.

"OK, will you get your boss then please?" I requested politely.

"I'm sorry sir, I'm on my own, I can't leave the door unattended."

"Well phone him then?" I suggested.

"I don't have a phone on me sir, it plays havoc with the metal-detector."

"Well press your emergency button?" I tried.

"That's only for emergencies sir, I can't use that."

I saw Betty limp over to the security chief's office, stick her head around the door and speak a few words. He appeared at the door and called over briefly.

"That's OK Fred, it's been cleared, just tear up the security bag so it can't be re-used."

"Yes sir." Fred neatly sliced open the bag with his key (which apparently did not play havoc with the metal-detector) and handed me the clock box. "There you go sir." The tone that he used, suggested that he was doing me a favour, and that all his prevarications had only been in my imagination. I admired his skill in apparently moving on effortlessly, but wondered if there was actually resentment underneath - it certainly sounded as if not.

I walked through, picked up Betty on my arm, and we proceeded on down the corridor to her office.

"Ah, good morning you two," greeted Alex as we walked in. "I wondered if you might not be coming in." Heading for the coffee machine, I noticed that Alex had added two plain new mugs to the collection.

"Alex, they are hideous," exclaimed Betty when she saw them. "I wish you'd let me choose."

"Oh, they were cheap," Alex defended himself. "And one of them might not make it through the day anyway," he added mysteriously. "What have you got there, George? Oh, the clock - better late than never I suppose."

"Don't be rude, Alex." said Betty. "George has been through the mill getting that in here!"

"So, how easy was it to get the *mugs* in through security?" I asked, inserting the batteries into the clock, and setting it accurate by my phone.

Alex shrugged. "They're only *mugs*." He looked at the easy-to-read clock face. "Nice."

Strangely, his approval lifted my spirits. Or maybe it was the first aroma from the coffee that Betty had handed me, or maybe it was just *us* three all being together again, but suddenly I was looking forward to yet another hugely interesting day.

Betty was reading the latest entries in the 'Lab Logbook' - in which all the experiments get formally written-up. (Though I gathered there was a formal Logbook, which GCHQ had access to, and a real Logbook, which got *all* results written in it.) "George told me about the fun you guys had yesterday afternoon - the results seem quite decisive. Did you actually eat that steak for supper?"

"No, I put it in the organic recycling bin," replied Alex. "I didn't want to have to try to explain it to Petra. But I'm sure it would have been fine - I should have given it to George, rather than waste it. You would have eaten it George, wouldn't you?"

"I guess so," I replied. "I would have trusted you if you had said it was edible."

"So, what do you want to do today, Alex?" queried Betty. "It seems like we are up-to-date on most of our to-do list."

"Well," replied Alex, "I thought it might be a good time to explore the paradox about changing the past."

Betty raised her eyebrows. "Are you sure, Alex? You've been very concerned about the paradoxes up until now."

"Yes, I know," replied Alex. "But we can't put off resolving these issues indefinitely, and with yesterday's negative result from the future pictures, that has cleared up a lot of the worry. Also, George was proposing, yesterday, how a change to the past could be planned to have a minimal, controlled effect, which got me thinking about very simple well-controlled experiments. So let me tell you what I propose, and then you can see if you agree it is constructive and safe."

"I'm all ears," said Betty enthusiastically, settling back in her chair, her ankle resting up on the desk.

"Right," continued Alex. "So the basic plan is that at 11 o'clock, I will activate a retrospective zap to crack a mug at 5 minutes to 11. Thus, presumably, we would have already seen the mug crack at 5 minutes to 11. Presumably, we then sit there for 5 minutes, with the broken mug, before I activate the retrospective zap. But, the paradox, clearly, is that during that 5-minute interval, I could decide *not* to activate the retrospective zap, even though I am already looking at the mug that was broken by it."

"OK," interrupted Betty, "so you would have to perversely decide not to activate the retrospective zap, in that example, otherwise you wouldn't test the paradox. But then the mug probably wouldn't be broken at 5 to 11, so you still wouldn't get to test the paradox? ...Ah, I see, so, the only way you could successfully test the paradox is if you *deliberately* decide to act *paradoxically* - so if you see the mug *broken*, then you *don't* send the retrospective zap, and, on the other hand, if you see the mug *intact*, then you *do* send the retrospective zap."

"Exactly," said Alex gleefully. They were both smiling broadly. "Do you get it George?"

"Yes, sure," I replied. "But what might happen? Because the paradox seems to imply that what we see as the end-result doesn't make sense?"

"Well, that's the whole point," replied Betty. "We *don't* know what would happen, and we want to find out. Some people have argued that nature will appear to 'conspire' to prevent such a paradox. So for example, if we see the mug as broken, and therefore Alex decides *not* to send the retrospective zap, one of us would perhaps fall over and accidentally press the 'Activate' button to send it anyway! Or, conversely, if we see the mug as intact, therefore Alex intends to *send* the retrospective zap, then he might get an urgent phone-call that means he has to leave the room, or maybe the equipment mysteriously breaks down, or maybe the parameters were entered incorrectly, or maybe the mug wasn't quite in the right position to get zapped! Personally I don't buy that argument, but it is a prominent view."

"Nor do I," put in Alex. "There is another possibility, and this is what I think will happen. We see an intact mug. I decide to be perverse and press the button to send the retrospective zap. But that does actually change the past. So, as far as we *remember* in the changed reality, the mug *was* cracked from 5 minutes ago. And we are left wondering why I pressed the button, when the perverse thing to do, the way of creating the paradox, would have been to *not* press the button. Of course, knowing that the paradox might work like that, we would actually be wise to the reason."

"So," I probed, still a bit unsure of that explanation, "what would be the reverse of that?"

"OK," replied Alex, "so, we see the mug as *broken*. Therefore, I decide *not* to press the button to send a retrospective zap to break it, so that I can create a paradox. But my decision *changes* the past, including our memory of what we saw. So as far as we then remember, the mug was always *intact*, and we are left wondering why I *didn't* press the button to zap it. Again we would probably be wise to the reason, because we have already previously considered how the paradox might manifest."

"Well, OK," I argued, "but I think there's a fallacy there, because in that last example, the mug started off as broken, but you never pressed the button, so why should it appear as broken in the first place?"

"Well you've got a point, George, replied Alex. I'm not going to try to defend that theory too far, but I think the repost is to argue that *'no action'* and *'action'* and *'intention'* all have the same implications and effects on consequences."

Betty laughed, but I was unsure why.

I did not fully understand that answer, so I asked Alex to repeat it, and I memorised the words, so that I could think about it again later.

"So," continued Alex, "has anybody any other thoughts about what might happen?"

"Well," replied Betty, "the other obvious outcome might be that we can *not* change the past at all. So, you can send your retrospective zap, but the mug just sits there resolutely intact. Don't ask me where the zap goes though. Maybe it cracks the mug in that instant that it arrives, but because the rest of the past has already happened, the mug remains intact thereafter. Or maybe it starts another timeline in which the mug is cracked…? Anyway, I would have suggested that we have a wager on the outcome, but Alex has probably already had a look at the future, so he can cheat," she quipped.

We all laughed.

"So what do you think then?" said Alex, "Shall we do it? The experiment, not the wager! Do you think its safe?"

"Well," replied Betty, "it does seem like the consequences are limited to this room and us, and none of the consequences that we have theorised seem very dire. I think the equipment mysteriously breaking down was the worst outcome. So I say yes, let's go for it."

They looked at me. "I don't think I am qualified to express an opinion - I only half-understand your theorising. But I must confess, I am aching to know the outcome."

\* \* \*

And so it was that Alex set up the parameters on the computer screen to send a retrospective zap, back 5 minutes in time. We had decided that he would either press the 'activate' button, to action that retrospective zap, at 11 o'clock, *or* he would press the button to turn the equipment off, at 11 o'clock, whichever would apparently create a paradox. That of course depended on whether we saw the mug as, intact, or cracked, during the preceding 5 minutes between 10:55 and 11 o'clock. One of the plain new mugs was accurately positioned on the cardboard box, vulnerable to a zap, and the door to the equipment room was left wide open so that we could watch the mug the whole time. And the new clock was placed prominently on the desk so that we could be constantly aware of the exact time. We were ready well before time, so we made a round of coffee. Fortunately, we still had enough mugs thanks to Alex's purchase.

"God, I love this job," said Betty, as we all waited the interminable last few minutes, leading up to the exciting, critical moment. As the last few seconds finally ticked off toward 10:55, we all gathered at the door to the equipment room, watching the mug to see what would happen.

At precisely 10:55 there was a zap, I jerked back slightly, still shocked by the zap, even though it was half-expected. And the mug did change. I was aware of seeing it both broken and intact simultaneously. There were some sighs of awe and surprise from my colleagues, and then I started to feel slightly queasy as I found it difficult to focus. I seemed to be seeing a blurring of Alex's arms as he gesticulated.

"Superimposition," muttered Alex, "well I'll be damned!" But his voice had a slight echo to it, reminiscent of how it sounds when one is losing consciousness under anaesthetic. I felt slightly fearful, and a little queasier. The mug was not changing so I decided to go back into the office and sit down. I glanced back at the mug as I turned and saw it completely intact, but then in a mixed state again. It was only then that I realised that I was seeing both Alex and Betty in double vision, and feeling quite faint, I retreated to my chair. But as I sat down, I noticed that I was seeing myself in double vision as well, actually that I seemed to have two bodies, moving very slightly out of sync. I closed my eyes to try to clear my head - I was having memories now of when I had been young, and taken LSD, that panic could come very easily. Then I heard Alex speaking, initially with an echo, but then the echo disappeared.

"Don't worry George, we are experiencing two superimposed realities, it will be over in another 4 minutes. Take a deep breath, keep calm. Betty,

George, if you are seeing the mug as broken come over to the main door, but if you are seeing the mug as intact then go over to the control computer." I opened my eyes and amazingly saw one Alex walk to the door and another Alex stride over to the computer. Betty looked startled, her eyes wide, then she seemed to smile with realisation, and one of her followed over to each Alex.

"But I can see both!" I argued in a strangely echoey tone, not understanding.

The Alex from the door came over to me, and held out his hand to me. I responded with my hand, and one of the hand images from my double vision connected solidly with his hand. He pulled me hard, up and over toward the door, and then I saw that the two images of me had completely separated. I was standing with Alex by the door, looking back at another me, who was still sitting in my chair. And *that* me, sitting in the chair, could look back at the other me by the door. Strangely, amidst the profundity, I felt a little embarrassed at how I looked. Now understanding the separation, the sitting me got up, but awkwardly, knocking the chair slightly out of position, so that the chair too, now showed two versions. That me stepped over to the computer to join the other Alex and Betty. I was simultaneously aware of the view from each position I was in, and aware of slightly different thought patterns going on. I found, though, that I was able to shift the bulk of my attention from one to the other, and that focussing on one, helped to allay the feeling of sickness to some extent, although I was still fearful.

"So," said the door Alex, who seemed to be in charge, "we should only be able to interact physically with those versions of our colleagues in the same version of reality." He shook my hand vigorously. Over by the computer, the other Alex put his arm around my shoulders in a reassuring hug. As he released me, I moved forward to give Betty a hug, but unexpectedly my arms went right through her. I winced and tensed, not understanding. A similar scenario unfolded by the door.

"Betty!" growled Alex crossly. "This is not the time for pranks!" The two Bettys ran across the room to change places, passing through each other and laughing manically, before giving very reassuring, properly physical, hugs to the men. From the computer I glanced back to the mug and saw that it was intact. From the main door I could not see through into the equipment room, so I took a few paces over and looked - it was broken. Betty was now trying to do a pretend mirror dance with herself, I could not help but laugh at the difficulty they were having, and the laughing went a long way to driving out the fear. Alex, responsible as ever, pushed my chair back into alignment with itself, obviously fearful that I might try to sit down in the wrong version of it, and hurt myself.

I felt like a sip of coffee might help sober me up, so I went over to my mug, still half-full. I paused, before I picked it up, thinking it through. There appeared to be just the one version of my mug. But I now understood that if I picked it up, it would leave behind the other version of my mug for the other version of me, who incidentally was queued behind me. There was of course no need for queuing, and so, realising that, the other version of me walked through me, and picked up his version of the half-full coffee mug, leaving mine intact for me to pick up. At last, I felt I was getting the hang of it. I noticed Alex watching me slightly anxiously. I smiled back at him to indicate that I was feeling better now.

"So," I started, still needing some reassurance, "at 11 o'clock this double reality will end?"

"Presumably," he replied, "as soon as I, or someone, irrevocably decides to press one or other button, then the superimposition of possibilities will collapse into a single reality. Presumably!"

"But will we be able to remember this?" I asked.

"I assume so, because whichever version of your brain survives, that brain will have been forming these memories during this 5 minutes."

"Survives!" I echoed. "So one version of us dies?"

"Well, it just won't exist any more, in a sense it never did exist; or it will never have existed."

The versions of us had all got mixed up again by now, so I put my hand out to feel whether this Alex was physical to me. My hand passed through his arm. He smiled.

"So," I said sadly, "only one of us having this conversation will survive?"

The other Alex, who had been listening to the conversation laughed, "Seems so," he said, "let's hope its us."

Betty meanwhile had been acting to herself, reciting lines and making poses and gestures. Clearly this was a once in a lifetime opportunity for an actress to observe closely the exact effect that her performance was projecting, and she was modifying and retrying.

The other me had been standing at the equipment room door looking at the two-state mug. My attention swung back to that version of me as I became aware that he(I) had an exciting idea.

I turned from looking at the mug and excitedly grabbed the nearest Alex's attention.

"I just thought," I started, "that there is another way that the superimposition can end."

"Go on," encouraged Alex.

"Well, if one of us moves the mug out of the line of fire of the zap, then it could not be broken," I said.

"Nice try," replied Alex, "but its too late. The zap has either already happened or already not happened, four minutes ago. You can move the mug if you want, it won't make any difference."

"Duh," I slapped my forehead, "of course." I felt cross with myself for being stupid, and rather took it out on the two-state mug. I had meant to push the intact mug to one side, but caught the largest piece of the broken version awkwardly, with my palm, and cut myself. There was a trickle of blood.

"Oh dear," observed Alex, "I have a dilemma. To maintain the superimposition I need to have no bias about which button I press at the end of the five minutes. *If* it was an injury of life-and-death magnitude, then I suppose I would morally have to abandon the impartiality to save the other you, which is healthy and intact. But its not that serious is it?"

I pulled my handkerchief out of my pocket, and wrapped it round my palm to stem the blood. I felt a tinge of annoyance that Alex's concern was about his experimental impartiality rather than my health. "No," I answered, "its not a deep cut. But talking of bias problems, what if the two versions of you both want to survive. Which one gets to press the button? The longer this goes on, maybe each will develop a more separate identity? Perhaps one of the versions of you will press a button prematurely rather than disappear?"

Alex nodded and smiled. "What about you?" he asked. "Are you feeling a separate identity from the other you over there? - Are you envious of his intact palm?" I switched my attention back and forth between the two versions of me to test Alex's proposal.

"No," I decided. "It feels like I am doing two things at once, but not really a separation of *me* into two *people*. So if one of me would cease to exist, it would just feel like I stopped doing one of the things I am doing." Alex nodded again.

It was just at this point that we were unexpectedly interrupted. The main door opened and in walked Harriet. "Oh," she exclaimed, "what the…" She looked around, open mouthed. Both versions of Alex, responsible as ever, started over toward her, but the trailing one gave way

"Hi Harriet, can you just sit down in this seat please, for a couple of minutes till we finish this experiment. There's nothing to worry about."

"Oh," cut in Betty, "can't we let Harriet have a double too?"

"No time," replied Alex looking at the clock, "we finish in 65 seconds."

I spent the last minute practicing shifting my attention from one double of me into the other. There was a certain knack to it. It wasn't that one became unaware of what the other double was doing - there was continual awareness of both, just like driving, and thinking about something completely different. But the focus could definitely be shifted from one to the other. I am not sure what I was practicing for - I did not expect to have to use the skill again, but it was helpful in becoming more comfortable in this strange state.

"OK everyone," announced Alex, as the clock was ticking up toward the 11 o'clock landmark, "at the moment I still have an open mind about which button I will press, but I will choose one when the clock reaches 11."

"Should we do anything?" I asked. "Like make sure we identify with the version that will survive?"

"I don't think it should be necessary to do anything," considered the other Alex. "Of course we still don't know for sure that the superposition will end when I choose, but I will be very surprised if it doesn't... and worried!"

We all watched as his finger hovered over the buttons on the screen. In the end he chose and stabbed the 'Activate' button and I fancy the doubles disappeared just a fraction of a second before the press, but anyway, as we looked around, there was suddenly just the three of us, and Harriet, sitting in the chair, her mouth a big 'O' shape. I stepped over to look into the equipment room. The mug was indeed just simply broken, and it had a smear of red blood across the largest fragment. I had my handkerchief round my palm, also stained with blood. There were jubilant high-fives between the three of us, before we shifted our attention to Harriet and what to say to her.

"So," Betty began, "coincidentally, we all have identical twins, and we thought it would be fun to get them together...?"

There was laughter.

"It's OK," said Harriet, "you don't need to explain anything to me. I completely accept that what you do is top secret, and I won't ask any questions or tell anyone what I saw." She had removed the hair band from her ponytail, and tossed her long blond hair loose, before retying it as she spoke. "I must say you guys are totally amazing, what you can do, wow. I apologise for walking in at an inopportune moment - I will knock in future."

"Oh, there's no need to apologise," Alex reassured her. "I guess we should have put a notice on the door, but to be honest we didn't know that that was going to happen anyway. Look it's difficult, Harriet. We would be happy to share more explanation with you, but we have been told not to. You know what this place is like. Its very considerate of you to say that you don't need an explanation."

"Shall I tell you why I dropped by?" Harriet put in quickly. "Then I'll leave - I'm sure you must have a lot of debriefing to do after *that* experiment. So... our intelligence caught only the tail-end of something that is quite important to us, and when I was discussing it with my boss he told me to come and see if you could help us. What he said was that you guys could take photos of the past - of yesterday and the day before, so to speak. He swore me to secrecy by the way! I thought he'd gone bonkers, and so I was a bit embarrassed to come and ask, but after what I've just seen I wouldn't put anything past you guys. Is that correct? Can you really take photos of the past? And could I use that to find out the details of what we missed?"

Alex and Betty looked at each other.

"Well yes," replied Alex. "We were told that you wouldn't be made aware of that particular capability, but you clearly have been told, so I see no reason why you shouldn't use it. Our boss is not around at the moment, I would need to clear it with him, - actually I'll phone him, but I'm sure it will be fine. How about you come in half an hour early this evening, and we'll show you how to use that capability?"

"God, that is *amazing*," said Harriet shaking her head gently. "I'm a bit lost for words. How is your ankle today by the way, Betty?"

"Oh, it's a lot better," replied Betty, coming over to give Harriet a hug. "Actually I'd pretty much forgotten it with all the excitement."

"Yes, *and*," I added, "you actually *ran* across the room in the middle of all that!"

"Good," finished Harriet. "So I'll get out of your hair now, and see you later on?"

"Actually, one other thing," put in Alex. "Have you thought how you will explain the existence of past photos to your colleagues? It probably wouldn't be a good idea to spread the knowledge of this capability?"

"Yes, don't worry," replied Harriet. "As far as anyone else is concerned the photos will have been taken last week or whenever. There won't be any questioning." She opened the door to leave.

"Great," replied Alex, "see you later then."

As the door closed there were sighs of relaxation, and the coffee machine was switched on again.

"My god, that was extraordinary," began Betty. "Did you get what was happening, George? Because it was unresolved whether the mug was broken, or not, for those few minutes, because it was unresolved, *both* possibilities for the mug had to exist *simultaneously*. And because there were two simultaneous possibilities for the mug, there had to be two simultaneous versions of us seeing the mug in each of it's two states - broken and intact."

"Yes, but," I asked, "why did the two versions of us do *different* things - surely, at the beginning they were both seeing the same thing - the mug broken and intact, superimposed? So why did they separate and do different things?"

"That's a really good point, George," stated Alex enthusiastically. "In other circumstances, our versions would probably not have separated, because both versions would be aware of seeing the dual-state mug, and would both have the same reactions to it. Neither version would realise that one version was seeing the mug intact, and one version seeing it broken. *But*, serendipitously, the zap only happened in the reality of one of our versions, and we all know that, even though we expect it, we always startle, or duck, or raise our hands to cover our eyes. Those reactions are reflex and instinctive. But because the flash and zap sound only happened in the reality of one version of us - the version which experienced the mug being cracked - that instinctive movement and reaction only happened for *one* of the versions of us. As soon as I saw the small separation of my two bodies, I realised what was happening. I found that I could switch attention to one or the other arm position, and accentuate the different movement, and consequent position."

"Oh, I get it now." I replied. "I began to feel ill - sort of like motion sickness, probably both because I thought I was seeing double, and because I couldn't keep centred, with the slight differences in body position. That's why I went to sit down."

"Right," continued Alex, "so one version of me came over to you and took hold of your hand. I knew that *that* version of me would have a physical connection with one or other version of you, so I led you over to the side of the room to facilitate you separating. I hope that was helpful - I didn't want to see you feeling ill unnecessarily for the whole 5 minutes?"

"Yes absolutely," I replied. "It still took me a minute or so to lose the panic, but I'm grateful you did that. Did you facilitate the separation in the same way as Alex, Betty?"

"No," she smiled, "I must have reacted to the zap by jerking my head slightly sideways, so I found two different views of the mug, and worked on closing one pair of eyes to get a feel of that body, and worked on the movement from there. Oh, we haven't checked the mug, it should be properly broken." She rose to go and see.

"I already looked, it is bloody and broken." I said.

"George, there's no need to swear? Oh!" she realised what I meant as she saw the mug. "How selfish I am. You've done so much to help me with my ankle, and I hadn't even asked you what happened to your hand. Let's have a look." She insisted on taking me along to the communal coffee machine, where the first-aid box was stored, and cleaned and fixed up my hand with a large plaster.

When we returned, Alex was already writing up the experiment in the 'Lab Logbook'. "So, Alex," I asked, "the reason that Harriet didn't experience a double was simply that she didn't see the mug?"

"No, I don't think so," he replied. "There are two possibilities. The first possibility is that the double is created at the moment that the person first sees the mug. But the two doubles would not necessarily separate then, because it would just feel like there is *one* person seeing two superimposed versions of the mug. However, the other possibility, which I think is more likely, is that *everyone* has a double during those five minutes, but again none of them, apart from us, would separate. And the clue as to why that is the most likely possibility, is that your chair got moved, and we saw that there were two versions of that - one for each timeline, so to speak. So, if there were two versions of the chair, there must have been two versions of everything. So, it seems likely that there were two versions of the entire universe superimposed during that period. And that rather suggests that the idea of the multiverse - the hypothesis that there is a separate version of the universe for every possible variation of events - is very plausible. I certainly wouldn't be surprised if there is a another version of the universe, in which I pressed the *other* button, and our doubles are right now enjoying themselves in a duplicate version of the office, perhaps wondering if *we* exist?"

"Cool!" said Betty. "Wouldn't it be amazing if we could communicate with them?"

"Mmm," agreed Alex. "That's a similar challenge to when George was proposing about changing the past *temporarily*, and getting back some information from that past, *whilst* it was changed. That would need a lot more thinking about."

"Anyway," added Betty, "did you find it difficult to keep unbiased about which button to press?"

"No," replied Alex, "you just have to commit to being unbiased. Bizarrely I used to practice that when I was young - I would walk toward a tree, keeping completely undecided about which side of the tree I would pass on, until the very last second."

"Misspent youth!" muttered Betty. "Anyway before you rush to write-up these results and publish in 'Annalen der Physik', I think there is a flaw in the experiment - I don't think we have addressed the paradox, even if we have discovered the joys and thrills of superimposition."

"What do you mean?" retorted Alex.

"Well, let me first ask you a question, Alex. When you went to press the button at the end, were you aware of which version of you went over to the computer to do it - the broken-mug version or the intact-mug version of Alex, so to speak."

Alex was silent for a minute, taking the question seriously, and thinking back over the event. "No, I wasn't aware of which version went to do it. I could have worked it out of course, by looking at the mug, or by touching the George who had the bandage, whom I knew was the broken version. But when I decided to go over to the computer to end the experiment, it was just the nearest version of me who did it, for convenience."

"Good, OK," continued Betty. "I was a little worried that what I am going to say might disabuse you of your naivety in being able to choose in an unbiased way. But it sounds as if that won't be the case."

"Stop prevaricating," said Alex pleadingly, "and tell me."

"OK, well when the *broken* version of Alex went over to the computer to press a button, he could *only* press the 'Activate' button to send the zap and break the mug. Suppose he had instead intended to press the button to turn the equipment off, then *he* would no longer exist in the ongoing timeline, in which the mug stays intact. So *who* would have pressed the button? It can't have been *him* because *he* doesn't exist in the *extant* timeline, which we must assume is complete and intact. It's the paradox avoided again!"

"But," I put in, "couldn't he just disappear as soon as the button was pressed?"

"No," explained Betty. "It's the moment the *decision* is made about which button to press, that the inconsistent doubles seem to disappear. And that decision, when it's beyond doubt, occurs just a fraction of a second before the button is physically pressed. Did you notice that the inconsistent doubles disappeared just before the button was pressed? So, in the paradoxical case we are considering, the inconsistent double would be gone before he could *physically* press the button to annihilate himself."

Alex was raking through his thick dark hair with both hands. He nodded. "You're absolutely right, Betty. I wonder if we could challenge the paradox by telling him to press the wrong button?"

"But that's why," continued Betty, "I asked you whether you were aware of which version of you was which, at that point in time. Because it's actually the choice of *which double* is to press the button, that is the key, not the subsequent illusory choice of button. But, so long as you can maintain the naivety or impartiality about which version of you gets to press the button, then the superimposition is still possible."

"Mmm…, this is complicated," muttered Alex, "Excuse me, I need to think." And he walked out of the room.

"He's gone to the toilet," remarked Betty. "He does that if he needs to think without people around him talking. *My* head is spinning a bit too, from all this hypothetical reasoning. Let's talk about something else for a while?"

"Right," I agreed, "So, you were acting some drama lines in the middle of all that - what were they?"

"Oh," she replied, "yes, I realised that it was an ideal opportunity to observe how the lines come across. I could do it on video, but this was much more useful because I could observe from all angles, and change the manner as I went along. I am auditioning for the part of Eleanora in Strindberg's 'Easter' play next week."

She adopted a breathy but unhesitating tone. "*Now bear this in mind, that one person can see what another cannot, therefore be not so certain of your eyes. I was going to speak of the flower on the table: It is an Easter lily which belongs in Switzerland, and has a chalice that has absorbed sunshine; therefore it is yellow, and soothes suffering...* Do you know it?" she asked.

"No," I admitted, "I once watched a Strindberg, not that one, but it was so morose."

She laughed. "Yes, Strindberg has that reputation. But this particular play is beautiful. It is set in a tortured family that is wracked by guilt and disgrace, because the father has gone to prison for appropriating orphans' inheritances. The daughter, Eleanora, that I want to play has - how can I describe it - an over-ethereal, other wordly quality - maybe mentally unbalanced, maybe psychically gifted - its left ambiguous. Indeed, she has spent time in a mental asylum, but has escaped it, still fresh, honest and spiritual. She is a sort of catalytic heroine, helping the rest of the family to move through the ominous shadows of guilt and shame, and eventually transcend those shadows, as the result of an act of forgiveness, reconciliation and generosity. Hence the parallel with the Easter story, although the play is not at all religious. It will be performed the week running up to Easter - I hope you'll come?"

"Definitely. It sounds like a difficult part to play?" I suggested.

"Yes," she continued. "you don't get to meet people like Eleanora these days - they generally get medicated. But for me, it's *the* part I've always wanted to play, except when I was very young and wanted to play 'Alice' in Wonderland. I'm not that keen on Shakespeare."

"What about Pinter?" I asked.

"Well, I do think Pinter is profound. But whenever I have been to a performance, the audience always seems to laugh and giggle in completely the wrong places. Like they think the little gaps and pauses in the dialogue make the characters look like simpletons, to be laughed at. So I could never act in a Pinter play because I would get cross and shout at the audience. I suppose if I were a really good actress, I should take it as a challenge to convincingly portray those gaps as pensiveness or whatever, but... I've always wondered what Pinter thought about the audience reaction - he must have sat in on live performances."

The door opened and Alex walked back in. "Who must have sat in on live performances?" he asked.

"Pinter," Betty replied.

"Oh," said Alex. He had obviously been focussing on the logic of the experiment and was surprised we had not been.

"Did you get some peace and quiet to think?" asked Betty.

"Yes. Except when those two kids from down the corridor came in for a couple of minutes - I won't tell you what they were talking about. Anyway, having thought through what you said about the paradox around the disappearing double pressing the button to annihilate himself?" Betty nodded. "The doubles did indeed disappear just before the button was pressed on this occasion, so we can conclude that the *fixed intention* to send the zap was enough to establish the disappearance of the out-of-place doubles. But that doesn't mean it would be the same if the double chose the button to annihilate himself. It might require him to *actually* press the button to establish the disappearance of himself. In the first case, the *intention* was enough to cause the disappearance, as long as it was definitely going to be carried through. In the second case, the existence of the double is required right up until the button is pressed, before he can disappear. For him, the button pressing is the *action*, which is required before the disappearance is effected.

Betty placed the back of her hand on her forehead in theatrical mode. "Uh, I made an *assumption*! Yes, I admit I did assume that the ill-fated doubles would *always* disappear just before the button press; Worse, I assumed it from just that *one* observation. So maybe the alternative that you suggest would happen. But then we would be left with an inconsistency in the timeline. A zap was sent, but no-one, who is actually left *in* the timeline, sent it."

"True. Its untidy, not scientifically aesthetic," replied Alex. "But that's no worse than you saying that the double simply can not press the button to annihilate himself - that's tautological. Why can he not press it? What stops him? I guess we knew that we were likely to be left with some unsatisfactory detail one way or the other - it is a *paradox* we are looking at, after all. Anyway, the good news is that we can resolve this easily. If we repeat the superimposition a number of times, then statistically, a double must press the button to annihilate himself sooner or later; or he won't, in which case your theory is right."

"Cool," said Betty enthusiastically.

"The only practical problem with that," I put in, "is that we don't have enough mugs." There was some laughter.

"No problem," said Alex, "we can use plastic cups from the communal coffee machine - they won't survive a zapping, not so dramatic as a mug cracking," he pointed to my hand that had been first-aided, "but safer… I'll go get some cups."

He left the room and Betty and I exchanged glances. "I think we could be here for some time," she said. "The trouble with a theory that something *can't* happen, is that anyone who disagrees, can carry on claiming that we haven't repeated the experiment enough times to sufficiently discount the statistical possibility, that it still might happen sooner or later!"

Alex was back with a dozen plastic cups in a moment, but we had to wait impatiently for a half-hour before the particle cloud was prepared and ready for another zap run.

"OK," said Alex, "I'm setting it for 1 minute this time - we don't need to superimpose for a full 5 minutes to test this."

"Do you think we should put a 'Do Not Disturb' note on the door this time?" asked Betty.

"No, don't bother," replied Alex, "the only other person with fingerprint access is Bowen, and he's away today. OK, counting down ten seconds to superimposition from now."

"Wait," shouted Betty, "we haven't put a cup in there yet!" I grabbed at the cups and ran into the equipment room, placing one down on the scorch line across the cardboard box, which also sported some spots of blood from my earlier accident. Fortunately, we had already binned the fragments of broken mug.

"OK, ready," I shouted back, as I backed fearfully away from the impending zap, colliding with Alex who had come to the equipment room door to observe.

The crack sounded, knocking the plastic cup a few inches to one side, and the plastic caught fire. I jerked involuntarily at the sound, and, aware of seeing both the whole cup and burning cup, I struggled to switch my attention from one view to the other, to get a sense of the two copies of myself. Looking back I saw that Alex had already separated his two doubles, so I grabbed towards his arms to connect with one and pulled myself toward him, which did the trick of separating me completely. I then checked back to work out which of my doubles was seeing the intact cup, and which, was seeing the burning cup. I saw that the burning plastic cup had now set the singed top of the cardboard box alight. There was an acrid smell of burning plastic.

"Whoa," exclaimed Alex, "Betty, turn the machine off quick, or the smoke alarm will trigger, and security will come rushing in."

I saw the valuable opportunity. The version of me that could still see the intact cup grabbed the version of Alex that was physical to me. "No, *you* do it!" I barked at the *other* version of Alex. He looked slightly surprised, but rushed back into the office, pressed the button to turn the equipment off, and promptly disappeared! The fire was gone. So was the smell. And so was the version of Alex who had pressed the button.

Betty, who had not bothered to dissociate her doubles this time, was sitting serenely on the far side of the office observing and smiling. "You bugger, Alex, you were right again," she laughed. "…Except about zapping a cup not being as dramatic as zapping a mug!… So evidently someone *can* press the button to annihilate themselves. That leaves a couple of loose ends though," she continued. "Who, in this timeline pressed the button to turn the machine off?

"*George* did," replied Alex triumphantly. "Just as surely as if he had used a long pole to push the button, instead of his finger. He just used my double to carry out *his* instruction. And as you pointed out, my double *couldn't* disappear until he had *actually* pressed the button, despite the fact that he had already *decided* to do it."

"Mmm… OK," said Betty.

"So what was the other loose end?" demanded Alex.

"In a parallel world, we left our doubles to explain to security why we had started a fire, and set off the fire alarm?" she quipped.

Alex laughed. "Maybe! Fortunately that's *their* problem, and there's nothing we can do to help."

"Actually," Betty persisted, "I'm still not convinced that would explain the hackneyed paradox where you send a zap back to kill your grandfather before your parent is conceived. OK, so you disappear and so does the equipment. But, in the extant timeline, it would still leave a *zap without a cause*."

The strange expression, invoking echoes of a thoroughly unrelated cinematic title, caused laughter.

"Well, that's certainly not an experiment *I* am willing to try, however much the loose end bothers you! In fact, I can't see why anyone would ever want to do that experiment - maybe that's why it's not a paradox?" he joshed.

"Now who's being tautological?" protested Betty.

"Oh no, let's talk about it later, Betty. I've had enough mind-bending logic - I need some lunch right now. That was a long morning's work. Did you bring in sandwiches - it was your turn wasn't it?"

"Oh sorry, Alex, I forgot. George kindly brought me in his car to spare my ankle."

"Never mind," said Alex, "let's all go out for a meal, it will be good to get out of the office, it's been so intense this morning."

And so, I drove us all into town where we had a long lunch, talking about everything except the morning's work, which was not only a security requirement, but also a respite from what felt like quite an emotionally draining morning. Alex seemed in especially good spirits after getting resolution on some tricky physics, which he had been anxious about attempting for some time. And though there was still some friendly rivalry between Alex and Betty over whose theories prevailed, the atmosphere was one of friendship and success. Alex had two, maybe three glasses of wine and decided he was going to follow Betty's example of the day before, and take the afternoon off. Then he remembered that he needed to phone Bowen, to clear Harriet's request of earlier, to take pictures of the past. It was amusing to hear Alex, usually a paragon of patience, talking to Bowen, always awkward, with half a bottle of wine clouding the communication. Alex became quite animated at Bowen's dithering over what was a straightforward enough request, obviously already OK with the military. Betty was laughing so loudly that I was worried Bowen would hear her. Then we dropped Alex at his home, and I drove Betty back in, so she could modify the control software, ready for Harriet to attempt some photos from the recent past.

*     *     *

Harriet, when she arrived, was still treating us like sorcerers. Not surprisingly, she had been taken aback by what she had seen earlier in the day, especially since she had not been offered an explanation, and had felt obliged, by the etiquette of secrecy, not to ask for one. She looked around the office furtively for doubles before settling down to learn, from Betty, the very simple technique of specifying the required past time and date on the computer.

"So," asked Harriet, "how far back can we get photos from - a week, a month?"

"Well, there's no actual limit," replied Betty.

"So I could even get photos from the First World war?" Harriet pushed.

"Would you want to?" responded Betty, surprised.

"Yes, I could write an amazing military history book," suggested Harriet keenly. "Ah, is that why you are on this team, George? - To get accurate photos of history?" she added.

"No," I said, "I've only been here three weeks, so this is all completely novel to me too. I am as stunned by all this as you are. In fact for the first few days I was unsure whether it was real, or whether Alex and Betty were running some elaborate scam." I exchanged a wry smile with Betty. "But there's no way we could chronicle history by this technique, because we'd never be able to acknowledge how the photos were obtained. We'd never be able to use the photos as evidence or illustration. I wrote my books the old-fashioned way, with research." I was a little surprised at the laxity of Harriet's suggestion, so, not sure how seriously she meant it, I added, "Of course, the need to keep this technique secret is the overriding concern. I gather the military would rather not use the technique at all, than risk it getting exposed."

"Sure, I understand that," Harriet nodded reassuringly. "But could you go *way* back, and photo the Iron Age or the Stone Age?"

"In theory, yes," replied Betty. "But the mathematical model gets much more complicated, or approximate, if we wanted to go back that far. The shape of the Earth has changed, the continents have drifted. Friction from the pull of the moon on the oceans, would have changed the lengths of the day and year. If I remember correctly, somewhere back in the time of the dinosaurs, the day was 23 hours long and the year was 385 days in length. Excuse me for being able to recall numbers - it's just a benign affliction that I suffer from! But to answer your question, we haven't tested the extremes yet, because we have only been able to actually *do* this for a few weeks. In fact as soon as we could get decent photos, you were called in, Harriet."

"Can I ask one other question?" asked Harriet. "Can you photo things away from the Earth - so for example a satellite, or even the surface of the moon?"

"Well, we could," replied Betty, "but it would require a specific and accurate mathematical model to predict the position of any particular satellite at a particular time, but yes it could, with some work, be done."

I was a little concerned that Harriet was carrying the questions too far, and that Betty was too amicable to refuse to answer. "You're asking a lot of questions today, Harriet," I suggested gently.

"Oh, sorry," she replied. "I think I've only been trying to understand the limits of what I am working with. I haven't asked anything about this morning's spectacle, and I won't, because it's not within my remit."

"Yes, don't be rude, George," Betty castigated me.

"Oh… OK," I backed off politely, leaving a defensive riposte, about *'the Moon and the Stone Age hardly being a part of military remit'*, half-formed and unsaid. I remembered Betty jokingly telling Alex not to be rude, earlier in the day, in defence of me. This time it had not seemed so much a joke, but I understood Betty well enough now, that she would speak her mind plainly, but still be friendly and affectionate without reserve.

We waited whilst Harriet keyed in the timing, and coordinates, for her first try at retrospective photos, to make sure she was happy with the process, and then left her to her evening shift, with assurances to phone us if she had any problem.

As I drove her back, Betty suggested we get a takeaway and heat it up later. We were both still fairly satiated from the big lunch. I had been researching the local musical entertainment and had found a concert which appealed to me the following night. "So, Betty," I asked, "the Brodsky string quartet are playing some Shostakovich at the Pittville Pump Room tomorrow night. Would you like to come along with me to listen to it?"

"Oh George, I thought you were never going to get round to asking me out!" she purred. "Yes I would love to come." As always, Betty sounded quite earnest, but it was difficult to know whether she was playing, or sincere, especially now as I was driving, and unable to pay attention to her face. However, the fact that she had agreed to come was enough to put a smile on my face.

"So which of the cycle are they playing?" she asked.

"The last three," I replied, "- thirteen, fourteen and fifteen."

"Oh brilliant!" she enthused. "Thirteen is my favourite. But fifteen - that's the funereal one isn't it - and you were the one earlier saying that Strindberg is morose!"

"Well there's a big difference between moroseness and profound melancholy," I retorted.

Betty laughed and considered for a moment. "Yes, you're right George, they are quite different." There was a pause in the conversation. "…But there's something you should know, George," she continued, "I don't sleep with someone after a first date… And especially if my mind is aching with profound melancholy," she added pensively. "So we had better stop off at your apartment to collect your toothbrush now, so we can do it tonight, instead!"

She had timed the last comment to coincide with me starting to pull away from traffic lights. In my surprise, I got the balance of clutch and throttle all wrong, and stalled the car clumsily. She laughed warmly and long, as I quickly restarted the car and drove on. I pulled over the car as soon as I could find a space and embraced her strongly. I realised I had been holding back on my feelings for her for some time. I loved her, of course. She was a spectacular, multi-talented woman, who always made life seem fun, and interesting, and insightful. And she was always caring and affectionate to those around her. How could anyone not love her? She did play games though, and I suddenly wondered for a second if she was serious. I pulled away slightly and looked into her eyes.

"Yes I am serious," she whispered, as if able to clearly read my transient doubt.

Back at her house, she changed into an evening dress and sat at the piano. It seemed that she found this a vital and integral part of her day - playing in the morning before work, and again after she arrived home; important for her to express a more profound side of her emotions.

She flicked through a pile of sheet music that she had lifted from the piano stool. "OK, I'm going to play Enescu tonight - can you turn the pages for me please? - because I don't know it all off by heart. He was a relatively modern composer, but he wrote this suite in what he calls *'le style ancien'*."

I was not adept at reading music or page turning, but managed to keep up with Betty through the Prelude and Fugue, which she executed precisely. But when the Adagio came, a slow piece that was poignantly beautiful, and which she played almost at Lento pace, the tears started to roll down my cheeks. After that, the finale was furious and frenzied, with notes spraying from the piano, and I found it impossible to follow the written music, but by now, I was sensitive to Betty's slight nod that signified when she had taken in the end of the page and wanted the next.

After the piece ended, we retired to the sofa, her head on my lap, to savour the stillness that comes after serious music. I closed my eyes; the remembered juxtaposing echoes contradicting, but somehow complementing, the calm in the room. We stayed like that for a long time. She may even have drifted off to sleep for a while. It felt close to perfection - I could not remember ever being happier. When she eventually stirred and stretched, I stroked her cheek as she looked up at me. I ran my fingers along the contours of her body. We made love on the sofa, not waiting for bedtime.

# Chapter 8
# A 20th Century plastic cup, and a late 19th Century bulldog

### *FRIDAY 2nd December*

I had slept very deeply and only woke to the sound of Betty playing her early morning recital. Actually, some of it was clearly practice, rather than recital, but a delight to relax to, all the same. I lay in the soft bed watching the wind swaying the branches of the trees outside the window to its own rhythms, independent of the music, as the dawn light slowly grew. Again, I felt the touch of perfection.

Judging from previous visits, I had suspected that Betty avoided cooking, using takeaways or going out to eat, but my suspicion was dispelled when she produced a superb Eggs Benedict with smoked salmon for our breakfast.

Despite the leisurely start to the day, we still arrived into the office around nine. Alex was there already, sitting, thinking. "Good morning you guys," he greeted us, looking from Betty to me and back again - did he know somehow? I hid a slight blush by attending to the coffee machine.

"So, Betty," he started, before she even had her coat off, "suppose we sent a *delayed* zap into the past to change the past. Then sent a *delayed* quench to revert the past back to its original version. And then, projected a cloud to take an image of the changed past, obviously arriving *before* the quench, of course. Do you think we would get an image from the temporarily changed version of the past?"

"Whoa...," she replied, "that was a bit involved. So what is the aim?"

"To get an image of a *temporarily changed* past," he replied.

"Oh, I see," she concurred, "so the problem is, if you change the past, then the observer in the original version of the universe is also changed, so he wouldn't know to take an image before the past got reverted, and he wouldn't be able to pass the image on to the reverted universe, even if he did."

"Yes."

"So go through it again, how you propose to get round the problem?" she requested.

"OK," Alex started again, "So suppose we want to zap something in the year 1900 to make a change. We know we can send that zap, in the morning, with a delay so that it won't be actioned until say, 12:00 our time. And we know we can cancel out that change to the past with an anti-particle zap, also sent in the morning, and we can delay that, so it is actioned at say 12:30 our time. Now if we then try to take a picture, which we also delay, and also send in the morning, so that it will be actioned at 12:15 our time, will we get an image of the changed past?"

"Mmm... I get what you mean," said Betty, "so the first zap will instantiate a different history, because the anti-zap is not actioned concurrently. But the first unknown is whether the anti-zap would still be actioned, in a changed universe. It might not, because everything initiated by the original universe might be nullified. Or the anti-zap might only be actioned against the original universe that it was created in. Anyway, if we assume that the anti-zap *would* work, then it's possible the image would work too - you're thinking that the cloud to take the image is entangled with our cloud back in the original universe, so the decoherence has to deliver the image to us? However, at the time the image is taken, the past has already been changed, so we might not even exist to receive the picture. I think the answer is that we have only just begun to scratch the surface of knowledge about timelines, and the possible parallel timelines, so we cannot yet predict the answers. And frankly, it's too dangerous to try, because if the change doesn't get successfully reverted, then we are stuck in a changed history, and we might not even be here, with the equipment. However, we don't need to wonder about it, or risk zapping 1900, we can just do the experiment on a plastic cup in the equipment room today."

"So you think it's worth trying then?" questioned Alex.

"Sure, there's a real chance it might work, and it would be a profound bit of science to know that we can get an image from a changed past, an alternative history. But for god's sake don't start zapping 1900! Do it on plastic cups, they are made to be disposable, but the entire history of the nineteenth century isn't!"

Alex grinned, and looked at me. "Looks like your idea of a 'minimal impact change' is not in favour today, George." I hoped Betty would not ask me to clarify my idea of a minimal impact change, because, from her previous comments, I suspected she would consider it reckless. But Alex continued, "Can you run that Betty, whilst I carry on with the writing up and stuff?"

"Sure," she agreed. "George, will you please write '20th Century' in large letters on this plastic cup, with one of the marker pens, and place the cup on the guillotine?" I was happy to oblige, and positioned the cup carefully on the cardboard box, across the centre of the scorch mark. "So we need to activate three runs, first a zap to hit the cup at 09:30, but delayed for three hours. Then, an anti-zap delayed for an extra 10 minutes, but again to hit the cup at 09:30. And finally an image to be taken at 09:35, but delayed by an extra 5 minutes. And we need to reverse the polarity of the connections for the anti-zap run. The three hours delay gives us enough time for the equipment to prepare and cool three runs, so we should get our image of an alternate timeline of the plastic cup, or not, at lunch time."

"I'll go get a couple of cups of water in case the cup and cardboard box catch fire," I offered.

"Good point, George, thanks. It shouldn't happen, because the anti-zap and zap are both scheduled to hit the plastic cup at 09:30, but if you stand by at that time, just in case the anti-zap doesn't work on the altered timeline."

Mundane as these minor roles were for me, I very much enjoyed being involved. So, after only a short wait, I was standing ready with my miniscule water supply, as fire-fighter, at 09:29. But, a few minutes later, we were all happy that there was no fire, indeed nothing to be seen at all. And that presumably meant that the zap and anti-zap had cancelled each other out correctly, even though at this time we had not even sent them, they were just firm and definitive intentions. But we would not find out until lunchtime if we had obtained an image of an alternative timeline of the cup, during which it had been zapped.

I felt a bit awkward about hanging around in their office, after being so close with Betty the previous night, so I decided to retire to my own office until lunch, realising that I had actually done very little of my own work, writing my book, during the last week or two. I soon became engrossed and forgot about the pending results.

*  *  *

And so it was that Betty came in about lunchtime, grabbing me by the arm. "Come and see what we have got, George," she enthused. She led me back into their office and showed me the new picture. It was unconvincing, in the sense that the plastic cup had been reduced to a couple of mangled blobs, so that the message *'20th Century'* was no longer visible to prove the heritage of the melted plastic mess, (though Betty claimed she could see a bit of black marker pen on one of the melted bits). But the image also showed some extra scorch marks on the top of the cardboard box, and an extensive damp mark on the box, where, presumably, another version of me had doused the burning plastic. But importantly, when I checked in the equipment room, the cardboard box top bore no signs of extra scorch mark, or damp, although the latter could have dried out. And, of course, the '20th Century' cup was still intact. Even being rightly sceptical, the balance of probability seemed to be that the new image was indeed of an alternate timeline of that cup. As Betty remarked, it was a pity that we had not sacrificed a real mug, which would probably have retained visible parts of the marker pen message on the fragments, proving the verity of the experiment beyond doubt.

The weirdest knowledge though, was that apparently I had doused the burning cup, in a portion of time, of which I had no memory. "So does that other reality, the alternate timeline, still exist and continue?" I asked Alex.

"We can't know for sure," replied Alex. "It may be that the anti-zap caused it to become redundant, and it ceased to exist, so it had only run as a separate timeline for a few minutes. Or it might be that it is still a valid timeline in itself, and we, due to the anti-zap, are effectively, now, an altered offshoot of it. I can't imagine there is any experimental way to find out, I would need to do some deep thinking about that.

"But I tell you what," he continued, "now that we know that a temporary alteration of history works OK, why don't you spend the afternoon seeing if you can accurately locate that dog of yours. Then maybe we can have a go at the experiment you described." Betty narrowed her eyes questioning what we were talking about. I explained the idea to her, at length.

"So," she summarised, "you want to kill a dog to make a statue disappear?" She did not sound impressed.

"Well, yes, temporarily," I supplied.

"Tough on the dog?" she suggested.

"But we'll resurrect it with an anti-zap?" I proffered, hoping it was some amelioration. "It'll only be dead for a short time, then it'll be alive again. Well actually, of course, it won't, because it's been dead over a hundred years now, but you know what I mean." I could see that Betty wasn't wearing her usual smile, so, assuming she was an animal lover, I was struggling to justify the infliction of suffering on an innocent dog.

"Yes, I know what you mean," she said flatly.

I saw there were tears in her eyes, so I kept trying, "I mean, the dog must have suffered when it actually died naturally, anyway, so we are only bringing forward the suffering, perhaps even making it a quicker death."

"I don't care about the bloody dog," she snapped. "What about if the anti-zap doesn't work for some reason? Have you thought about that?"

"Well, in that unlikely event, we'd be living in a timeline which is only very *slightly* different from now - that's the point of designing a minimal impact change."

"Different how?" she asked shortly.

"Well, Elgar's works and biography would be very subtly changed, and the wooden statue of the dog wouldn't be there."

"And?" she persisted.

I was not sure what she was getting at. I shook my head.

"And," she said bitterly, "we wouldn't have spent that evening together on the river bank by the statue. Geez, George, the story of the statue was inspirational to you as a kid, a different you might not even *be* at GCHQ. Does our relationship mean *so* little to you?" She stomped out of the office. I was nonplussed.

"Give her a few minutes," said Alex. "I hadn't realised that you two had got together. By the way, I liked the line about the dog being resurrected, although it's actually been dead 100 years," he quipped. I tried a weak smile. Actually, I was mostly touched that our relationship did mean a lot to Betty, though I was bemused as to why a very low probability hypothetical was so important to her. I was not going to chase her into the ladies', so I did give her a few minutes. She returned, and shot me a sulky glance.

"I'm sorry," I started, "I hadn't really given much thought to the possibility of getting stuck in an altered timeline."

She nodded, and put her hand on my arm. "No, my mistake," she offered. "I am very fond of the little dog statue because, to me, it reminds me of the first time we got close. But after thinking about it, I realise, for you, the statue has always been there. For *you* though, although it's an interesting artefact, it doesn't really have anything to do with *us*. So I was wrong to berate you."

"Oh I see," I gave her a quick hug. "Does that mean its OK for us to go ahead with this experiment, or shall I think of something else?"

"Good grief, yes, go ahead," she said. "Never let it be said that a woman's histrionics got in the way of science."

I was absolutely unsure to what extent she was being serious or acting.

Nevertheless, I spent the afternoon trying to get an accurate fix on Dan the bulldog, on the day before he fell into the river. It was harder than I had imagined. I knew the address where Sinclair the organist and his dog had lived - 20 Church St, Hereford, and I knew the house was still intact - I had walked past and seen the plaque outside. So, the coordinates were fairly easy to work out from an online plan of the area. And I knew the date in 1898 that I wanted to target, but my first attempt at an image came out very dark, with almost no detail. I had to call in Betty's help, and it turned out that it was not my fault. With the time coordinate over a hundred years ago, much longer than had been tried before, there was clearly a time calibration error, and we had no idea whether it was hours, days or even more. Worse, there was no obvious way of checking the date in the pictures. This first, dark image had clearly been taken at night-time, so I subtracted 12 hours and tried again. Whilst the equipment was preparing, I worked out the coordinates for 'Big Ben' - reliable since the 1850s - at least I could get to know the time of day accurately.

The second attempt at picturing the house was much more helpful. Though partially obscured by some object, the image was of a kitchen, though no person or dog was in sight. I reasoned over the plans where the other rooms were likely located, and adjusted the target coordinates by the appropriate number of metres, to try another room.

This time, whilst the equipment was preparing, I mused over the kitchen - a substantial range cooker, lots of cupboards, plates displayed on racks, pots and pans hung in a row, in the old-fashioned way, a mangle. I found memories of my grandmother welling up. What an absolute delight to be able to look into the past in this way. Of course, photography was already established by those years, so we do have records of kitchen style, although most early photos were actually posed portraits. I was, in point of fact, looking at a time, two years before the introduction of the famous 'Kodak Brownie', which first put photography into the hands of non-professionals.

I was disturbed from my historical reveries by Betty asking about arrangements to meet up for the concert that evening. I was relieved that her possible reservations about what I was doing had not put our 'date' in jeopardy. We decided that she would drive and pick me up in her Cabriolet, and we would eat after the concert.

The next image gave me an enormous stroke of good luck. I had found Sinclair's study, though he was not in attendance. In front of the far wall stood a large, rather ornate roll-top bureau with a leather-inlaid writing surface. Facing the bureau was a finely proportioned wooden study chair with a swivel seat. Both the seat and back were covered in leather with stud work decoration. On the bureau itself, there were two piles of neatly stacked papers and a few stray documents. Unfortunately, none were legible from the angle of my picture. However, on the top shelf of the bureau stood one of those oak perpetual desk calendars, which were so popular around that time, with three windows showing the weekday, day and month. The information was on scrolls, and these were turned by hand each day, using wooden knobs on either side. The two small windows indicated 'Tuesday' and 'April', and the large window showed '12'. I had in fact been aiming for Friday 15th April, so the calibration was about 3 days out. Even though the year was not shown, it *had* to be 1898, otherwise the weekdays would have been different. I felt a thrill of excitement in pinning the date precisely, but I kept the revelation to myself, determined to also establish the exact time, with an image of 'Big Ben', before I presented the data to Betty. I was sure that as a mathematician she would be delighted to be able to refine the temporal calibration of the equipment, in the same way that I was charmed by the antiques I was witnessing.

To my surprise, the image of 'Big Ben', as on Tuesday April 12th 1898, was satisfactory at the first attempt. The mapped coordinates were easy to obtain, and I had been wise enough to back away from the grand clock tower, and elevate the view sufficiently to get a clear result, though the tower was slightly too far to the left, and too low to count as a good composition. I was thoroughly elated with the afternoon's work, though I had only just managed to complete the last image before Harriet was due to arrive for her evening shift on the equipment. As I suspected, Betty was full of enthusiasm when I showed her the two defining pictures, and the upset of earlier was purged by our mutual enthusiasm. She resolved to re-calculate the temporal calibration on Monday morning, whilst I would continue trying to track down the bulldog.

*    *    *

The 'Pittville Pump Room' turned out to be a resplendent stone building, fronted by a long colonnade of pillars, and topped with three statues. There was a massive lawn with trees to its front, and though unfortunately the evening was cold, we walked, hand-in-hand some way back onto the lawn, to admire the architecture. I imagined that in the summer the lawn would be an idyllic place to sit. The interior was no disappointment - more Ionic columns, chandeliers and a beautiful, decorated domed ceiling. I had entertained no expectations of the venue, and it felt like another gift, in a perfect day - I gleefully anticipated researching the history of the place.

The music was of course stunning. At the interval, we felt invigorated, but spoke little. At the end, the profound melancholy of the final funereal string quartet silenced us both. There were tears in my eyes, and Betty sobbed quietly whilst we walked slowly around the lawn in the darkness, savouring the silent echoes. But it was a very pure, clear sort of sadness, enhancing rather than sullying, the perfect day that I was having. At length Betty drove us to a small Italian restaurant where we both ate Betty's recommendation, Porcini and truffle linguine, accompanied by a bottle of Syrah. When I told her I was having a perfect day, she smiled broadly. When I asked her if she felt the same, she explained that she felt blessed every morning when she awoke, that she enjoyed *every* day. It was one of the things about Betty, which was so endearing.

\*        \*        \*

## *SATURDAY 3rd December*

The next morning being Saturday, Betty was in no hurry to do her piano practice, so we lay in bed, chatting, until mid-morning, when she fixed us brunch. I was enjoying being with Betty enormously, and beginning to take her for granted, so it hit me in the pit of the stomach when she said I had to go. She saw my shock and explained that she had already invited Harriet over for the weekend.

"We have something really good together, George," she said softly, "and we'll get together again soon, but I have to spend time with other people too, that doesn't change anything that *we* have." I recognised that Betty was a free spirit; it was part of what made her such a beautiful person, so I knew I had to give her that freedom without begrudging it. I beamed back, hugged her and left. I walked home with a smile on my face, enjoying the bracing air, and called in at the library on the way.

## _MONDAY 5th December_

On Monday morning, I resumed the search for the dog. I reasoned that the dog would most likely be in the kitchen or the study. So, I rotated the image locations, and varied the times of day. I also made the pictures low resolution so I could get more pictures done each day. But it was frustrating. I caught occasional glimpses of people - a woman and a man, presumably Sinclair himself - in one or two of the shots, but no sign of the dog. I began to wonder if the dog was maybe confined to the garden, so I started including some pictures within the garden as well. I pondered how very much more efficient video would be - I could probably have panned around the whole house and garden in two minutes. By the end of the day I had a nice collection of pictures around the house, albeit low resolution, which gave me some satisfaction to peruse as a historian, but still no sighting of the dog.

I was still processing the final image when Harriet arrived for her evening shift. Betty greeted her with a hug, and I happened to notice looking round, that, as they released, Harriet ran her hand down across Betty's butt in a way that looked slightly more than accidental. I looked away. Betty had not said anything about her weekend with Harriet - had they been rather more than friends? I felt a slight pang of jealousy, but dismissed it, remembering that Betty's freedom was part of her attraction. Nonetheless, I had missed being with her the last couple of days after the wonderful time we had had at the end of the previous week. "So Betty," I boldly suggested, "would you like to go out to eat this evening?"

"No can do, I'm afraid George," came her reply. "Monday evening is my amateur dramatics group - we'll catch up later in the week. In fact I need to get straight off now." And she picked up her coat and left. Harriet smiled at me, giving nothing away. But of course, she perhaps did not know that Betty and I had an intimate relationship. Or had Betty told her? It was beginning to feel a little tangled. I small-talked with Harriet for a few minutes, and then left her to it.

## _TUESDAY 6th December_

My frustration of the previous day had dissipated and I set about searching for the dog with renewed enthusiasm. I felt sure he could not elude me for much longer.

Soon after lunch I got lucky - the dog was lying on the kitchen floor in the middle of the afternoon. But it was at that point I started feeling some guilt and doubt. It suddenly seemed more real that I was proposing to inflict suffering on the animal. I had begun to feel that the idea had run away with itself, and the danger of interfering with history began to make me feel anxious. The whole idea had really been intended as a vehicle to discuss the possible mechanism with Alex. I had not really expected him to propose actually doing it. Nevertheless, I started varying the spatial parameters to try to place the image right on the dog. I got advice from Alex on this - I thought it better not to ask Betty since she had initially seemed a bit squeamish about zapping an animal. By the end of the afternoon, I had the coordinates exact for what would be, in effect, an assassination.

I showed Alex and Betty. Betty seemed concerned, she reminded Alex of the mantra *'Just because you can, doesn't mean you should'*, and asked him to justify the reason for the experiment, but otherwise she was silent. Alex replied that we had indeed already demonstrated changing the past by zapping a cup, and subsequently, successfully reversed that zap. However, he proposed that it was valid, indeed desirable, maybe essential, to explore whether a very limited change on a *grander* scale, outside of the lab, but with minimal consequences, could be achieved. He also felt that the experimental change to the past was reasonably safe because the counter-zap was sure to return the timeline to its former structure. He was however thoughtful, and wanted to ponder the idea until the next day before definitely agreeing to try it.

# Chapter 9
The Moving Finger writes; and, having writ, Moves on: nor all thy Piety nor Wit Shall lure it back to cancel half a Line, Nor all thy Tears wash out a Word of it.

Omar Khayyam

## <u>WEDNESDAY 7th December</u>

The next morning Alex seemed to have cleared any doubts he had had, and he laid out the plans for the experiment, making sure that Betty was also up to speed on the precise schedule.

The experiment was to follow exactly the same sequence as the pilot test we had done on a plastic cup. Firstly a zap to hit the dog, using the exact coordinates I had found the previous day. Then, after changing the polarity of the equipment, an anti-zap, to cancel out the zap, restoring the timeline to its original state. And finally, an image of today, where the wooden statue of the dog currently stands, using the coordinates we had previously worked out for that. The zap would be actioned with a delay of 3 hours, and the other runs with corresponding delays, so that the zap, image and anti-zap would occur in that order separated by a few minutes, at around 12:00 our time. The 3 hours delay allowing us to prepare and action all three runs on the equipment. Although the anti-zap would actually *happen* last, we had to *action* the image run last so that the equipment was available to receive the picture. Assuming the runs happened in the same way that they had on the plastic cup, we would expect to experience nothing out of the ordinary happening, but get an image from the temporarily altered timeline.

As we waited for the equipment to prepare the first particle cloud, Betty was happily explaining that yesterday evening she had been given the part she wanted in the upcoming production of Strindberg's 'Easter Play', whilst Alex was comically dreading her getting stuck in character, which was a conceit he often used to rib her.

About an hour later, we were ready to action the first run. I saw Alex hesitate on the button, and go back to double-check his calculation of the time coordinates again. I think we all realised that what we were about to try was a step more risky than the previous experiments, even though the same sequence of runs had been successfully tested on a plastic cup. There was a rumble of thunder outside. Betty shivered. Alex smiled at her. "Its in the weather forecast for today, Betty," he stated. "It's not an omen."

Betty shook her head. "Such a thing never occurred to *me*. Who are you trying to convince, Alex?"

Alex pressed the button decisively. At that point, I knew that the dog had been condemned, but it was all very impersonal - I imagined that if we had had to actually witness the zap on the dog, we might have been more reluctant.

*   *   *

A few moments later, the door opened and Bowen came in, with Fred trailing behind him. "Miss Gosmore, your drug test of 9th November has come back positive." He almost spat the words out, without preamble, and appeared to be suppressing a smirk. "The use of drugs is incompatible with holding security clearance, so you have been suspended. You have to attend a disciplinary hearing with HR in the main complex at 11am on Friday." He thrust the sheet of paper he was holding into Betty's hand. "Please get your personal belongings, and security will escort you off the premises."

Alex rose to intervene. "Hang on Phil, don't be hasty. There must be some mistake."

Betty meanwhile was studying the piece of paper with a quizzical look on her face. "Oh," she said finally, "THC. Oh yes. My brother was offering round hash cookies at his birthday party the weekend before. I ate one - that's all it was. It was a really nice afternoon actually. It's no big deal. Surely you don't expect me to refuse my brother's hospitality on his birthday?"

Bowen was red in the face. "Miss Gosmore, you are suspended. Please get your coat. Security will see you off the premises." He stepped back forcing Fred to take the lead.

"I'm sorry Miss," Fred apologised, and gestured to her coat whilst rolling his eyes, out of sight of Bowen.

"Oh, for God's sake," Betty grabbed her coat, and rolled her eyes within full view of Bowen, before flouncing out, followed by Fred.

"We'll fix it, Betty, don't worry," Alex called after her. Alex followed Bowen back into his office and slammed the door. He was clearly angry and rattled. I heard raised voices. I sat back down and finished my coffee, not knowing quite what to think. Betty was right of course - that it was trivial. Back in academia, it would have been a non-issue. And why the fixation on drugs when employees were free to get as drunk as they liked, as often as they liked - surely that would be even more of a security issue? I mused for a while. The voices were still raised in Bowen's office. Our door was still open so I used the excuse of closing it, to go over and see if I could hear what was being said. I could not. But looking down the corridor to the entrance, I saw that Betty and Fred were sitting side by side on the outer table still talking amiably. I shut the door and sat down to wait for Alex to come back. A few minutes later, I thought I heard Bowen's office door, but Alex did not appear.

I looked at the data on the computer screen. I was au fait with the procedure - no need to wait for Alex. I keyed in the coordinates for the anti-zap run. But I could not start this run preparing because the polarity needed to be changed on the equipment to produce anti-particles, to make it an anti-zap. That was still a hardware change - the wires needed reversing. I had seen Alex do that once, but I was not too sure which wires. It would have to wait for Alex.

After waiting another ten minutes, I was beginning to get a bit concerned. Although we had some contingency time built into the schedule, it was important to get the run started, otherwise there wouldn't be time for the image run, after the anti-zap, and the whole effort would have been in vain. I went over to Bowen's office to see if Alex was still there. Bowen said he had left about 10 minutes ago, probably to go over to HR. Then Bowen started a conversation about the importance of adhering to the rules. He seemed to want to convince himself, and I was not interested in becoming his ally, so I quit the nascent conversation as soon as I civilly could, and returned to the computer.

I waited some more, but it soon became clear that we had missed the window for doing three runs - the image run would have to be sacrificed to allow time for the anti-zap run, which was of course vital to restore the timeline. I felt a bit peeved at Alex, but I supposed that he was right that it was more important to try to sort out Betty's status. We could always repeat the experimental sequence tomorrow.

I retired to my office to read whilst waiting for Alex. I had got used to taking it for granted that Alex was always responsible and reliable, so it was with some concern that I looked at the time a while later, and saw that it was a few minutes past eleven. The anti-zap preparation urgently needed to be started if it was going to be ready in time to cancel the zap to the dog. Otherwise, we were in danger of completely missing the opportunity to revert the timeline. I wondered if I could switch the polarity myself. I went into the back room behind the equipment room, and looked at the connector block, where I remembered Alex making the changes previously. The screwdriver was sitting invitingly on top of the shelf alongside. But there were 10 wires into that connector block, and I had only a rough idea of the positions Alex had altered. It reminded me of the movies in which the hero defuses a bomb; certainly there was some growing anxiety in my stomach now. But, of course, Alex would be able to talk me through it. I phoned his number - it went to voicemail. I waited a couple of minutes and tried again, with the same result. Then I realised that Betty would also be able to talk me through, or indeed Mike, though I did not have his number. I phoned Betty. Thankfully, she answered straight away.

"Hi George, I'm sorry about that nonsense earlier, but I was talking with Fred, and he…"

I had to cut her off. "Betty, sorry, its urgent," I started. "Alex has not come back, and I need to reverse the polarity for the anti-zap, otherwise there won't be time for the anti-zap run. Which wires do I swap on the connectors?"

"Oh shit," she exclaimed. "Right - it's the two wires which come from behind the synchrotron."

"I don't know what that is - give it to me in layman's terms."

"OK, sorry, you can see a large metal wheel-shaped case behind and to the right of the connector block - it's the two wires which come from behind that, they come across the top of it."

"Ah, OK, I see them, stay on the phone. I'm going to put it down whilst I swap over the wires." At that point, I heard the office door, and quickly stepped back to see that it was finally Alex. I felt a surge of relief.

"Alex, quick," I shouted. "You need to swap the two wires ready for the anti-zap preparation - its already 11:20!"

"Oh Geez...," he responded, quickly bounding into the back room without taking off his coat. He deftly grabbed the screwdriver and switched the polarity. I immediately ran back into the office and pressed the button to start the preparation, but I could see from the screen that we were short of time for a full run.

"Betty's on the phone," I said retrieving it from the back room, whilst Alex took his coat off. "It's OK, Betty, Alex is back, we've done the polarity change and started the preparation."

"Let me talk to Alex," she said.

Alex took the phone. "Hi, Betty....What....Well I was with HR trying to sort out your mess....No, I thought George knew how to do it....Look, I wasn't the one who upset the apple cart...Oh not now, look I'll talk to you later." There was clearly some tension between them.

"So," Alex started, sitting down at the computer, "how much time do we have?"

"There's not enough time to fit in the anti-zap run before the timeline gets altered," I stated, panicking slightly.

He noted down data from the screen and did a quick calculation. He still seemed reasonably calm. "There's not enough time for a *full* preparation, but we can get away without a *full* anti-particle run. We only need to generate and project enough anti-particles to eliminate the bulk of the original zap cloud, so that it is below the threshold at which it goes unstable and zaps. In other words, to reduce the zap to a normal image cloud, which wouldn't have any effect on the dog."

I sighed with relief. "So how long do we need before you activate then?" I asked.

"Well its difficult to calculate exactly, all the time we've got really - so I'll run it up to the very last few seconds before activating." he replied.

We both settled back to wait. "I'm sorry to have put you in a jam like that, George," he said. "Once I had finally got into HR, it wouldn't have been politic to walk out, saying I had an urgent experiment. I hadn't realised how late it was getting, and then the traffic on the way back was all jammed up. Oh dear. I should have been more careful."

"It was my fault too," I said, "I got engrossed in reading instead of watching the time - I should have phoned you and Betty much sooner."

"Oh God, I switched my phone off when I was in HR, didn't I," realised Alex, pulling it out of his pocket and turning it back on. "I guess we all get a wake-up call from this charade. Still, we should just have enough time in the end."

"Yes, I was beginning to seriously contemplate what life would be like if we had missed the deadline, and ended up in the altered timeline. Do you think it would be much different Alex?"

"Well *I* don't know," replied Alex. "You're the historian. I thought you were assuring me there would be minimal collateral change, apart from the wooden statue and so on? But even if the overall story is almost the same, there would undoubtedly be timing and positional differences as the tiny changes wash through as a cascade of consequences. People arriving a few seconds earlier or later, parking their car in a different place and so on."

"Mmm, yes," I mused, "I suppose I was thinking more personally. I mean Betty said I might not be here at GCHQ because the statue was inspirational to me as a child, so it might change the course of my life radically. But it was only one of many artefacts and stories that my dad showed and told to me, so I'm not sure she's right. It's just that it's the only story she knows about." Alex nodded. There was a pensive pause.

"So what did HR say then," I asked.

"They didn't say much at all, but they did allow me to voice my opinions, and they made notes. I guess it depends mostly what Betty says on Friday. It depends how much she wants the job - she tends to be very impatient with stupidity, though she can be very persuasive if she tries. But at least I don't think they'll take much notice of Bowen's attitude, after what I said."

"Do you think I should go and talk to them as well?" I proffered.

"No… No offence, George, but you haven't been here long, it wouldn't carry any weight. But I'll ask Harriet to have a word - the military do have a lot of influence."

"Well, we're down to the last five minutes before the point of no return," announced Alex, looking at the data on the screen. "But I dare not activate the anti-zap yet, it still needs to build up as much capacity as possible. I'll let it build till about 2 or 3 seconds before the last moment. God, this is much tighter than I'm comfortable with."

My anxiety was beginning to grow again at Alex's comments.

"I'll say goodbye then," quipped Alex, "just in case we do get stuck in the altered timeline, and you don't work at GCHQ anymore?" But neither of us laughed. One way or another it did not seem funny.

A few seconds later I began to become aware, faintly at first, that there were others in the room. Alex was still focussed intently on the data on the screen. "What the hell?" he exclaimed as the screen gradually became unreadable with an alternative set of data simultaneously displayed, superimposed, on top of his data. As my focus cleared, I realised there was another version of Alex sitting in one of the other chairs.

"Superimposition!" I shouted at Alex, as if I were raising a fire alarm. Though indeed it seemed no less serious. My heart started thumping. The alternative Alex looked very alarmed. I glanced around. There was another *me*, standing close behind, also looking very alarmed. He was rubbing his jacket sleeve, I noted inappropriately. I rose and used my arms in a calming fashion. "There's nothing to be alarmed about," I announced loudly in an attempt to reassure them. "You are experiencing a superimposition of timelines, of possible events. It will only be temporary." But the alternative Alex was clearly protective of the controls of his computer. He lunged forward at Alex, but of course passed through him without making contact. Undeterred he stabbed the 'off' button of the computer. For a second my heart stopped. Was that our chance gone? - Our chance of beating the point of no return.

"Ha!" grunted my Alex. The action of the alternative Alex had merely resulted in him turning off the *alternative* timeline computer. Alex could now read *his* screen clearly again. "The fact that *we* are still here," Alex blurted at me, "confirms that we still have enough time. But the fact that *they* are here, confirms that it must be extremely close - I will leave it until the *very* last second." The other Alex had rushed out of the office door.

I sensed an opportunity. I turned to the alternative me. "Could you please help me with some comparative information?" I fished my phone out of my pocket. He was still wide-eyed with amazement, but complied when I indicated he should do the same. I quickly keyed in *'statue of bulldog dan'* to google, and got him to do the same. Top of my list were two references to the statue on the river Wye, but top of *his* list were references to Yale Bowl in New Haven, which houses a large bronze statue of another bulldog Dan. A good start. I thought it only fair to point out the differences to my double. I keyed in *'list works elgar wiki'*, and he followed my lead. It was a long list. I scrolled down impatiently to the Enigma variations. He followed suit. I could spot no differences - Elgar had still dedicated the thirteenth to Sinclair. I would have loved to hear it. Was the content very different, or were the so-called *inspirations* to a creative work mere fiction? Further down the list, I noticed with relief that *'Pomp and Circumstance'* was listed. It is, clearly, a major influential work. It was written a couple of years later, and I had been somewhat in denial that my change to history would have affected it.

I knew I had very little time left. *'wiki enigma var XI'*. In his list, a mention of Sinclair and his faithful dog, but *no mention of a fall in the river*. Bingo. I felt elation. My double looked simply bewildered but was clearly taking note of it all carefully.

I looked over to Alex with a big smile on my face, which disappeared almost instantly as I saw the troubled expression on his. A moment or two later he stabbed the activate button. My double disappeared, as did the chairs from different positions in the room. I sighed with relief. But Alex was raking his hair and sweating slightly.

"That was surprisingly useful, Alex," I started saying enthusiastically. "I got loads more information than I would have got from one of our pictures. But scrolling down lists to find something quickly on a smart phone is frustratingly slow. Next time, I'll make sure to choose targets that are top of the list." I was joking, using the phrase *'next time'*. I knew that the superimposition had been dangerous, and unintended, and could not be part of a well-executed plan.

But Alex did not smile. He sat in front of the screen with his hand over his mouth, not looking up. "I think we may have messed up very badly." His voice sounded strained.

"What do you mean?" I asked. "The superimposition has ended and we are still here in the same timeline."

"Can you just go and find out if the security guys are OK for me please?" he asked in reply. I remembered that the other version of Alex had left the office and not returned - what had he said to security? But surely, Alex could smooth that over - why was he looking so sombre?

I found Fred on his own, slumped in a chair, in the late stages of a panic attack, still breathing heavily. I ran to him, put my hands on his back and chest and encouraged him to breathe slowly. I realised I felt some affection for the man. It was a minute or two before he had calmed enough to speak.

"Oh God," he wheezed, "I had some sort of hallucination… near scared me to death…. Please don't tell anyone…I might lose my job…I don't know where he came from… but this other guy was dressed in security uniform… at first I thought he had come from the main building… then I saw his face was just like mine… that scared me… thought he was an impostor and we had trouble… but then *he* looked shocked… he pressed the emergency button *himself*… so what on earth was he wanting here?… but backup still haven't arrived… then Alex came out… and started talking to him… but that means it can't have been a hallucination doesn't it?.. unless Alex was a hallucination as well… Oh God… then Alex saw me and gave me a strange look, and he got out his phone and starting talking to someone… then the weirdest thing…. I thought I should grab the metal detector as a weapon just in case… not much of a weapon I know but… there were three on the table - he must have brought one in with him… and I went to pick it up but it wasn't solid… my hand went right through it… so I suppose it *was* some sort of hallucination… nothing like this ever happened to me before… but nobody came in or out… I swear…. security wasn't breached…"

I felt a need to reassure him that it was not just him alone experiencing these strange events, but I didn't want to give any indications that would point to our office as the source.

Then at that moment, a couple of security guards arrived running, at the front door. "Fred, they've had some strange happenings on the main door compromising security. Have you had any problems here? We need to lock down and check everyone."

Fred seemed immediately relieved that it was not just *his* door. He found the strength to stand and started to tell his story to the security guard. The other guard turned to me. "Could I see your security pass please sir?" I showed him. "Would you mind returning to your office while we check everyone who's in the building, please sir?" I welcomed the opportunity to be relieved of responsibility for Fred, and the opportunity to report back to Alex, and try to understand what had happened - the phrase *'strange happenings at the main door'* had struck a chill in my stomach.

When I got back to the office I was surprised to see Alex slumped in front of the BBC news on the computer screen. I briefly related Fred's experience to him and warned him security were coming round to check everyone. He nodded but did not reply. He looked very stressed - his brow was creased and his face - usually full of energy - had collapsed. "So what has happened?" I asked straightforwardly.

He looked up briefly, and drew a long breath. "So, last week, when we caused a superimposition, it was limited to this office - the cup, broken or not, was *only* visible to us. But this time, the superimposition relates to changes *outside*, and from a hundred years ago, so it is global, it has affected pretty much everyone, and I fear the consequences may be awful." He pointed at the TV report. The newsreader was stating that the attack, which had caused confusion and a temporary shutdown at their studios, they now understood to have also affected other media outlets. *'Facts were still sketchy, but somehow mass hallucinations had been caused, though the effects seemed to have stopped now.' 'The cause was unknown, but a nerve gas attack was suspected.'* Though now another correspondent was arguing that gas attacks could not be easily coordinated across multiple sites.

The security guard came into our office. He recognised me, but still asked to see both security badges. We showed them. "It's not just here," I informed him. "The BBC and other sites have been affected."

"What do they think caused it?" he asked.

"They don't know, they're talking about gas attacks I think," I stated, knowing that I was being deliberately misleading, driven by a gnawing guilt in my stomach. I was dreading him asking us complicated questions about what our experience had been, why we had not called security, and what Alex had seen at the door - it was actually of course the double of Alex at the door. And I was worried Alex himself was not now motivated to give plausible answers, maybe he would even own up to causing the chaos?

The security guard opened the door to the equipment room and its back room, and checked to see that there was no one else in there. "You'll both have to stay in here until we've checked all the offices and labs, but the lockdown shouldn't take more than a few minutes," he informed us. To my relief he then left without asking any further questions.

The news report was now showing footage of a pile-up on the M62. At first, I did not make the connection. Then the horrid realisation dawned. People would have been driving at speed, unexpectedly and suddenly images of other vehicles would have intruded - close by, or maybe directly in front. Panic and sudden braking, inevitable crashes, injury, death.

Sickness, regret and guilt were churning at my stomach and throat. I went out to the coffee machine to get some cups of water. I set one down in front of Alex, but he seemed in a state of shock, and did not acknowledge it. The news was reporting an aircraft crash close to Gatwick. Alex's phone rang. For a few seconds he appeared oblivious to it, then he responded.

"Yes Petra,... what?... Oh no... Right... I'll come to the hospital now." His voice was breathless. "A car hit the side of my wife's car, one of my kids is injured, I have to go to the hospital, George," he explained, suddenly animated, grabbing his coat and leaving me alone.

*'Multiple pile-ups on all the motorways'*. I felt shivery, and pulled my jacket closer round me. *'A state of emergency has been declared by the government'*, The pain in my stomach was forcing me to lean forward. *'Other countries also affected by chaos'*. The news broadcast had shifted to listing and detailing the catastrophes rather than speculating on the cause. *'All motorways have now been closed for at least 24 hours.'* I did not want to hear any more, but I was mesmerised and unable to stop listening to the unfolding reports of disaster. *'Hospitals overwhelmed.'*

My phone beeped. It was a message from Betty. *'Meet now usual place.'* My head cleared a little. It felt immediately better to have somewhere to go, something to do, however small a purpose. Presumably she knew? Though it would be difficult being with her - usually it was the sweetest thing - but now that would be soiled by our complicit guilt. Tears came to my eyes.

By the time I got to the front door, I had composed myself. Fred was listening to the radio news. He was clearly grateful for my attention to him of earlier. "Hello sir, have you been following the news? Whatever it was, has been happening all over the place."

But I did not want to get involved in conversation. "Yes, Fred, no need to worry about your own sanity. But I need to get home now, and check everything is OK," I lied.

The cold air outside was a relief. It seemed to clear away some of the anxiety that was hurting inside me. I strode to the car and drove off toward 'our hill'. I was relieved to see no signs of carnage on the local roads, though there were several vehicles that looked like they had either had a scrape, or parked hurriedly. Overall, the roads seemed eerily quiet. Driving out into the countryside was a relief - nature seemed unperturbed.

After a few minutes, I pulled up behind Betty's Cabriolet at the gate to the field. I trudged up the hill toward her. She was huddled in a blanket following events on her mobile. She waved in acknowledgment, but without warmth.

"So tell me quickly why it happened, George," she spoke in a business-like way.

I sat down next to her. "There wasn't enough time for a full anti-zap run, so Alex ran the preparation up to the very last second before actioning it. The superimposition occurred for the last couple of minutes - presumably because it was touch and go whether the original zap would get cancelled."

Betty nodded. "I assumed so. I'm surprised Alex didn't just abort the run at the first sign of superimposition. That way, it would have been just an ineffectual blip."

"But then we would have been stuck in the altered timeline." I replied.

"So would you rather live with *this* mess?" she barked, impatient with my slow understanding. "Listen George, we don't have long to fix this, and *you* have to do it, because I can't get into the office at the moment - I am suspended."

The words *'fix this'* crackled through my brain, returning hope to the vocabulary of my consciousness. "We can fix this?" I echoed incredulously.

"Yes," she confirmed, "but we don't have much time, security will be on our case all too soon."

"Why, surely they have no idea it has anything to do with us?" I argued.

She sighed deeply again at my lumbering, measured comprehension. "Harriet witnessed superimposition last week? She will inform the powers that be. I have messaged her to come here to see me as soon as she can. I will try to buy us some time. I will try to persuade her to let us attempt to fix it, before she informs the authorities that the likely source is our lab. But it will be difficult. Her loyalty is to the authorities, and it would be difficult for her to explain to them why she delayed before telling them. Indeed she may already have spoken to them." I felt my new-found hope begin to ebb away. "That's why you have to move fast, George." I nodded my understanding of the urgency. "You have to eliminate the discovery of the i-vector from the timeline," she continued.

"But, how do I... do... that?" I said it slowly because the truth was beginning to dawn.

"You have to eliminate Alex at a time before he discovers it. You have to prepare a zap to hit him about two years ago."

"But is there no other way?" I protested, dreading the very idea.

"Well," she continued coldly, "its no use zapping *me*. Although Alex is very generous in crediting me with working out the actual meaning of the i-vector, I suspect he, or one of his other colleagues would have got there eventually. But without Alex, I would never have conceived of the particle research - I am not a physicist."

"That's not what I meant," I protested.

"And its no use zapping *you*, before you came up with this damn Schrodinger's dog idea. Sooner or later we would have stumbled into making the same mistake. The i-vector equipment is just *too* dangerous, without understanding all the ramifications and effects."

"Isn't there some way we could just send back a message warning of the danger?" I proffered, even though I knew it was impossible.

"We can take pictures of the past, but we can't send messages back," she said bluntly.

"Alex would agree with this," she continued. "It is a sacrifice. We have to do it to avoid all the suffering that has otherwise been caused today. It's ghastly to have to kill a good friend, but it is our duty to humanity. It is rational. I sent Alex a message to come here as well, but he hasn't responded. How is he?"

"He was certainly devastated," I replied. "Just slumped in a chair staring at the news. Then Petra phoned and said one of their kids had been injured in a traffic accident, so he rushed off to the hospital."

"Oh," Betty sighed, showing some compassion for the first time.

"So wouldn't it be kinder to ki.., to eliminate Alex before he has his kids?" I suggested.

"It would, George, of course it would, but I don't know where to find him at that stage of his life. Look, I've written down the coordinates of his office back at the university where we used to work, before we came here to GCHQ. She handed me a piece of paper. I've thought through the timing, and I want you to target November 10th, 2 years ago. That's a Monday, so if by any chance you don't catch him that day, keep trying consecutive week days. But those coordinates are worked out so that you should get an image of his chair, hopefully with him in it. Use low resolution pictures so that you can get them done quickly. You then need to adjust the coordinates to get right on top of him, check with another low resolution picture, before preparing a zap run. He usually worked regular hours, so try maybe 10 am to start with. If we are lucky, you should get him in the image first time. OK?"

My mouth opened, but I found nothing to say. Betty had obviously thought it all through. And I could find no reason why she was not right.

"OK," I nodded. "You know what else this means, don't you?"

"Yes," she said softly. "We will almost certainly never meet. We are also sacrificing our relationship." She pulled me close and hugged me hard, but only for a few seconds. "But go *now*, George, quickly," she said, her voice finally faltering with emotion. "There is not much time to get it done."

I stood, turned away and strode back toward the car, tears running down my face. I knew I should not look back.

But, as I reached the gate, I heard Betty shouting to me. I turned. She was running down the hill toward me. "Wait, George, wait!" I desperately hoped she wasn't going to drag out this excruciating goodbye. But there was something different in her voice.

"Something you said George," she panted, … "about sending back a warning message… you remember Alex tried an image of the future last week, when I was out here board-kiting with Harriet?… can you remember what future day he targeted?"

"Uhm…," I considered for a second, "he said a week ahead I think, so that would be today. But it didn't work, you remember?"

"It didn't work *last* week because there was no future to image *then*, but it *might* just work now that the future has caught up. What time of day was the target for the picture?"

I shook my head. "He didn't say."

"Damn," she banged her head with her palm, "I read the 'Lab Logbook' but didn't pay enough attention. The image was to be of the usual wall in the equipment room though, I remember that."

"Yes, because he wanted me to remember to bring in the clock, before today, and put it on the table there. I presume, in order to record and verify the date and time."

"OK, George, listen carefully, *new plan*. Go back to the office quickly now. I am going to write a warning message on my phone, and email it to you, while you are driving back. Immediately you get in to the office, print off the email and pin it up in the same position on the wall, where the newspaper is now. Damn, I suppose the image that he tried to get is low resolution."

"No," I cut in, "It's definitely high resolution. Alex got called in to Bowen's office and delayed for ages, while that run was preparing, so the preparation went on longer than intended. I remember Alex remarking that it would be a high resolution picture."

"Great," she continued, "In that case, I can make it a detailed warning message. Print it out in Arial font, size 14. I know that will be legible in high resolution on the wall, provided the light is on, of course. That's important, George."

"Then read the 'Lab Logbook'," she added in a more subdued tone, "to find out whether we have got the message up on the wall, before the target time, or not." We had both become enthused with the new plan. But the truth was that we might not meet the deadline time, to attempt the message. And even if we were in time, we did not know whether it would work as we were hoping. "So, if we are not in time, then you have to proceed straightaway with the plan to eliminate Alex, as we agreed earlier. But if you get the message in place before the target time, you must then wait until after the target time to see if it worked. If the warning message gets through to us last week, then we would have acted differently, the timeline after receiving the message will be different, and presumably, we would avoid today's horrible mess. But if you are still there and remembering what happened today, then that means the warning message didn't work, the current timeline is still running, and the past was not changed to eliminate today's catastrophe. So *then*, you must go ahead with the plan to eliminate Alex. Is that all clear George?"

"Yup, so..., Go back... Print message... Arial 14... Lights on... Pin up message... Check log... I'll phone you to let you know at that point, anyway."

"Yes please," she kissed me quickly. "*Go now.*"

\*     \*     \*

This modicum of hope had done wonders for my motivation. The nightmare feelings had subsided somewhat, and I drove back with purpose. There was still the danger that security would be searching for us already, so I drove furtively past the entrance, and glanced in to see if there were any signs of trouble. It looked like Fred was still on his own, so I parked up and went in.

Fred was still glued to the radio news and its sombre cataloguing of disasters. "Hallo again sir," he checked my badge cursorily. "They say the death toll is in the tens of thousands now. They still have no idea what it was though." I gulped at the former revelation, but his attention to the radio made it easy for me to avoid a long conversation. I went on through to the office, sitting straight down at the computer. Betty's email had just arrived, so I set it printing immediately. Amazingly, she had managed to type about five pages of a detailed warning message in the short time I had been driving back. I picked up the five sheets of paper from the printer and opened the door to the equipment room.

But what I saw almost made me buckle at the knees with shock. As it was, my stomach convulsed and I vomited behind the door. Alex had clearly returned, and had hung himself, using his belt, from one of the ceiling struts. I looked away, not wanting to witness the strange open eyes, his lips were very dark and his tongue was slightly protruding. Confusion and panic descended on me. I went back into the office and sat down heavily on a chair, trying to get my breathing back to normal. What should I do now? How did it affect the plan I was supposed to be executing? Betty had been very clear. I was grateful she had set it out in steps. I was supposed to be working quickly. No, I did not think it made any difference to the overall plan. It just compounded the nightmare. I had to just carry on. I went back into the equipment room, my eyes avoiding the horror of Alex's limp, heavy figure. I carefully unpinned the newspaper pages from the wall and pinned up Betty's warning message in their place. Fortunately, my vomit had only soiled a corner of one page. As an afterthought, I turned the clock upside down, in the same manner that people used to do with the Union Jack, as a warning sign, in the days of the Empire.

I kept repeating the steps to myself - Return... Print... Pin Up... Lights On... I had automatically switched on the light-switch as I entered the room. OK, Logbook, next. I returned to the office, closing the equipment room firmly behind me, and pulled out the 'Lab Logbook'. I flicked back the pages until I had Wednesday 30th November. There was a lot written for that day. First the high-speed filming of a spark, and a zap. Then I found the details of the attempted future image - my finger traced through until I found *'Target Time: Wed 7th December 17:00'*. Right. It was now 16:07. We had set up the message in time! I breathed a long sigh of relief, but then the ugly scene next door came back into my mind. First, I would message Betty on the phone. I pondered telling her about Alex, but decided against it - there was no point in upsetting her. I texted *'Target 17:00 Phew'*.

Then I decided the next job was to clean up the pool of my vomit in the equipment room. I badly wanted to go to the gents anyway to wash out my mouth and freshen up my face, so I went and got a pile of paper towels at the same time. I made a reasonable job of cleaning up, and disposed of them back in the gents. A text came back from Betty: *'I'm freezing, getting dark, still no Harriet, hack light switch on, start locate Alex x'*. I looked at the time, still only 16:14. It felt like it was going to be a very long hour to wait until 17:00. She had put a kiss on the end of her message - why had I not thought to do that? Or was it an accidental duplication of the last 'x' in Alex's name? No, Betty was very precise. *'start locate Alex x.'*

Yes, I could start a run with the coordinates Betty had written down, to try to locate Alex two years ago. I pulled the scrap of paper Betty had given me, from my jacket pocket, and keyed the coordinates into the computer. I started the run preparing.

I needed to keep busy. What did she mean *'hack light switch on'*? I had already made sure the light was on. I heard some voices in the corridor. A degree of panic set in. Should I hide? I began to realise that the presence of Alex's dead body in the next room *did* complicate matters. Otherwise if security came looking for us, I could simply have gone with them, and left the message to look after itself. But they would be bound to check the other rooms. Then there would be lengthy unwanted activity in the equipment room, which might block the message. They might even remove the message, thinking it was a suicide note. They might turn the light off on leaving. Ah! Was that what Betty meant - *'hack the light switch'*? Make it stay on?

The voices passed by the door, off in the direction of the exit. I breathed again. Should I move the body? It would be very difficult emotionally, and physically. And I had nowhere to sensibly get it out of sight, anyway.

OK the light switch. I could probably manage that. I went to get the screwdriver from the cabinet top next to the connectors, averting my eyes from the unpleasant sight as I passed by. But seeing the screwdriver reminded me that the polarity was *still* reversed from the *anti-zap* run we had done. Damn, I would have to reverse the polarity back again, and redo the run that I had started in order to locate Alex two years ago. I went back to the computer and cancelled the run, back to the connectors to adjust the polarity to normal, (at least I was now clear how to do it), and back to the computer again to restart the run. Now, the light switch. I unscrewed the plastic faceplate from the wall. There were two wires feeding in to the switch. Presumably, all I had to do was connect the two wires together and the lights would be permanently on? I was aware that the wires were live. I fetched my leather gloves from the office. If I got this wrong, and the lights went out for any reason, the message would be unreadable and it was game over. Was it worth the risk? I decided I *would* try. I carefully unscrewed one of the terminals and pulled the wire out of it. There was a small spark as it separated, and the lights went out. A moment's panic. But then I realised that obviously the lights would go out when I disconnected a terminal. I carefully loosened the other terminal screw, pushed the loose wire into it, and tightened it again. The lights came back on. I tried clicking the switch. The switch made no difference, the lights stayed on. Success. I screwed the plastic faceplate back to the wall, hiding the hack.

It was now 16:25. The pressure had reversed since earlier. Then it had been a rush to make sure the message was ready in time for the future picture. But now there was nothing to do except wait, and hope for no interference. I waited. I ran through in my mind what I might say if security came. I waited some more. Just 10 minutes to go. My phone beeped and made me jump. It was a text from Betty: *'MP'*. What did she mean? I went through the permutations... Oh, Military Police. That did not sound good. Should I leave or stay? I decided to stay, to try to manage the encounter, and protect the message. I hoped they might not come before 17:00.

Voices and footsteps in the corridor. The door was opened by Fred, allowing in two very burly MPs. The first soldier had a couple of photos in his hand. "Yes," he checked the photos, "this is one of them." He addressed me, "Command want to talk to you sir, you have to come with us." I rose from my chair compliantly. But the other soldier was already routinely opening the equipment room door to search in there. There was a profanity. "The other one's in here, Sarge, but he's hanged." He checked Alex's body more intimately than I had had the courage to do. "He's dead. Shall I cut him down?"

I found my voice. "Can I suggest you leave that room untouched for the forensic people?" I put in politely but firmly.

He looked questioningly over to the Sergeant who nodded. "Yes, let's get this one back to command, pronto." he said. I glanced at the computer screen - it was 16:58. They marched me out and down the corridor toward the main entrance. Fred followed us. I felt elated that the room was clear and intact, with just a minute or two before the warning would be imaged. But I felt very scared of what lay ahead. If, indeed, *anything* lay ahead, I mused.

## Chapter 10
But there's one great advantage in (living backwards), that one's memory works both ways.
*Alice through the looking glass*

*So, the story now reverts back to WEDNESDAY 30th November. As I have already narrated, the morning had been filled with high-speed video-recording of a spark and zap. Betty had taken the afternoon off to go kite-boarding with Harriet. Alex had started the preparation of a particle cloud for the very first attempt at an image from the future. He had admitted feeling guilty about excluding Betty from this epic experiment, but was anxious that she might not be able to resist the prank of causing a paradox by subsequently changing the content of the future picture. After some soul-searching, he finally actioned the attempted image.*

Seconds later the stream of data came up on the screen. Alex scrolled the numbers up and down, examining the technical characteristics of the picture. "Wow, we *have* got a picture," he stated, clearly surprised. He had earlier stated that he doubted that it would be possible. We sat back to wait for the image to process.

It was a ten-minute wait, during which we pondered what the content of the image might be. It was in the equipment room, of course. I know we expected my clock to be in the picture, but I had not really thought about what else we might see. Perhaps us? - a kind of holiday snap from the future, or a welcome message, or even the winning lottery numbers? When the image finally appeared on the screen, it was a horrible shock. Down the left hand edge of the image was Alex's apparently dead body, hung presumably from the ceiling, his lifeless eyes open and staring, his face grotesquely bloated and tilted to one side. Looking over Alex's shoulder, there was a lot of text on pages pinned to the wall, which was not immediately readable on a single computer screen, and I thought I glimpsed the clock in the bottom right, though it seemed wrong somehow.

"What the hell...," Alex barked. Alex jerked back in shock, banging his head against mine, then immediately leant forward and snapped the screen off. I had found the fleeting glimpse of the image sickening, but it must have been much worse for Alex. He jumped up and strode about a bit. I didn't know what to say - I had no idea what this meant, but I was curious to read the text, once Alex had calmed down enough - perhaps we could cut the appalling part out of the image, so we could read the rest.

Alex's shock had turned to anger. "Its one of Betty's pranks," his voice was stressed. "She's obviously used Photoshop to make the image, and coded it in the software to show up when we try a future picture," he expounded. I remembered the prank she had played on me with the man in the flat cap by the river.

He picked up his phone and called Betty. "You have a sick sense of humour, Betty," he almost shouted down the phone. "How could you think something like that is amusing?... What...No, the future picture... Don't lie... Oh, Go to Hell," he ended the call abruptly. He seemed close to tears now. "I can't trust her, George, she's a menace sometimes. Always playing games." He slumped into a chair. I went over and sat next to him.

"It doesn't seem like the sort of thing Betty would do," I proposed gingerly. "Are you sure it's a hoax?"

"Oh, so you're suggesting its a *real* picture?" barked Alex scarily.

"Well, perhaps we should read the text to see what it says?" I suggested tentatively. I had never seen Alex this angry.

"No," he snapped, "we're not buying any deeper into her prank."

"Oh, OK," I had to back off.

"In fact I'm deleting the picture," he added, leaning forward, typing into the keyboard on the other computer.

I decided to retire to my own office for a while. It was uncomfortable trying to talk to Alex in this mood. As I sat down in my own office, a call came in on my phone. It was Betty.

"Hi George, I just had a really weird call from Alex. Are you with him? What's going on?" she asked, sounding very concerned.

I felt confused, not sure whether Betty was being devious, as Alex would have it, or genuine - perhaps Alex had overreacted to the ghastly image of himself. I decided the only thing I could do was to be straightforward myself. I explained what had happened to Betty.

"Well, I'm a bit miffed that he did the experiment without me there," she admitted. "But the image sounds really scary, I can't quite imagine what... how that could be. And you didn't read any of the text?" she checked. "I'd better come straight in and see what's going on."

"Actually, " I suggested, "I would leave it for a while - Alex is really angry and upset, and he still firmly believes you are pranking him."

"Oh, Oh... OK, George. I'll come in later then. Actually, we are having a brilliant time here - Harriet's going to let me have a go with the kite-board in a minute. We'll sort it out later - don't worry."

"OK. I'll see you later then. Take care if you're trying the kite-board." I still wasn't totally sure if she meant sort out the tension between her and Alex, or sort out what the image meant, though I was getting a gnawing feeling in my stomach that this was no prank, that the image was real, and that something was badly wrong in the future."

Then I remembered that Alex had deleted the image - did that mean we could never find out what it meant? After thinking it through for a minute or two, I realised that we could do another future image tomorrow, targeted to the same time, to get another copy of the picture. That was assuming that Alex would countenance doing it - it had clearly given him a dreadful shock.

\*       \*       \*

It was about half past five when Harriet and Betty arrived back. I was still in my own office. I had been in to see Alex once on the premise of asking him a question, to see how his mood was. He seemed to have immersed himself in some other experiment, and had not mentioned the fracas of earlier.

They came into my office first. Betty had had an accident coming off the kite-board, and had twisted her ankle. She was hobbling along on one foot, being ably, and perhaps too willingly, supported by Harriet on the other side. I felt a fleeting irritability toward Harriet for putting Betty in danger, but Betty dismissed the injury as slight and 'well worth it for the fun'. We settled Betty into a chair with her foot supported on the only other chair. Harriet and I went into Alex's office.

"Betty has twisted her ankle," I started. I was relieved to see a look of concern sweep over Alex's face - his anger toward her must have subsided. "She's OK, she's in my office," I assured him. "Harriet's a little early, but when you are finished up, perhaps you can come in to my office and talk through this afternoon's experiment with her." I was needing to be circumspect because Harriet was standing there. He sighed rather deeply, but nodded.

"OK," he confirmed, "I'll just be a couple of minutes, then Harriet can take over."

I walked back into my own office. Betty was already keying into my computer. She was propped with her elbows on the desk, and her leg still supported on the chair beside her. "Oh, I forgot to say that Alex deleted the picture," I told her.

She smiled up at me disdainfully. "The software makes an immediate backup of pictures - you don't really think I'd leave something important unsecured? Anyway, why would he delete it if he thinks it's a fake? - obviously I would have the original."

"I guess it's an emotional gesture from him," I suggested, "it's a disturbing image. He said he'll be a couple of minutes. Can you make sure it's off the screen before he comes in?"

As the image appeared on the screen, Betty gave a little gasp of pain and I saw her eyes tear over. It convinced me that she was not pranking, even though I knew she was an accomplished actress. "Oh... I see what you mean," she said in a small voice. "Let's make a copy without the gore." She was using some sort of image editing software, and scrubbing out the offensive part of the picture. I knew we would need more chairs, so I left her to it, and went back in to delay

Alex if necessary, and to requisition a couple of chairs from his office.

A few minutes later, Alex and I entered my office humping along a chair each. The printer was busy. Betty looked at Alex, but he would not meet her eyes.

"It is really horrible, Alex, I'm so sorry. Please don't think that I would do something like that." She held out her hand to him and started to cry. "I really don't want you to think it was me."

"So you're telling me it's real?" Alex's voice was cracking. "I can't look at it."

"I know," said Betty softly. "I've redacted it from the message - the message seems to be some sort of warning about things going badly wrong." Betty gestured to me to fetch the printed message from the printer. There were three copies, but Alex shook his head, so Betty and I read it through silently. Parts of it were technical, the concept of superimposition I had not yet experienced. It was clearly written by Betty, and she had stated so at the end, sending her love back to us.

I looked over to Betty when I finished reading it through and noticed that she was trembling. She winced and adjusted the position of her ankle on the chair. "So," she began, in a wobbly voice, addressing her remarks to Alex, "it is written by me in the future. It warns that the changing of the past, by using the zap, can result in a temporary superimposition of the extant present with the altered present, which can cause widespread disastrous effects. It is an attempt by us, in the future, to change the way things unfold, by giving us this information now, to help us to avoid the carnage and bedlam that apparently we accidentally caused… in the future." She held out the spare copy to Alex. "There is nothing in it about the image of you," she added to reassure him. Alex looked over to me. I nodded to reassure him that everything Betty had said about the message was correct.

He took the sheets of paper and started reading. He got to the end and went back and re-read it. "So, a message from the future," he looked at Betty very intently. She was still trembling and tearful. I picked up her coat from the floor where she had dumped it when we sat her down, and put it over her. She smiled up at me weakly. "Well, it seems plausible," he continued, clearly struggling to integrate the mind-boggling nature of the proposition, and still lurching between belief in hoax, or truth. "And it makes certain predictions," a pause, "so it can be verified or falsified in due course," another pause. "But one suspicious thing," he went on, "it says that you were suspended for failing a drugs test, so how could you have put the message on the wall?" He shot a questioning glance at Betty.

She furrowed her brow. "*I* don't know," she answered with irritation.

"Betty," said Alex with exasperation, "if this is one of your games, I swear I will... "

"What, hang me?" shouted Betty, bursting into tears.

Alex exhaled sharply. "Alex," I put in, "if its any help, the clock was in the picture. But the clock is still at my home at the moment, so Betty couldn't have faked that."

Alex looked at me intently. "Unless you are in on this game too? Or maybe Betty bought another clock like it? - Betty saw it the day her niece came to your place?"

"And another thing," I added, "the message mentions assassinating the dog on a particular day, - that was something I only started thinking about this lunchtime - I haven't told Betty anything about it as yet."

"It could have occurred to Betty as well," countered Alex. "You talked to her about the story behind the statue didn't you?"

Betty sighed in an exasperated fashion. "So," she asked, "how far in the future has this message come from?"

"Next week," I put in.

"*Next week, Jesus!*" Betty repeated, surprised. "That's a lot of new experimental ground they, or we, covered in a week. Wait a minute, does the clock in the image show the exact time you targeted for?" We all turned the last sheet round to look at the time on the upside-down clock.

"Yes, it does," confirmed Alex.

"So, there!" Betty declared brightly. "If I had tried to fake the picture, how could I have known what time in the future you would target?"

Alex thought for a moment. "You could have put in some computer code to read the target time, and some clever image processing to draw the appropriate numbers and letters into the clock outline."

Betty started laughing through her tears. "Alex, this is getting ludicrous. As you said earlier, there are experimental predictions in this message, which can be verified, so let's just drop this *ridiculous* argument for tonight. We can start doing experiments tomorrow to prove for you whether it's real or not." Her voice softened. "Actually, no, I'm sorry, it's not ridiculous. I can imagine that if it were me in that horrible picture, I would be in denial too. George, will you help me get home please - I can hardly walk on my own." She stood awkwardly, and I put my arm around her, and her hand on my shoulder to walk her out. We left Alex sitting there still musing over the message.

## *THURSDAY 1st December*

The next morning we started on a slew of experiments, which I think were both a part of Alex's plans anyway, but were also implicated in the warning message from our future. Zaps and anti-zaps, superimposition and deliberate paradox were explored, just as I have previously described. Except that all experiments were carefully confined to the office and equipment room, and the office door was always kept locked with a 'Do Not Disturb' sign hung on the door handle, in recognition of the warnings in that message. The mood always became bright when new experiments were in progress, and it was difficult to say at what point Alex actually became convinced of the validity of the warning message. I think once the superimposition had been experienced, and its implications thought about, it actually became irrelevant whether the message was real or fake - the warning itself became very relevant and important, and I think there was some sense of relief that we were shielded, by fore-warning, from making a huge mistake.

## *FRIDAY 2nd December*

Thus, I was a little surprised when Alex called us to meet on the hill on the Friday evening.

"In my opinion," he started, as we huddled together in blankets, "the balance of probability is that the alleged message from our future is real. All the experimental results are consistent with what it says, and the warning in it is undoubtedly valid, and massively helpful. In my mind, it still remains a possibility that Betty could have predicted the experimental results, and I note, by the way, that she still has not yet been suspended, though the message says she would be?" He paused and looked at Betty, who just shrugged. "But there is a hugely important issue that we need to address if this message is true. Namely, that when we get to next Wednesday, then whatever is pasted on the equipment room wall at that time, will be the message sent back to ourselves the previous Wednesday. In other words, if that image is different from the image that *we* received, then the past will be changed, yet again."

He stopped talking at that point. I admit I had not considered that issue, though I imagine Betty must have thought it through.

"Yes," Betty took up the thread, "and for obvious reasons we don't want the same picture, we don't want Alex in it like that. So, we have to accept that the past *will* be changed again. And unless we are careful, the past will keep changing every Wednesday and we, or some alternative versions of us, will spend the rest of eternity repeating this week in different ways."

"Unless," Alex picked it up again, "unless we fake the image of me, in fact, fake the whole image on to the wall, so that it looks exactly the same as we experienced it?"

Betty laughed gently - the irony was palpable. "I think it would be difficult to fake it, to make it look three dimensional and so on. Unfortunately, we don't have access to last week's computer to programmatically insert an image, in the way that you originally thought I had counterfeited it. To fake it, we would have to stick a piece of paper on the wall, which carried the image of you, and a piece of paper carrying the image of the message. But unfortunately, if it was examined and found to be fake, then the whole message might well be rejected."

"But have you actually examined the image in detail?" responded Alex. "We might already be in receipt of a faked image - this might not be the first iteration of the loop in time."

"No I haven't, that's true," said Betty thoughtfully, "your adverse reaction was, understandably, so severe, that I immediately redacted the image, and I haven't looked at the original since - I don't *want* to see it again either. But if you think it's a good idea I will examine it in detail tomorrow."

"Well, lets consider the alternatives first," suggested Alex, methodically. "In order to prevent the past getting repeatedly changed in different ways, it is first and foremost important that the image is reproducible, and re-displayed exactly as it was originally received. And I would suggest that our version of the message should *state* that it must be repeated *exactly*. The fact that the message, which *we* received, does not include that instruction, is a clue, in my opinion, that it may be the original message, done in haste, in response to the stated disaster. If there had been time to consider the ramifications, as we are doing now, then the writer of that message would surely have included the instruction to repeat the message exactly."

"That's a very good point," Betty replied crisply, raising a finger in recognition. "Indeed, if it was intended to be repeatable, then why would they put that horrible image in, which would be very difficult to reproduce? In fact, why include that image at all - did they think we wouldn't take it seriously without the gore?"

I realised that we had only seen the 'gore' for perhaps a second each, and had integrated it in our minds as an unwanted part of the message. "Perhaps," I suggested, "that horrible part of the *image* is not part of the *message*. As I remember it from my fleeting glimpse, it was not an image on the wall, it was… in front of it."

Alex shuddered, but nodded. "In that case, I think we should be extremely grateful to those versions of us, who must have gone through a truly terrible time emotionally, but responded by giving us sufficient information to avoid the same catastrophe. But it also places on us, as first responders, the responsibility to get the *new repeatable message*, absolutely right. I suggest we drop the gory image, use the text pretty much as is, and add a paragraph at the end about exact repetition for the following week, including font style and size, and the precise position on the wall."

"I agree," said Betty, "but that also means we have to accept that *this* week, however we live it, is going to become redundant, superseded, non-existent, not included in the continuity of our lives. Because clearly, our revised message, particularly since it will not contain the gory part, will cause *this* week to be very different again, from last Wednesday onwards."

"A profound thought," replied Alex. "But that doesn't mean this week is unimportant - it is *critical* for building the future. How odd it is, that a decisive, vital week, will actually then be excluded from the flow of time."

"And," continued Betty, "while we are being so pompous and profound, there is one other question which bothers me. We are hypothesizing that this image and message is the first one, in response to the accidental disaster. So, that means that those versions of us, who were involved in the disaster, clearly *didn't* get a warning message from *their* future. But they must have attempted a future image on their Wednesday. Because preceding that, there was/is only the one timeline, everything was identical for them and us - indeed they were us. So what did *they* get in that first future picture?"

"Well we might be able to answer that," replied Alex, "by trying another future image targeted further into the future, though I'm a bit afraid of opening Pandora's box there," he sighed heavily. "Let's get through this week first."

"But," I interjected, "Wouldn't that future picture depend on whether the versions of us that went through the disaster, and their world, still exist as a continuing timeline. If they do, God help them, then we would get whatever message they choose to put on their wall."

"Well no," Alex explained, "we know that they are only *one week* ahead of us in time, so if we tried a future image targeting a month ahead, we would avoid them. And that's another reason that I think this message may be the original, written as a hasty response to the disaster. Because it suggests nothing about getting on-going, future messages from them, on alternate Sundays or whatever. In our position, considering it through as we are now, we might decide to include that? But then again, I'm not at all sure *their* timeline would continue, it may well cease to exist when the past is changed, which it has been, by their message. I suppose we will maybe get an answer to that conundrum next week. If we carry on remembering the gore after next Wednesday, then each timeline definitely survives. But if we don't remember then… We might be better able to approach an answer to that by an experiment zapping plastic cups in the past…" Alex trailed off and yawned. We were all cold and it was time to head back to the car, Betty limping along in the middle, one arm over each of our shoulders.

*   *   *

# Chapter 11
## and there came wise men from the east

### *THURSDAY 8th December*

We made a late start in the morning. We had had a lot to drink the previous night celebrating.

The last few days had been spent perfecting the *'essential-to-repeat-exactly'* message, and positioning it very precisely on the wall. But during those few days, there had been a sense of fear building. Fear that we might inevitably be living in a loop from Wednesday 30th November to Wednesday 7th December. Fear that every time the message was imaged from the 7th back to the preceding Wednesday, the intervening week would be changed, even by a tiny amount. And then we would be condemned to unknowingly live that week yet again.

But that had not happened. The target time of the future picture, 5 pm on the 7th December, came and passed as we held our breath. And we were living on. The sense of relief and freedom was palpable. The knowledge that we had done exactly what was needed to avoid the described catastrophe in the warning message, and to ensure future continuity, was exhilarating. We went out celebrating a new beginning. The new beginning was a set of hangovers.

Yesterday had also been the day of Betty's suspension of course. We had known it was coming at some point in the week, but we had also known that we had to act as if it was unexpected, so as not to arouse any suspicion. In the event, Betty's act was, of course, flawless and thoroughly convincing, but I had to choke back an urge to laugh.

It was only sad that, because she was suspended, we could not experience that critical moment, at 5 pm on the 7th December, all together. We had discussed getting together somewhere outside of GCHQ so that Betty could be with us, but we decided that it was more important to guard the equipment room, lest anyone should come in and inadvertently stand in the way of the message at the critical moment. It was also important to remove and shred the message immediately after 5 pm, in case anyone else happened to read it and start asking questions. However, we had managed to be together with her on the phone, at the countdown to the critical moment, like a detached and mistimed New Year's Eve celebration.

The new beginning was also tempered with humility, because we had been helped to avoid a dreadful mistake, that would have ruined ours, and many others' lives, and a determination that we should be thoroughly responsible and careful in our pursuit of the use of the i-vector equipment.

\*     \*     \*

"Do you realise," Betty said to me later, "that it's only two weeks to Christmas? Will you go back to Oxford for the holiday?" We were walking back down the lane to her place. It was a bracing evening with a clear sky, stars very evident as we got away from the lights of the town.

It was a straightforward question, but it made me face a bunch of issues which I had avoided considering. Despite my initial intention to return at the weekends to Oxford, I had not actually been home the last three weeks. And here, my relationship with Betty was very real and immediate; making my marriage, though not formally abandoned, feel very distant. "Well, yes, I guess I will," I replied after a moment's thought, "my son will be back from his first term at university, so it will be good to talk with him at length, I've only spoken to him on the phone a couple of times. I don't know whether my daughter will be coming over though, she's working on the west coast of America… But I will miss you." I pulled her closer. "What about you? Does your family get together?"

"Yes, very much so, and it's good fun. But I tell you what, how about a skiing holiday for the two of us, just after Christmas? A reward for persevering with the drudgery of present choosing and card writing?"

"Oh, that would be brilliant," I enthused, relishing the idea of pure mountain air, and snow-scenes, though in truth I had never actually skied before. Out of the corner of my eye, I noticed a dim and brief shooting star. "Hey," I added, "I've just had a cool idea. Suppose we target an image back two thousand years and get an image of the 'Star of Bethlehem', then we could print some Christmas cards with the real thing. No one would know of course. That would make the most amazing subterfuge - a sort of reverse fraud!"

Betty laughed, "Yeah, that would be beautifully devious. But I'm not sure we could get an image - remember the *'lights have to be on'*!" We walked on in silence for a minute. "Unless," she said slowly and thoughtfully, "unless we take the image from *above* the atmosphere - the starlight is much brighter up there, plus the much thinner atmosphere would allow the particles longer to register the light, before decoherence occurs. Yes, we could just use coordinates a few miles above sea level," she concluded excitedly. There was another minute of silence as we contemplated the ruse. "But," Betty finally added, "isn't there some doubt about when the Nativity actually happened?"

"Mm," I responded in mock arrogance, "but I'm an Historian, I should be able to sort out a problem like that!" We had arrived back at Betty's house and crunched our way up her gravel path.


## *FRIDAY 9th December*

Betty's disciplinary hearing was this morning, though she had seemed unperturbed at breakfast time. We had arranged to meet up at a café in town for lunch, to hear how it had gone.

But she strode in to the office late morning.

Alex beamed. "Does this mean you're back?" he asked.

"Yup," she replied, heading straight for the coffee machine.

"So what did they say?" he persisted.

"Well, I think they liked me," she started incongruously. "Basically they warned me that if it happened again I would likely lose my job. And I warned *them* that if they persisted with irrational, rigid and anachronistic employment rules, they would likely lose some of their valuable employees. So, we discussed the detail of the incident, and I think they had to agree that my behaviour was nowhere remotely near being a risk to security. Strangely, they asked me about the argument I had with Bowen a day or so before - I don't know why they were interested in that."

"Ah, that's probably because I mentioned it when I spoke to them," put in Alex. "It seemed to me more than coincidence that the 'random' drug tests came just a day or so after you and he had a big argument."

"Oh, do you think so?" replied Betty. "They did ask me why, if my naughty indulgence was very rare, and the random drug test was also fairly rare, why I thought the two had serendipitously coincided. I didn't have an answer to that - I told them I had just assumed it was an unhappy coincidence. But I got the impression they weren't asking for an answer, just encouraging me to think about it. But I can't see that Bowen could have triggered it - he didn't know where I had been, or what I had been doing, did he? I don't think I even spoke to *you* about it Alex?"

"No, you told me about the party, and told me a bit about your brother, but nothing incriminating," confirmed Alex.

"So that kind of sounds as if they are telling me they have eyes and ears on me all the time," deduced Betty, "scary, but we don't think that's true do we?"

"Surely not," replied Alex, but he looked suddenly uncomfortable with the thought. The conversation seemed to have come to an awkward end.

"Well," added Betty loudly, "after that ordeal with HR, I could do with a line of coke. Did you bring any in today Alex?"

Alex winced slightly. "No, not today Betty... Not *any* day." he added loudly.

I had not been a participant in the preceding conversation, but now I felt an urge to lighten the mood. I had done a bit of preparatory research on my Nativity Star idea the previous evening, and thought now would perhaps be a good time to present the idea to Alex, for his approval or not, since we were wary of doing anything too consequential after the dire warning message the previous week.

"Well it sounds harmless," was Alex's verdict, after listening to me describe the proposed Christmas card, "as long as you don't do any zapping back then, of course! Actually, *I've* had an idea for a ruse as well. Do you remember Stephen Hawking threw a party for Time Travellers back in 2009? But only publicised the invitation *afterwards*! I'm thinking we could get some sort of meaningful image from the party, and send it to him anonymously, just for fun?"

"Ooh," Betty cooed with appreciation, "that's a lovely idea. But, although it wouldn't change the past, unfortunately it might generate a lot of publicity, and of course an image from the past would link it directly back to us, for those few GCHQ people in the know, and I don't think they would be too happy about us advertising the fact that it's possible. So, unfortunately I think that would be far too risky?"

"Yes, of course you're right," agreed Alex. "I had originally thought about zapping one of his champagne glasses at the party - but of course that would change the past, and is far too audacious." Betty laughed her appreciation.

"Hey," added Betty, "how about instead we make a camping site for time travellers?" Her grin was met with puzzled expressions from Alex and I. "Just imagine, you'd look around and there'd be past tents, present tents and future tents!"

We both groaned, and she threw her head back laughing. I retired to my own office to start some serious research on the Nativity, which I then continued throughout the weekend.

*   *   *

## MONDAY 12th December

I was engrossed until lunchtime when Betty came and dragged me back into their office. "So have you worked out the date of the Nativity Star *yet*?" she demanded. I had been refusing to talk about it all weekend, until I had finished the research to my own satisfaction.

I took a deep breath. "Yes, well, to be honest it's a bit of a philological nightmare," I admitted. "It reminds me why I decided to specialise in *modern*, rather than *ancient* history."

"Whoa, hang on," interjected Betty. "What's philological? - that's not a term I'm familiar with."

"It's the study of written historical sources, looking at the linguistics, authenticity, working out the originals and so on. Because back then there was no printing, just hand-written copies, and people who were educated enough to make copies, tended also to be motivated to make changes, thinking they were improving texts one way or another." She nodded as she handed me a mug of coffee.

"So, to start with, all the gospels were written, starting at least 65 years after the Nativity, so they were not written by eyewitnesses - the disciples were all dead, and the earliest copies we have are revised third generation at best. The Nativity Star and Magi, are depicted *only* in Matthew, just *one* of the four gospels. Presumably, the disciples who passed down most of the information for the gospels, had only first met Jesus when they were adults, so were probably unaware of any events surrounding his birth anyway. So, it's more in the other contemporary historical records, and perhaps astronomical records, that relevant sources would have been used by the authors of the gospels, and indeed now, by researchers.

"In fact the current astronomical software is extremely useful - it enables us to check the appearance of the sky at any date, even 2000 yeas ago, in regard to the habitual periodic objects - stars, planets and regular comets. Although it can't situate one-off events like supernovae, or the irregular comets, of course. Fortunately, though, there are reliable astronomical records made by Chinese and Korean astronomers, from that time, which can be used to double-check any one-offs stated by the middle-eastern astronomers." Alex and Betty were both munching on their sandwiches, but fully attentive

"There has been," I continued, "an amazing amount of research on the subject of the timing of the Nativity Star already, which makes it very quick and easy to pick up the threads. I think the most important line in Matthew, and, for my aspirations, the most devastating, states that King Herod had not been aware of 'The Star', - we know because Herod is said to have been surprised by the Magi's questions. So, as one of the researchers, Gingerich, put it, *'it wasn't that there was suddenly a brilliant new star sitting there that anybody could have seen, but something more subtle.'* " I took a sip of coffee before continuing.

"So, that suggests that something, not obvious to the masses, but an astrologically meaningful pattern in the sky, was what was motivating the Magi. And that's where all the astrology and interpretation starts. And, unfortunately, the idea of a big bright new star that everyone can wonder at, ends. One of the most documented theories is put forward by Larson, though he is a committed

Christian, and consequently is highly motivated. Larson's interpretation is that in 2/3 BC there are a couple of astronomical events, which are indeed endorsed by astronomical software, which satisfy the biblical predictions. Namely that there was a triple conjunction of Jupiter on Regulus in 3 BC (King Planet meets King Star), in Aries (which apparently conveniently represents Judaea). And that, 9 months later, Jupiter, in 2 BC, made a very close conjunction with Venus. Those two planets, very close together, would certainly make a fairly bright object, which he interprets as 'The Star', and he ties it all together with established symbolism and predictions. But there are date problems with his theory, in that Herod is generally accepted to have died in 4 BC, whereas with Larson's theory, he would have to be still alive to receive the Magi, in 2 BC." Alex had narrowed his eyes, obviously following my logic carefully.

"Then there is another prominent theory that in 6 BC, the Sun, Jupiter, Saturn and the Moon, were all aligned in Aries, whilst a couple of planets were on exactly the other side of the sky. Again it's all about interpreting the symbology. But visually it's nothing special, since the Sun would outshine the other details, making them invisible." Betty adjusted her sitting position whilst picking up another sandwich.

"Then there are comets, Halley's in 12 BC, and another in 5 BC - this latter one, enticingly, would be in the southern sky, looking from Jerusalem, and therefore over Bethlehem from their point of view, with the tail straight up. But the prevailing wisdom is that comets were seen as portends of *doom* rather than an important birth, so they are generally dismissed as candidates, but I'm not so sure about that. There was a massively bright comet in 44 BC, just after Julius Caesar's assassination, coinciding with a festival to honour him. And that comet was accepted by the populace as signifying his *deification*." Betty had paused her sandwich, and was listening intently, sensing that I was approaching my conclusion.

"So, now, going back to the author of Matthew, was he creating a historical account, or a symbolic narrative? Around the time that Matthew was being written, there was a spectacular appearance of Halley's comet, in AD 66, and believe it or not, there was a delegation of Magi who visited Rome. Magi, by the way, means Zoroastrian priests - they were specialists in Astrology - rather than 'wise men from the east'. Although they would indeed have come from the East - Zoroastrianism extended from Iraq to India. So the ideas of *Magi* and *comets*, and perhaps the *deification* of Julius Caesar, would have been very much in Matthew's author's mind as he compiled the text. And that might also explain why the dates don't add up - Matthew's author would either have been unaware of, or just not had access to accurate records of when Herod died, who ordered the census, what sort of census it was, and all the other little loose ends that don't quite add up."

"So," I concluded dramatically, "I'm going with Halley's comet of AD 66 as the fundamental inspiration for the Nativity!" And I returned my attention to my coffee mug.

There was a moment's silence. Then Alex spoke slowly. "So you're telling us that you are going to get a *real* image of Halley's comet from AD 66, which you think was the *real* inspiration for the *fake* Nativity Story, and put that *real* image on Christmas cards which people will assume is a *fake* image of the *real* Nativity?"

"That's it," I nodded. They both collapsed laughing, and although I could see the tortuous nature of my scheme, I could not quite see why they thought it so funny. Eventually Betty came over and gave me a hug.

"Excellent," she declared reassuringly, still giggling.

"Yes, excellent," agreed Alex. "Beats my zapping of Hawking's champagne flute. Maybe I should teach you quantum physics sometime - sounds like you may have the right sort of brain for it! So, Betty, it's your turn. George and I have both come up with great ruses, how about you - a great ruse for Christmas? You're usually the most creative one?"

Betty widened her eyes and smiled. "Could we perhaps retrospectively zap my incriminating urine sample bottle? Preferably whilst Bowen is holding it in his hand?" Alex laughed but shook his head decisively. Not that Betty was serious in her suggestion. "OK, give me a few days to think of something else," she requested. Betty had no immediate reply, but looked happy enough to take on the challenge.

\*  \*  \*

## SATURDAY 31st December

Betty and I had decided to celebrate the New Year up on one of the snowy slopes above the skiing village, rather than drinking the evening away in one of the taverns below, crowded with noisy revellers. I could see a handful of couples, who had made the same decision, sitting around at various vantage points, waiting for midnight and the accompanying fireworks display. Although it was cold, and snowing very gently, the skiwear, I had discovered, was amazingly warm and comfortable. We had brought a bottle of liqueur with us as well, both for added warmth and celebration.

It was bringing back fond memories of the recent times we had sat with Alex, discussing private concerns on 'our' hill back in the Cheltenham countryside, watching the lights of the city below.

The Christmas card ruse had played out perfectly. The image had been stunning, authentic, in its treble-bluff way, though nobody knew as much, not even Alex's wife Petra, who had skilfully painted in, with remarkably few brushstrokes, a minimal silhouetted nativity scene on the bottom of the card beneath the Star, before I had them printed. My old friend, John Partridge, back in Oxford had commented, "It's not like you to send religious cards, George?" but he had to agree with me that the image was worth the apparent reverse-apostasy. It had been great to catch up with other old friends in Oxford, and even my wife, Marianne, had treated me like an old friend, rather than an errant husband, thus making Christmas with our children a pleasure.

And finally, here I was, enjoying the pure mountain air with Betty. It had been an amazing couple of months, full of fascination, intrigue and falling in love. She had, she admitted, failed to come up with a major ruse, as challenged by Alex. But it was like waiting for the other shoe to drop; I suspected she was cooking up something.

We cuddled up and talked of perfection, and relaxation, and contentment. "But there are a couple of things," said Betty, "in the back of my mind, which still worry me. One is that business of why the drug test happened when it did - so does it mean we are under much greater surveillance than we think?"

I glanced over at the only person who was on the mountain on his own, about a hundred metres to our left, on the opposite side of the piste. I had noticed him briefly before - wondering whether his aloneness was a sign of great strength of character, or an inability to bond with other people. But now, a third option crossed my mind.

"Maybe GCHQ," Betty was continuing, "are actually aware that we are withholding information from them about the zap capability - the ability to change the past, and maybe they are aware of our ability to get an image from the future, but they are just stringing us along, because it suits them at the moment. There could be serious trouble lying ahead for us - '*O, What a tangled web we weave, when first we practise to deceive*'," she added wistfully.

"I doubt it," I reassured her. "Why would they programme a drugs test and then give you no punishment."

"As a warning?" she shrewdly suggested.

"But wouldn't it be simpler for them to just verbally warn us that they are aware of our subterfuge?" I countered.

"Maybe," she agreed. There was a pause.

I thought of trudging across the snow to the alone man on the other side of the piste, offer him a drink, see if I could spot any recording equipment. But in the unlikely event that he *was* security, it was more probable he was keeping us safe from foreign agents. Anyway, better not to show *our* suspicions.

"So," I carried on, "what is the other thing that worries you?"

"Ah, oh, well, we know just how dangerous it can be to meddle with the past - the widespread human catastrophe that can be caused by accidental superimposition - I sometimes wonder how it might feel to suddenly see a car apparently materialise right in front of you at seventy miles an hour, on the motorway - terrifying. Well, *we* now know enough to keep the technology safe. But at some time in the future, some other scientist will also discover the i-vector, who knows when or where in the world? And he or she will probably make that fatal mistake. Maybe he or she will even change the past significantly and irrevocably. Maybe we will cease to exist.

"We ought to try to stop those things happening." she continued. "We have a duty to try to prevent that possibility. But so far I haven't been able to think of any *scientific* way of detecting i-vector equipment being used anywhere else. So, I suppose the best chance lies with the likes of GCHQ or other surveillance services. I know they think they have tabs on any scientists following Alex's old direction of research, but it's probably not enough. It's just so important. It's far more important than the army's silly photos. But we can't tell them how important it is, without admitting that we have been withholding information."

"Hmm," I acknowledged. "But it might be possible to let GCHQ in on the knowledge, at a later date, pretending that we just then discovered it?"

"Well, I don't know whether that would make me feel safer or not," Betty sighed. "If the ethical decision about whether to change the past, or whether to get weekly reports from the future, moved to a wider sphere of people... And I'm still not confident that our surveillance services would be able to smell out foreign physicists working under foreign security. And if they did, what would they do? - Tell them to be *very careful*? Or bomb the lab? It's all a bit intractable."

\*   \*   \*

The firework show started, the huge expanses of snow providing unusual backdrop reflections of the bursts of colours. "Happy New Year, George," she grinned, swigging from the liqueur bottle and handing it to me. The previous signs of worry in her face had, for now, dissipated.

"Yes, Happy New Year, Betty," I reciprocated, briefly seeing unexplained tears in her eyes.

She clicked a photo of the fireworks and snow on her phone, and texted it to Alex with a greeting. He texted back, reminding us that we were an hour ahead (on European time), and that we shouldn't send messages from the future, unless there was an emergency! He added a note to me saying that last year was all history now. I replied, suggesting that we needed to wait until the dust settles before declaring history. After all, someone might still change it!

\*   \*   \*

But that evening was the last I ever spent with Betty. When I woke the next morning she was gone.

At first I was not concerned - she was accustomed to getting up early to go and play the piano in the local church before breakfast. On the day we had arrived she had immediately noted the 'pointy church', as she described it. We had spent a couple of hours visiting the Gothic building with its magnificent interior, and she had quickly managed to make friends with the priest who had happily been persuaded to give her permission to play the piano there - she had assured him that she would only play 'suitable' classical music. As I love to do, I spent some hours reading about the fascinating history of the place, and during the evening, whilst we were gathered around the fireplace with some fellow skiers in the large chalet where we were all staying, Betty had asked me to recount the story of the church.

"Well, the history of the church really starts away over in Constantinople in the 10th Century," I began. "A devout Jew there had speared a statue of the crucifixion in an attempt to test the faith of the Christians present, but to everyone's astonishment, 'blood' flowed from the 'wound' in the statue. Unsurprisingly, the Jew immediately converted to Christianity on witnessing this sign. The Emperor Leo had the 'blood' collected into a vial which he secretly kept, in the Hagia Sophia Cathedral, as one of his most treasured belongings." I could see from Betty's face that she was appalled at the outrageously unscientific nature of the story I was telling, but I could also see that attentive smile she always wore when I was recounting stories.

"The Emperor himself was personally protected by his 'Varangian Guard'," I went on, "an elite collection of Knights from the northern Viking countries, including a Danish Knight called Briccius, who was well-favoured by the Emperor, particularly since he had once rescued the Emperor's daughter from kidnappers. But after faithfully serving the Emperor for many years, Briccius decided he wanted to return to his own country. He informed the Emperor, who told him that, because of his many years of exemplary service, Briccius could choose any one of the emperor's belongings to take with him as a reward. Briccius, after considering for a while, chose the vial of holy blood. The Emperor, who had not realised that Briccius knew about the vial, was reluctant, but finally agreed, and Briccius set off on the long journey north-west back to his homeland." The others round the fireplace were refilling glasses, but still paying attention.

"But, shortly afterwards," I continued, "the emperor regretted his generosity, and sent cavalry after Briccius to retrieve the invaluable relic. Briccius must have been aware of the pursuit - one of the accounts suggests a divine message - because he headed eastward, deviating away from his natural route. But he was pursued relentlessly and, realising that if the vial was in a wallet or bag it would be easily found, he adopted a drastic strategy of cutting a wound in his calf, and secreting the vial inside the wound. Reportedly the wound healed instantly, and he continued on his journey. But trying to cross the Alps in deep mid-winter, he struggled with pain and fatigue, and was finally overcome by a blizzard, dying in a snowdrift, near the Gross Glockner glacier - the spot, near here, is now marked by a small chapel." I paused briefly for another sip of wine.

"His body was found by farmers collecting stored hay, and they buried him where he lay. However when the farmers passed by later, they saw that his leg was now sticking up out of the snow, so they buried his body again. But this time, three ears of corn unseasonably sprouted from the burial spot. The farmers suspected a miracle and returned with a cart and oxen to transport the body down into the valley. Apparently when the oxen reached here, they refused to move any further, so the body was taken in to the local chapel. But before the priest managed to get the body buried again, the corpse raised its leg three times, and thus finally the vial was discovered, with a document describing its provenance. So Briccius was finally buried here, in Heiligenblut, which in German means Holy Blood, he was declared a saint, and the vial of 'blood' is still held in the church's sacrament house today."

"A tall story indeed," Betty had laughed, "but blood, snow, and death do form a very artistic trio." she had added wistfully.

*     *     *

Usually Betty returned from the church for a late breakfast, so when she still hadn't returned for some time after breakfast, I wandered along to the church to see if she was still at the piano. She wasn't there, and no-one I spoke to remembered seeing her that morning. I returned to the chalet and checked her ski gear - still there, then I went upstairs to our room - her suitcase and clothes were gone! I felt my stomach turn over - why had she left, before I woke, and without telling me? I sat down for a few minutes with a lump in my throat, trying to think it through and wondering what to do. Eventually I got out my mobile phone and called her, but as I had anticipated, the call did not connect. Then finally I noticed the letter - it was lying next to her pillow. She had written my name on the envelope. I didn't open it for a minute or so - I knew I almost certainly didn't want to hear whatever message was inside. But with heavy heart I eventually opened it and read.

"*Dearest George, First let me say how deeply sorry I am to have left without saying goodbye, but you will understand why as you read on. I love you, and have enjoyed enormously our time together the last few weeks. You know that I have always tried to live life to the full, but what you did not know was that I always had a limited time. I have known since I was young that I carried the gene for Huntington's disease, and that at some time the symptoms would start. I realised that it had started some weeks ago, when I involuntarily jerked and came off the kite-board on the hill, that day with Harriet. Since then my hands have lost control several times whilst I was playing piano, and I fell twice, skiing on my own in the mornings, whilst you were having your lessons on the lower slopes. I have no doubt. My time has come. My father, bless him, suffered enormously, and I have no wish to carry on living if I cannot be me, doing the things I have loved and enjoyed. I discussed this at length with my mother over Christmas - she understands what I have to do. By the time you read this I will be well on my way to Switzerland where they have a very accommodating attitude to assisted suicide - I know you will be distraught, but do not try to follow me to try to dissuade me, please respect my decision. I feel some satisfaction in knowing that the gene will now be eradicated from our family - both my brother and sister are clear. I know you will hurt, missing me, at first, as will my family and friends, but I do hope you will feel that I have added something to your life, not just given pain of loss. I was me - I lived as hard, fast and full as I could during my limited time. I did consider dying a more poetic and resonant death - with blood in the snow, like poor Briccius, but I think that would have caused us both more pain, so I have opted for the comfortable way out. I leave you with my dignity, and love for you, intact,*

*Betty xxx*

*P.S. I will check our hire car in at the airport - you will need to find a lift for yourself.*

I was stunned and devastated. I spent the rest of the day crying, slumped in a chair, staring out at the mountains, unable to move.

# Chapter 12
# The aftermath

### *TUESDAY 10th January*

I missed her dreadfully. I felt I had to resign my post at GCHQ, and return to Oxford, because it was now impossible to work back at the GCHQ office - she was so loudly absent. And for some reason Alex was now having major problems with getting the i-vector equipment to work at all. Bowen was frantic, but Alex didn't seem motivated any more. They talked about recruiting some more staff to work with Alex, but his sparkle was gone, at least temporarily. Alex and I vowed to stay in touch, but the security regulations mean that we would never be able to discuss the experiments again.

I found digs back in Oxford - I could not move back in with my wife, Marianne, not after the involvement with Betty. That time spent with Betty and Alex and the experiments had briefly injected some vivid colour into my life, but equally, now that those days were gone, life, for the moment, seemed achingly dull and purposeless. Betty had somehow released me from hanging on to the old academic comfort zone, but without it, or her, I felt lost. Maybe time will heal me, or maybe I have been privileged to mess about with time too much, for such a simple remedy to work any more. On the other hand, now that I have tasted adventure, I will be more inclined to search for it and invite it in - I know Betty would encourage me to do so.

*     *     *

### *MONDAY 16th January*

At the funeral they played that same beautiful piano piece, Enescu's

Adagio, which had moved me to tears the night that Betty and I had sealed our love. And again at the funeral it made me cry, but this time I cried with pain, rather than because of the music's beauty. Alex was grief-stricken too - he had known about her condition, (I suddenly remembered he had once used the expression 'doomed angel' though had never explained it), but he too, was unprepared for such an abrupt ending. At the funeral, Betty's mother had handed him a good-bye letter that Betty had prepared previously.

Kendall found me at the funeral, "Hello George, Grandma says I have to remember all the fun times with Betty now that she's gone - we had lots of fun at Christmas... *why* didn't she come back from holiday with you?" I broke down in tears at the directness of her innocence, fortunately Betty's mother scooped her up and talked to her.

*   *   *

## *TUESDAY 17th January*

The next morning a policeman came to my Oxford flat and told me that I was required urgently to attend an interview with MI5, and that he would drive me there straightaway. Not surprisingly, he was unable to give me any indication about what the security service wanted to know. On the hour and a half drive there I pondered what they might want from me. I had already given a detailed statement to the security people back at GCHQ, but I supposed that, since Betty and I had both been party to very sensitive information, they just wanted to dot the i's and cross the t's. Or were they wise to what we had concealed from GCHQ? - that caused me to feel a little guilt and anxiety.

On arriving at 12 Millbank, MI5's home in London, I wanted to stand and admire the stunning architecture - less than a hundred years old, but superb both in its solidity and style. However the policeman hurried me into the entrance, and from there another officer escorted me through a labyrinth of corridors to the relevant office.

I immediately liked his office as I walked in - next to the desk it had two filing cabinets, so often absent in modern-day offices. And he had a couple of open files on his desk. I guessed that some information is more secure on paper than in a computer. "Good morning Professor Tremaine, I'm Tom Wheatley. Please sit down." He gestured to a chair in front of his desk, and removed his gold-rimmed spectacles slowly as he spoke. He had an impressive but warm air about him. "I know this is not an easy time for you, but we are having to deal with this extremely serious matter. I already have your full GCHQ statement and a copy of your 'goodbye' letter from Betty Gosmore, and later on, one of my staff will go through all of that in detail with you, but first I want to ask you to do a formal identification of Miss Gosmore from a photograph please." I nodded. "I am afraid it is a photograph of the body in the coffin - you understand that because of the security issues, we felt we needed to take photographs and do a DNA check." I nodded again - he seemed to be in a hurry, and not looking for any responses from me. He reached into a manila A4 envelope, withdrew some large photographs and placed them on the desk to face me.

It took a little while to focus - seeing the coffin again brought back tearful feelings, and I had trepidation about seeing Betty in death. I looked at the face but somehow failed to connect. Of course embalmed bodies look different from real life, but… She was wearing her clothes…

"Take your time, please sir, no assumptions." I looked from one photo to another and back again.

"It *is* her clothes," I started, "but the face just doesn't look right. Her hair doesn't usually curl that way, and… the nose is the wrong shape. What on earth…? I don't understand? I've never looked at an embalmed face before - are they *very* different?"

"What about the body shape?" Wheatley prompted.

I looked again. I tried to imagine what Betty would look like lying in a coffin. "Its difficult to say," I replied, "but those rings on the left hand - Betty never wore rings. She disliked the implications."

"And they are not usually left on by professional undertakers," he added, bending over to look at the photo closely. "So, all things considered, are you confirming it's not the Betty Gosmore that you knew?"

"Well, I don't understand why, but as far as I can tell it's *not* her," I stated in a wobbly voice - my insides were tightening as I struggled to comprehend what the hell was going on.

He made a call on his phone. "It's a negative ID, Ben, pull out all the stops."

Someone arrived with a tray of tea and coffee, and he gestured for me to help myself. "So, to explain sir - can I call you George, now?" he asked, his tone shifting from formal to more sympathetic. I nodded shakily. I was feeling a bit dizzy, and lumbering to understand what all this meant. He responded to my rapid breathing by inviting me to retire to a very comfortable leather armchair in the corner of the office. "You just relax there for the time being George, it looks like we have a defector on the loose, abroad, and with knowledge of secrets which are a serious threat to national security. *You* know what those secrets are - I only know the category - which is very high. So as you can imagine we are taking this extremely seriously, and vigorously investigating a number of leads. Things may become clearer soon."

"What... Betty would never have defected," I protested. He nodded patronisingly, then went back to work at his desk. I suppose I should have not been surprised at his assumption - they did not know Betty, they just had this strange set of facts. Or maybe I was just being blind to the obvious?

I sank back into the armchair, closed my eyes and found myself drifting back to that time, just a few weeks ago when Alex had explained about the i-vector for the very first time - and how stunned I had been, unable to take it in. I had the same feeling now.

After a while Wheatley's phone rang and he spoke briefly to the caller, before talking to me again. "OK George, we have just received back the results from the DNA test of the body in the coffin - it does not make a family match with Miss Gosmore's mother - we took a swab from her last week, and nor is it positive for the Huntington's gene. So that confirms your negative identification, and makes the picture a little clearer."

I nodded that I understood. I adjusted my position in the sumptuous armchair and closed my eyes again. This time I drifted back to the early period at GCHQ when I was not sure whether Alex and Betty were genuine, or unfolding a sophisticated hoax, and Betty's confusing deadpan jokes about breaking into the military camp at Bovington. My body jerked slightly as suddenly I remembered the time in Bowen's office when Betty was arguing that *'The whole principle of successful deterrence rests on a level of transparency...'* - could she really have defected? No, it was just a heated discussion with Bowen about the value of pictures from the future.

After some minutes, he took another call. Then he turned to me again.

"So, George," he stated, "we have now checked all the flight manifests out of Salzburg on that day, and her name does not come up, nor on the following day. She didn't travel under any other name, or have another passport?"

"Not to my knowledge," I confirmed.

"We're checking the car hire now - was it in your or her name?"

"Mine," I replied. "Oh, and there was some damage to the car - the hire company deducted an excess from my credit card. I noticed it when I checked the card statement and phoned them to query the deduction."

Wheatley's eyes widened and he came over to where I was sitting. "Look, details like that are really important to us, George, you mean the damage was done before or after Miss Gosmore left Heiligenblut?"

"The car was fine before she left."

"So did they describe the damage?" he asked. "It doesn't matter if you can't remember, we'll get it from their records. But please do try to remember any detail, however small, that you haven't already told us?"

"I think they said the front wing was crumpled and scratched. I wasn't bothered about the money because it must have been a difficult and emotional day for her too - not surprising if she made a little mistake with the car."

"Well yes, but that damage might alternatively indicate that a malicious third party was involved. Until you said that, although I have to be open to all explanations, I was favouring the explanation that she had defected, of her own free will."

I leant back into that comfortable armchair and closed my eyes again. Now I was remembering that evening with Betty on the bank of the River Wye. She had pulled an elaborate practical joke on me, with the man in the flat cap, and then thoroughly confused me with a tirade of contradictory statements. I felt a tinge of that panicky confusion now, genuinely not understanding what was happening.

He fielded yet another call. "Well George," he sighed thoughtfully after putting down his phone, "we now have sight of your car hire documents from the hire firm at Salzburg airport. The signature on the return document doesn't match yours or Miss Gosmore's. So there is definitely a third party involved."

"Oh god," I sat up straight, finally feeling some clarity and alarm slamming home. "So she was *kidnapped*. I knew she wouldn't have defected."

"Possibly," he replied, "we still don't know for sure that she was coerced - the third party could have been a pre-arranged escort. On the other hand, damage to the driver-side wing, which they have confirmed, *is* what we would expect to see if another vehicle forced her to stop or go off-road."

"So how do we find her?" I asked naively.

"Well, our agent is working to collect the relevant CCTV from Salzburg airport. We might get a picture of the person returning your car, maybe even of the car or van he drove away in, if we're lucky. Then we might be able to track the journey they took using number plate recognition - its fairly good at the Schengen borders, unless they swapped vehicles of course. But frankly we haven't got much hope of actually *locating* her - they have had a two week start on us - they could have taken her anywhere in the world by now."

Another call. "So," he relayed to me, "we have found and talked to the clinic in Switzerland which Miss Gosmore had booked into, and they confirm that she never arrived - not too surprising, of course. They confirmed that she had visited them on previous occasions for consultations. But they have no knowledge of the coffin, so we are investigating now to find out by whom, and where that was despatched from. This was a really professional job - they obviously knew about Miss Gosmore's intended destination, they must have been monitoring her mobile phone or email conversations, and maybe more. Then they went to the trouble of faking the follow-through with a coffin and body, hoping we would never realise that our security had been breached. There's presumably a body theft or collateral murder too, in order to provide the decoy body. And, apart from trying to locate Miss Gosmore, we have a problem that security around GCHQ is evidently not watertight - there could be a mole, or some very clever espionage by the hostile party. I gather that very few people were aware of the special capability that you and she were working on, but it might be that the hostile party don't know exactly what that is - they may have just deduced that any workers in that annexe must be doing something special." He sighed. "We have a lot of work to do to understand how security was compromised, but we will sort that - it's what we do. However, unless MI6 overseas embedded agents can come up with any leads, I fear that we have lost Miss Gosmore to a fate rather worse than her planned death, if you get my meaning."

He spoke that last sentence softly and sympathetically, but I broke down in tears. I hadn't imagined that it could get *worse* than Betty dying.

Then suddenly I realised. "But we *can* find Betty - I mean using the special capability that we work on back at GCHQ, we should be able to locate Betty.'

His eyes widened in surprise, but he smiled broadly. "Bring it on then," he enthused.

I wondered how many past pictures it would take to track Betty's abductors across Europe, but it was definitely do-able. "Can I call Alex Zakarian back at GCHQ and get the process started?" I asked.

"I'm afraid he's here, just down the corridor right now, being interviewed separately," said Wheatley, "but when we finish here, we'll get you both driven back to Cheltenham. Here's my phone number," he handed me a card, "I need you to keep me posted on anything you do manage to find out. I will call GCHQ and tell them we need you reinstated there immediately."

It was another half hour before they re-united Alex and I. We hugged hard - it was only yesterday that we had been together at the funeral, but so much had changed since then, and now we were both highly motivated to do something about Betty's plight. We were unable to discuss anything technical in the open car on the way back, but I called Harriet from the car, and asked her to meet us when we arrived back. Alex also was able to reassure me that the equipment which had been malfunctioning when I was last in the office, was now OK - he had finally managed to trace the fault to a loose septum magnet housing, - I had no idea what that was, but I was relieved, because it would otherwise have been a show-stopper, not to mention Bowen's frantic mood whilst the machine was out of action. Harriet had apparently been catching up her work over the weekend.

*   *   *

I had no trouble getting in at the annexe door, indeed they had a security badge ready for me, and gave me the keys to my old flat - Tom Wheatley was clearly capable of pulling strings at GCHQ. Thankfully Bowen was away. We sat down with a coffee and explained to Harriet what the new situation was.

She was clearly shocked - she sat back with her hands to her mouth, and tears in her eyes. It had echoes of two weeks previously, when I had explained, with emotional difficulty, to both Alex and Harriet about Betty's heart-wrenching decision.

But we were now determined to get on with the search. I suggested that we work three shifts to get the maximum number of pictures each day. Harriet said she would explain to her boss why this needed to take priority over all but the most important military pictures, and get him to speak to Tom Wheatley if necessary. I showed them on a map exactly where our hire car had been parked, and stated that Betty had most likely left sometime between 01:00 am and 07:00 am on the 1st of January.

Alex explained what he called a binary chop method. Firstly get a picture from the middle of that time period to see whether the car was still there or not. Then narrow it down again with a picture in the middle of the remaining period when the car was still present, and so on, this being the fastest way to home in on the departure time. Harriet agreed, but said the military called the method by a different name. We knew it would be dark apart from the few streetlights, so we set the parameters accordingly. We also aimed to do low resolution pictures so we could do them more quickly.

And hence we started. The first picture, timed at 04:30 showed that indeed the car was still there - although the light was poor, I could just make out the shape and position of our car. Alex set up the next picture for 05:45. The wait was very frustrating. But finally the image came through, and we could see Betty's car had now left. So Alex split the difference and started setting up for 05:07, but Harriet, who had bothered to study the picture in detail, as she was accustomed to do, told Alex to hold fire. "Look," she pointed at the picture, "a van that was parked a little further up the road has also gone, but all the other vehicles are still there. I think there is a good chance that the van is the pursuit vehicle, and took off after Betty. It's not likely that many other people would head off in the middle of the night after New Year's Eve. I'm thinking that maybe if we do a close-up of the van's number plate, we have a short cut."

"Brilliant," I enthused.

"Well," considered Alex sounding dubious, "I'm not certain we would be able to read the number plate in that light."

"But we could take a picture from the previous day," countered Harriet, "when it was still light, the van would probably still be there?"

"Yes," I injected, "but even if we got the number plate, I'm not sure we could be confident enough that it is the hostile vehicle, to pass it on to MI5 - it would be awful if we set them on a wild goose chase, and then they wouldn't believe us the next time we gave them information."

"OK, let's narrow it down some more then," concluded Alex, keying in 05:07. Another wait. Car still there.

"It looks like she's timed it to leave at first light," commented Harriet. "That's going to make the next stage a bit easier if we have better light. Oh, this reminds me of my work placement when I was scanning CCTV footage all day, trying to pin down incidents!" Alex set the picture time to 05:25. I was beginning to feel some excitement rising, amidst the frustration of the waits between the images.

The next picture choked us all up. We had a picture of Betty bending over at the boot of the car, presumably loading her case. The image was not really clear enough to see that it was Betty, but it was compelling. Harriet hurried off to the toilet, I think she needed to have a cry. Alex set the target time to 3 minutes later at 05:28. When Harriet returned, she changed the location coordinates, panning them up and back, so that the next picture would give a wider field of view, showing a longer stretch of road, now that we expected the car to be on the move.

We were into mid-evening at Cheltenham now, but none of us really wanted to leave. Petra called Alex to see where he was, but he apologised to her that he had to work late that evening. Harriet insisted that she would work through the night, as she was used to doing, and explained what she thought was the best strategy for the next phase, assuming that the car now drove off. Of course we knew the route Betty would take to the airport, about a two and a half hours drive. Harriet explained that she would iteratively estimate the speed that Betty was driving at, and so calculate the time it would take her to get to a next target spot a few miles down the road. In that way Harriet thought she could monitor the drive with the minimum number of pictures. Also Harriet had changed her mind about the poor light - she thought she could begin monitoring the car, or both vehicles, more easily in the dark from a substantial elevation, maybe half a kilometre, discerning their position from their headlights, as if bright dots on a map.

When the 05:28 image finally came up on the screen, Betty's car had gone, but ominously, the van that we had suspected, was just pulling out. I began to feel some dread about seeing the next set of pictures, especially with the excruciating wait between each of them, so, on the pretext of practicalities I decided to head back to my Cheltenham apartment. I needed to get something to eat - we had both missed lunch in London, and I also needed to buy a toothbrush from somewhere, as I had left Oxford not expecting to be staying away. I knew I could rely on Harriet to efficiently manage the next episode of pictures. Alex could still not tear himself away from the unfolding story, so I said I would get some sleep and take over in the morning.

*　　*　　*

## **<u>WEDNESDAY 18th January</u>**

The next morning I woke with a start. I had had trouble getting to sleep, but had then slept deeply with vivid dreams. The previous day's drama ran through my head in a flash. I was impatient to get in to the office, but, forcing myself to be practical, I grabbed a breakfast in a café on the way.

As I entered the office, I saw the whole distressing story laid out in pictures across one of the desks. Harriet was tired by now, and Alex had finally been persuaded to go home in the early hours. Harriet talked me through it. The van - Harriet had now identified it as a Volkswagen Transporter Panel van - had followed at a distance for only a few miles, then whilst still on the quiet local roads, had driven alongside and forced Betty off the side of the road. There were several pictures of the brief melee, still in poor light, as Betty was forced into the van. I felt anger rising inside, and frustration that I could not be there to do something to help. Though I knew that, had I been there, I would probably just have been despatched as collateral damage. One of the, apparently, two men was pictured getting back into Betty's car, and another picture, shortly after, showed the two vehicles driving away in convoy. Harriet had got a good picture of the van's number plate, but she had not yet managed to get identifiable pictures of the kidnappers because the light, at that point in time, was still poor, and they were bundled up in hats and scarves - the temperature was well below zero.

"So I need to go home and sleep," Harriet said, tired and ashen faced. "I guess you now need to track the van on towards the airport; or until it gets light, so that you can get pictures of those bastards' faces. They are only averaging about 35 miles per hour on the minor road. Here are the coordinates and time of the incident. I'm sorry, George, this is awful. Betty was the last person in the world to deserve such treatment, and it's so frustrating that she has been at their mercy for two weeks already, before we even found out." She left looking dejected.

I decided to phone Tom Wheatley straight away.

"Oh, good morning George," he began, "I'm afraid we had no luck with the hire-car CCTV - the abductor was all bundled up in warm clothing - scarf, sunglasses and hat, - so impossible to get a useful facial shot, and he wore gloves signing the release slip, so no fingerprints either."

"Ah, right," I replied, "but I phoned you to say that we have identified the abductors' van - it was a Volkswagen." - I gave him the details that Harriet had written down.

"Good grief," he sounded both shocked and impressed, "how did you manage that, are you sure about this, George?"

"Yes," I assured him, "I am 100% confident, though I am not allowed to tell you why, or how."

"Good man, George," he laughed, approving of my security rigour. "But if your technology is that good, I am wondering why MI5 don't have access to you on a routine basis - I see from the short security clearance list of personnel in-the-know, that the army already has access?"

"I couldn't possibly comment," I joked, knowing only the popular parodies of political power in the higher echelons.

He laughed again. "OK George, I'll run that plate through the Schengen system, and I'll let you know what we find." He ended the call.

It was barely ten minutes later when he rang back. "Hello again George, yes, well that plate is Romanian as you realise, the van belongs to a hire company in Bucharest there. It was clocked crossing the border into Hungary at 11:24 on the 1st of January, then crossing into Romania at 15:15. I can't say I'm surprised - they were presumably heading for a Black Sea port - from there it's a short hop to hostile territory. We can probably get the Romanian police to check when the van was returned, but, that doesn't really help much. I have to be honest with you, George, there is almost no hope of getting Miss Gosmore back, unless sometime in the future, assuming we find out who is holding her, we can organise some sort of prisoner exchange. But much more worrying for us professionals in the security umbrella, those secrets have probably been extracted from her already. You presumably understand better than I do, the implications of that?"

I was choking on the phrase 'extracted from her', and couldn't reply for a moment.

"George?, you still there?"

"Yes, I understand," I finally managed. "But can you let me know the exact location of one of those border crossings please?"

"Oh, OK, well the van crossed the border on the A4 autobahn in Austria, which becomes the M1 in Hungary."

"And the precise time?" I asked.

"Um, let's see… The Schengen database says 11:24:07 am CET - that's Central European Time. Do you want the other crossing as well?"

"No, I think that's enough to work on, thanks," I replied.

"OK, well keep me posted on anything more you find out. I may well see you in Cheltenham sometime over the next few days - we will be descending on GCHQ for a security investigation and review after this fiasco - there have been some angry voices raised, as you can imagine. Bye then, George."

I had realised that there was no need for me to try to tediously track the van to the airport now. MI5 had given us a short-cut - we knew where and when to spot the van at the border, in daylight. I wasn't as adept as Harriet with coordinates, but I worked at google maps, locating the autobahn and the border, then switched to aerial view and finally 'street view' to find the gantry on which the cameras were mounted, and wrote down the coordinates. Then I realised that I was stumped on the height above sea level, so I had to phone Harriet for advice - fortunately she had not yet gone to sleep. I corrected the Central European Time to GMT, and started to key in the numbers to the computer, backing the coordinates away and up to get a broader view of the autobahn.

As I waited for the picture to process I realised that at that time that the van was crossing the border, was about the same time that I discovered Betty's letter. My throat and stomach tightened again.

The first picture attempt was not bad, but it took another to actually spot the van, and another 4 or 5 adjusting the coordinates clumsily to get a good daylight close-up of the two men sitting in the front. I hated those cold, hard faces. My anger was palpable. I sent the pictures to Tom Wheatley.

I was just pondering what to do next, when Alex arrived, refreshed from a good sleep. I brought him up to date, and recounted what Tom Wheatley had said about the hopelessness of getting Betty back. I knew we could now easily get a picture of Betty in the back of the van, but I was scared of the feelings that would evoke, and there didn't seem to be any purpose anyway.

But a plan *was* forming in my mind - I wondered if the same had occurred to Alex. I wanted to discuss it in private, but it was pouring with rain outside, so going out to 'our' hill was not an option. I put some music on one of the computers, getting a very quizzical look from Alex, and turned the coffee machine on to create even more ambient noise, then I spoke quietly. "I think we should use a zap to intervene in the past Alex."

He nodded. "I know that *seems* the obvious course of action, but the warning we had from our future selves made it very clear that there is huge danger in doing that - when they tried, it accidentally caused mayhem."

"Yes, but as far as I understood that message," I countered, "it implied that the catastrophe occurred because there was doubt about *whether* the change would get actioned or not, so superimposition occurred until actioning the zap was decisive."

"Yes, you're right, it did sound that way," agreed Alex, "and it does make perfect logical sense that it should work like that, but…"

"And it's not just to save Betty from suffering," I continued. "Wheatley said that they would have probably extracted the knowledge from her by now - it will be only a matter of time before there is functioning i-vector equipment in hostile hands, they may have already started building it."

Alex sat back into his chair and raked his hands through his hair, clearly anguished by the dilemma of trying to weigh-up the right thing to do.

"And," I continued pushing, "we need to do it now, because the place will be crawling with MI5 and security people in a day or two - Wheatley said they were about to descend on the place, and things may then get so tight that we don't have the freedom to action it anymore."

Alex was quiet for a second or two. "OK, lets do it then, but lets plan it very carefully - we're only likely to get one shot at it. What are you thinking?"

"Well it's no good taking out just *one* of the kidnappers, the other could still carry it through. We could disable the van, but then they might just steal another vehicle. And obviously trying to blow the door off so that Betty could escape is pure fantasy, but I can't help it going through my head."

At that moment Harriet arrived. Alex and I looked at each other. She was keen to be brought up to date, which I did, except for our latest musings.

Then Alex drew a deep breath and said to her "Look Harriet, we need your opinion - you have military training, so here is a hypothetical situation, and we would like your judgement on what is the best course of action. Suppose you have a weapon, say a handgun, no, maybe a more potent type of gun, and you could be anyplace and any time along this unfolding kidnap, but you could only take *one* shot to best solve the problem, where, when and what would you shoot at?"

Harriet looked somewhat puzzled by the question, and looked at us both quizzically as if we playing some inappropriate fantasy game.

"No, please take the question absolutely seriously, Harriet," pleaded Alex in his most convincing tone.

"OK, so, one shot, anytime, anywhere?" she repeated, checking. We nodded. She sat back in her chair, removed the hair band from her ponytail, and tossed her long blond hair loose, before retying it, as she pondered. It was a routine I had noticed her do before when she got fascinated by something one of us had said. We quietly let her think for a full half minute before she replied.

"Well since it's only one shot it has to be decisive - shooting only one of the abductors is no use. So in order to take out all the abductors, we need to shoot the driver at a moment when the van will definitely go out of control, destroying the van and hopefully any other abductors too. And obviously that has to be before Betty is in the van. So, you know that those mountain roads have hairpin bends, and during the first 10 or 12 minutes of their journey, the van driver is pushing the speed a bit to catch up to Betty who had a 2 or 3 minute start. Well I would say their most vulnerable moment is on a flat piece of road, while the driver still has his foot on the throttle, just before he would start braking for the upcoming hairpin bend. If the shot to the head causes him to jerk, then we want his foot to be on the throttle not the brake. So, considering the van is racing a bit to catch up to Betty, there's a very good chance it will crash right over the barrier at the hairpin bend - those barriers are quite low. Even if it doesn't go over, it should certainly crash, and as long as the van is un-driveable, the kidnap would be prevented. Also it would be best to do it whilst they are still some distance behind Betty - we don't want her to see the crash in her rear-view mirror and go back to help!"

Alex and I looked at each other - we were impressed by the clarity of the clinical, comprehensive military assessment.

"Wow, thanks Harriet," said Alex, "that's really helpful. Now I wonder if you would mind letting George and I have the equipment to ourselves tonight?"

"No way," she protested, "I want in, if you're going to try something like that, you need my expertise. I want to see it done right, for Betty and country. So *can* you use this equipment as a weapon?"

Alex and I looked at each other again. It *would* be easier with Harriet on board, and fortuitously, because of the way in which we would be changing the past, Harriet's, and hence the military's, knowledge of the zap weapon would be lost, in the same way that the i-vector know-how extracted from Betty would be lost. Hence our concealment of the weapon from the military would still be intact in the nascent future.

"OK, well it looks like we are all in then," concluded Alex. "Yes Harriet, we *can* use it as a weapon - we just put a lot more energy in, and project it right into the target rather than in front of the target as you do when you are taking a picture. It causes a nasty disc-shaped explosion about 1 metre wide. So, one refinement to what you suggested - if you can choose a place where they are driving roughly northward or southward, then the disc of energy, which always projects east-west as you know, may be wide enough to encompass both the bastards' heads."

Harriet nodded, and smiled at both of us in turn, then brought up a military map of the area onto the computer screen in front of her. She started searching for a suitable piece of road to make the attack. Harriet was very painstaking - she insisted on taking several overhead pictures separated by a few seconds each, so that she could work out exactly how fast the van was travelling at each point along the road. That way she could be confident exactly where the van started braking. Then, having chosen a time and place, we ran into trouble. The light was so poor that it was difficult to discern from the pictures precisely where the cloud was being positioned inside the cab of the van. But fortunately there was just enough reflection of the headlights by the surrounding snow, that we were finally confident that the cloud was intersecting the driver's head and upper torso, and also intersecting part of the passenger's head.

Alex keyed in the parameters to form a maximum density particle cloud. We now settled down to wait a full hour for the cloud to prepare. It was past midnight now - this final phase had taken a long time to get exactly right. It was only at that point I began to feel slightly squeamish about what we were doing.

"So one very important point," Alex, as always, was thinking it through methodically, "when, after the hour, the preparation is complete, we must action it *immediately*. There must be no hesitation, we have to be completely committed to doing it. I'm sorry Harriet, it's too difficult for me to explain the reason and the science behind that, just believe me how important it is." I knew he was taking every precaution against causing any superimposition.

Harriet nodded. "I'll do it. It's a military operation. I'll press the action button as soon as the status goes green." I was glad she had volunteered. Although I felt nothing but anger and contempt toward the kidnappers, still I would not like to have pressed the button. We settled down to a coffee.

"Wait a minute," said Harriet, a while later. "If we change the past so that Betty does *not* get abducted, what happens to us now, I mean we wouldn't know about the kidnap, so how… that's very confusing?"

Alex and I both laughed gently. "Yes," he replied, "it *is* confusing - best to think of it as kind of instantaneously rewinding time back to when we intervene to knock out the van, and then starting time again, from that moment."

"Oh, I see, OK," Harriet acknowledged, "but that means we won't remember any of this evening, anything about the kidnap?"

"That's right," Alex confirmed, "It will be as if it had never happened."

"That is weird, I feel like I am in a dream," commented Harriet.

"In a sense, maybe we are," said Alex thoughtfully.

The conversation moved from this to that subject as we waited for the hour to pass, but as the last few minutes were counting down on the computer screen, we fell silent. Thankfully there was no sign of any superimposition.

"The sad thing is that, although this will save Betty from a lot of pain, it can't bring her back to us," Harriet sounded wistful as the last few seconds ticked down.

"No, but she will die comfortably, just as she chose. Rest In Peace now Betty," I whispered as Harriet reached forward and pressed the activate button.

*   *   *